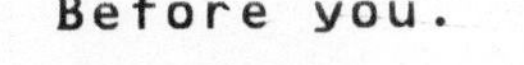
Before you.

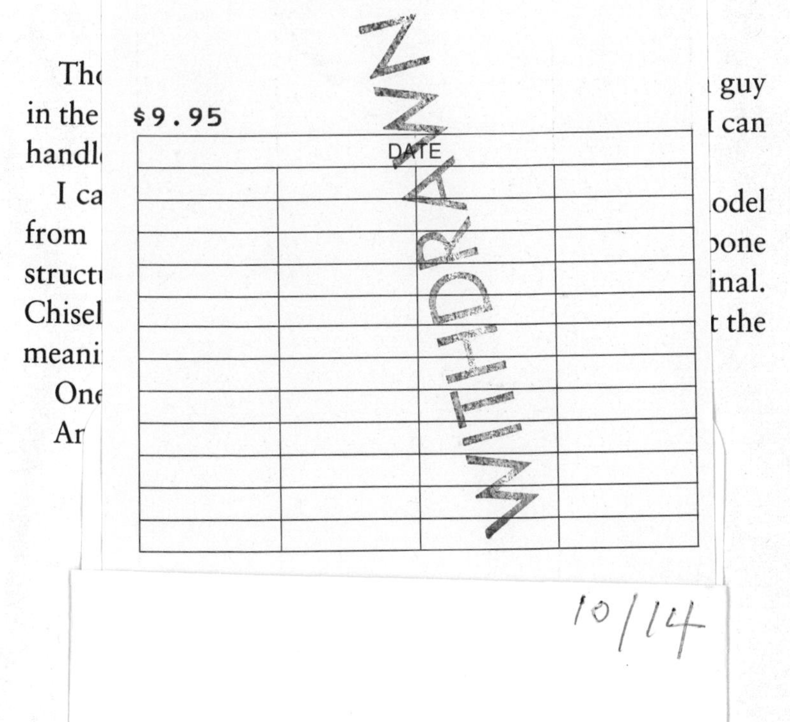
$9.95
DATE
WITHDRAWN

AMBER HART

KENSINGTON PUBLISHING CORP.
www

KTEEN BOOKS are published by

Kensington Publishing Corp.
119 West 40th Street
New York, NY 10018

All Kensington titles, imprints, and distributed lines are available at special quantity discounts for bulk purchases for sales promotions, premiums, fund-raising, educational, or institutional use.

Special book excerpts or customized printings can also be created to fit specific needs. For details, write or phone the office of the Kensington special sales manager: Kensington Publishing Corp., 119 West 40th Street, New York, NY 10018, attn: Special Sales Department; phone 1-800-221-2647.

First trade paperback printing: August 2014

10 9 8 7 6 5 4 3 2 1

ISBN-13: 978-1-61773-116-7
ISBN-10: 1-61773-116-1

First electronic edition: August 2014

ISBN-13: 978-1-61773-117-4
ISBN-10: 1-61773-117-X

1
faith

My closet is a place of secrets.

This is where I change into Her, the girl everybody knows as me. Searching through hanger after hanger of neatly pressed clothes, I find the outfit I'm looking for. A black knee-length pleated skirt, a loose-fitting white top, and two-inch wedge shoes. Looking good at school is a must. Not that I do it for me. It's more for my dad's reputation. I have to play the part.

I am stuffed into a borrowed frame. One that fits too tightly. One that couldn't possibly capture the real me.

"Faith," my stepmom calls. "Are you joining us for breakfast?"

There is no time. "No," I reply, my voice carrying downstairs.

I quickly dress for school, catching my reflection in the closet door mirror. Waking sun shines off my hair, highlighting a few strands brighter than the rest. Everybody has a favorite body part. Mine is my hair, which is the fiery-brown of autumn leaves. My best friend, Melissa, swears my eyes are my best asset. Ivy-green, deep-set, haunting. Like they go on forever.

Speaking of Melissa, her horn blares outside. *Beep,*

beep, pause, *beep*. That's our code. I race downstairs, passing my dad, stepmom, and little sister on the way out.

"Wait," Dad says.

I sigh. "Yes, Dad?"

He glances at my outfit, pausing at my shoes. If it were up to Dad, I would wear turtleneck shirts and dress pants with lace-up boots forever. The perfect ensemble, it seems. As it is, I dress conservatively to protect his image. I'm eighteen. You'd think he'd stop cringing every time he saw me in anything that showed the least bit of skin.

"Hug," he says, waving me over.

I hug him. Place a kiss on my five-year-old sister's jelly-covered cheek. Then, grab a napkin to wipe the sticky jelly from my lips.

"Bye, Gracie," I say to her. "See you after school."

She waves a small hand at me and smiles.

"Take this." Susan, my stepmom, hands me a bagel even though I already declined breakfast. It's poppy seed. I'm allergic to poppy seed.

As usual, I don't put up a fight. My frame feels especially uncomfortable at the moment. It's always the same thing. I learned early on that it's easier to go with the flow than to be different. Different is bad. Standing out attracts attention, something I try to avoid at all costs. Unfortunately, being the dance captain makes that more difficult.

"Have to go," I say, shoving the bagel in my bag.

The screen door swings shut behind me.

Melissa waits in my driveway. We live in a modest, yellow-paneled house in Oviedo, Florida. The majority of the people here are middle class. We fit in well.

"What's up?" Melissa smiles. "Took you long enough."

"Yeah, well, you try waking up late and still looking as good as I do," I joke.

Melissa whips her blond hair into a ponytail and puts her red Camaro in reverse, careful not to hit my Jeep on the way out. I have my own car, but since Melissa lives three doors down, we have a deal where we alternate driving to school. She takes the first month; I take the second, and so on. Saves gas.

"You look smokin'," Melissa says, lighting a cigarette.

I roll my eyes.

"Liar."

She's always hated the way I dress.

Melissa laughs. "Okay, true, the clothes need to go. But your hair and makeup are flawless. And no matter what you wear, you still look beautiful."

"Thanks. You, too," I say, eyeing her tight jeans and sequined top. Melissa is effortlessly beautiful with her sun-freckled face and athletic build.

"Prediction," Melissa begins. This is something we have done since ninth grade: predict three things that will happen during the year. "Tracy Ram will try to overthrow you as dance captain, once again, but you'll keep your spot, of course, 'cause you rock. You'll quit dressing like an eighty-year-old and finally wear what you want to wear instead of what society dictates is appropriate for a pastor's daughter. And you'll come to your senses and dump Jason Magg for a hot new boy."

Melissa always predicts that I'll dump Jason, has done so since Jason and I began dating freshman year. It's not that she doesn't like him. It's just that she thinks my life is too bland, like the taste of celery. What's the point? she figures.

"First of all, I do not dress like the elderly," I say. "And second, I don't know what you have against Jason. He treats me nicely. It's not like he's a jerk."

"It's not like he's exciting, either," Melissa says.

She's right. What I have with Jason is comfortable, nice even, but excitement left a long time ago.

"Prediction," I say, turning to Melissa. "You will not be able to quit bugging me about dumping Jason, even though last year you swore you would. Despite your doubts, you *will* pass senior calculus. And you're going to win homecoming."

Melissa shakes her head. "No way. Homecoming is all you, girl."

I groan. "But I don't want to win."

Melissa laughs. "Tracy Ram would have a heart attack if she ever heard you say that."

"Great," I say. "Let her win homecoming."

We grin. Melissa and I have been friends since kindergarten. Memories come to me suddenly. I'm in elementary school, and it's sleepover night at Melissa's. In my overnight bag, I carry a small stuffed bunny, my steadfast companion since forever. People would laugh if they knew, me carrying around a stuffed baby toy, but Melissa never tells. Fast-forward to middle school. The braces on Melissa's teeth are still so new that the silver catches the light from the fluorescent fixtures when she smiles. The headgear is huge, cumbersome, and no one lets her forget it. But I relentlessly defend my friend. She's so beautiful, can't they see? Sometimes I leave flowers stolen from a neighbor's rosebush at her locker when no one is looking. That way people will know that she is loved. High school. Melissa and me, same as always.

"What do you want to bet?" Melissa asks.

Whoever gets the most predictions right wins.

"Hmm," I say. "If I win, you have to quit smoking."

Melissa almost chokes. "Pulling out the big guns, are we? Okay, then. If I win, you have to break up with Jason."

"Deal," I say, knowing that she won't win. She never does.

Melissa purses her lips and gives me the stink eye. She knows I have a better chance.

"Faith, I will find a way to break you out of your mold," she says.

I laugh, partially because of the determination in my friend's eyes, but mostly because of the absurdity of her statement. Everybody knows that girls like me never break free.

2
diego

"Diego, *vamonos*."

I can't help the frustrated sigh that escapes my lips, hurled at *mi padre*, my dad, like a gust of wind that threatens to flatten our house of cards. It's my fault. I should have built something stronger with the cards I was dealt. But I didn't. I didn't know how.

"Go away," I say. "*Vete*."

I'm not planning to attend school today.

In fact, I didn't plan to be in the States at all.

"*Vamonos*. Let's go," *mi padre* repeats in his heavily accented voice, yanking me off of the couch. "You will not miss senior year."

He has this new thing where we have to speak English as much as possible now that we live in the States. I almost wish I weren't fluent. Several summers in Florida, and I am.

With a grimace, I pass him, reluctantly moving toward my room. It feels like my feet are sinking, like I'm walking over sticky sand instead of thick, dirty carpet.

How did I get stuck in this place?

I open my dresser drawer and pull out faded jeans, a white T-shirt, and my Smith & Wesson.

"No," *mi padre* says, grabbing the gun.

I take a step toward him, challenging. He does not back down.

"This is why we left," he says.

Hypocrite. Under his bed is a similar gun, waiting. Just in case. But he's also the one who taught me how to fight. I'm bigger than he is, but he has more experience. And the scars to prove it.

Not that I haven't been in countless fights myself.

"Fine," I say through clenched teeth, and turn toward the bathroom.

The hot water heater goes out after five minutes. The tiny two-bedroom apartment—this hole we now call home—is the only thing *mi padre* could afford. It's not much, but it's inexpensive. That's all that matters. The plain white walls remind me of an asylum. Feels like I'm going crazy already.

Our jobs keep us afloat. They're our life vests, our only chance of survival in a sea of ravenous sharks. *Mi padre* found a job with a lawn crew a couple of weeks ago. Not many people would hire him with his scarred face and tattooed body. A restaurant offered me work part-time. Two shifts as a cook, one as a busboy. They promised a free meal every night that I worked. Couldn't pass that up.

"Don't be late for school or work," *mi padre* says as I step out of the house.

School's only ten minutes away. I walk, staring at the graffiti-covered sidewalk that stretches in front of me like a ribbed canvas. Latinos roam the block. It didn't take moving to the States for me to know that's how it is. The *gringos*, white people, live in nice houses and drive cars to school while the rest of the world waits for a piece of their leftovers. I'm trying not to think about how screwed up it all is when a Latina walks up to me.

"*Hola*," she says. "*¿Hablas inglés?*"

"Yeah, I speak English," I answer, though I'm not sure why she asks since both of us speak Spanish.

"I'm Lola." She smiles, sexy brown eyes big and wide. She reminds me of a girl I knew back home. Just the thought, the image of home, makes my guts clench.

"What's your name?" she purrs.

"Lola," a Latino calls from across the street. She ignores him. He calls again. When she doesn't come, he approaches us.

One look tells me he's angry. He has a cocky stance and a shaved head.

"Am I interrupting something?" he snaps.

What's this guy's problem?

"Yep," Lola says, turning her back on him. "My ex," she explains, brushing a strand of curly hair out of her face.

Perfecto. Just what I need. I didn't even do anything. Not that I'm going to explain.

"She's mine," the guy says, staring me down. "*¿Entiendes, amigo?*"

"I'm not your friend," I say, gritting my teeth. "And you do not want to mess with me."

Lola is smiling. I wonder if she enjoys the attention. Probably. I've met too many girls like her. She fits the type.

"You don't know who *you're* messing with," he says, stepping closer.

A few guys come out of nowhere, closing in on me. Blue and white bandannas hang from their pockets like a bad-luck charm. I know what the colors signify. Mara Salvatrucha 13 Gang, or MS-13.

I turn to Lola. Watch her smile.

This is all part of the game. What I can't figure out is if the guy really is her ex and she doesn't care that she could be getting me killed, or if he sent her to see how tough I am, to help decide whether he wants to recruit me.

I turn to walk away, but someone blocks my path.

"Going somewhere?" another gangbanger asks.

This whole time I wondered if I'd end up fighting at school. I hadn't thought about the fact that I might never make it there in the first place. I silently curse *mi padre* for hiding my gun. He wouldn't get rid of it completely, though.

"What do you want?" I ask.

The original guy laughs, looks me up and down. The number 67 is tattooed behind his right ear in bold black numbers. It only takes me a second to figure out the meaning. Six plus seven equals thirteen.

"What are those markings?" he asks, eyeing my tattoos.

"Nothing," I lie.

If they wanted to fight me, they would've done it already. This is a recruit.

"Where you from?" he asks.

I don't answer. Members of MS-13 stretch around the globe like fingers. They can easily check my past. I'm not gonna give them a head start.

"Swallow your tongue?" one of the guys asks.

I'm trying to figure out if I can win a fight against the five guys who surround me. I look for weak spots, scars, old injuries. I look for bulges that might be weapons. I'm a good fighter. I think I can take them. But at the same time, fighting will guarantee me a follow-up visit from MS-13.

Just then, someone speaks behind us. "Is there a problem?" a police officer asks from the safety of his car.

Everyone backs away from me.

"Nope," one of the gangbangers answers. "We were just leaving."

"See you around," 67 says, throwing an arm around Lola.

I turn my back and walk the last block to school. The police officer trails slowly behind, like a hungry dog sniffing for scraps. He leaves as I enter the double doors.

I think about what my dad said. *Moving here will give you a brighter future.*

His words sit heavily on my mind, like humidity on every pore of my skin. His intentions are good, but he's wrong. So far, moving here has done nothing but remind me of my past.

3
faith

"Hi, I'm Faith Watters."

Those are the first words I speak to the new Cuban guy in the front office. He grimaces. He'll be a tough one. I can handle it, though. He's not the first.

I can't help but notice that he looks a lot like a model from the neck up—eyes the color of oak, strong bone structure. Everywhere else, he looks a lot like a criminal. Chiseled, scarred body . . . I wonder for a second about the meaning behind the tattoos scratched into his arms.

One thing's clear. He's dangerous.

And he's beautiful.

"I'll show you to your classes," I announce.

I'm one of the peer helpers at our school. It's not my favorite thing to do, but it counts as a class. Basically I spend the first two days with new students, introducing them around and answering their questions. Some parents with kids new to the school voluntarily sign their kids up, but it's only mandatory for the international students, of which we have a lot. Mostly Latinos.

This Cuban guy towers over me. I'm five-six. Not tall. Not short. Just average. Average is good.

This guy's not average. Not even a little bit. He must be over six feet.

I glance up at him, kind of like I do when I'm searching for the moon in a sea of darkness.

"Looks like you have math first. I'll walk you there," I offer.

"No thanks, *chica*. I can handle it."

"It's no problem," I say, leading the way.

He tries to snatch his schedule from my hands, but I move too fast.

"Why don't we start with your name?" I suggest.

I already know his name. Plus some. Diego Alvarez. Eighteen years old. Moved from Cuba two weeks ago. Only child. No previous school records. I read it in his bio. I want to hear him say it.

"You got some kinda control issues or somethin'?" he asks harshly, voice slightly accented.

"You got some kind of social issues or somethin'?" I fire back, holding my stance. I won't let him intimidate me, though I'll admit, he's hot. Too bad he has a nasty attitude.

The side of his lip twitches. "No. I just don't mix with your type," he answers.

"My type?"

"That's what I said."

"You don't even know my type." No one does. Well, except Melissa.

He chuckles humorlessly. "Sure I do. Head cheerleader? Date the football player? Daddy's little girl who gets everything she wants?" He leans closer to whisper. "Probably a virgin."

My cheeks burn hot. "I'm not a cheerleader," I say through clamped teeth.

"Whatever," he says. "Are you gonna give me my schedule or not?"

"Not," I answer. "But you can feel free to follow me to your first class."

He steps in front of me, intimately close. "Listen, *chica*, nobody tells me what to do."

I shrug. "Fine, suit yourself. It's your life. But if you want to attend this school, it's mandatory for me to show you to your classes for two days."

His eyes narrow. "Who says I want to attend this school?"

I take the last step toward him, closing the gap between us. When we were little, Melissa and I used to collect glass bottles. Whenever we accumulated twenty, we'd break them on the concrete. When the glass shattered, the slivered pieces made a breathtaking prism of light.

I cut myself on the glass by accident once. It was painful, but worth it. The beauty was worth it. It's funny how the bottle was never as beautiful as when it was broken.

You will not shatter me, I silently tell Diego. *Somebody already did.*

"If you don't want to be here, then don't come back," I say.

A taunting smile spreads across his face. My first thought is that he has nice teeth, but then I scold myself for thinking about him like that.

"My name is Diego," he says, like he's letting me in on some kind of secret.

"Well, Diego," I say, "better hurry. Class starts in two minutes." I step around him to lead the way.

While we walk to math, I feel Diego's eyes on me. I don't know what it is about him. All the other confident students had nothing on me, and I swear I've heard it all, but he seems different. He shines. In a dark way. When he looks at me, I get a tingly sensation, like I'm being zapped by electricity.

It doesn't matter. He's rude. And besides, I have a wonderful boyfriend. Jason. Think about Jason.

"Quit staring at me," I say, glancing at him.

He laughs, and strands of black hair fall into his eyes. I imagine it's a little like looking at the world through charred silk.

"Why? Does it make you uncomfortable?"

He's messing with me to get under my skin, like a pesky little splinter.

It's working.

"Yes," I answer.

In his white shirt, Diego's skin is dark. Perpetually tanned by heritage.

I keep Diego's schedule out of his reach. He inches closer, no doubt to grab it and run. I try to concentrate on the newly painted beige walls and tiled floors. Every few feet hangs a plaque about achievement or school clubs or tutoring programs.

When we come to the door, Diego rests an arm on the wall and leans toward me.

"I have a proposition for you," he says in a sultry voice.

It's hard to seem unaffected.

"I don't do propositions," I say dismissively.

He grins, his mouth arching up like the curl of a wave.

"But you haven't even heard me out," he says.

"Don't need to."

He ignores my comment. "What do you say we forget about this thing where I follow you around like a little dog? And when the guidance counselor asks, I will say you were superlative."

"Big word," I mumble. This guy did not do well on his entry exams, but he says things like *superlative*? What's with that?

He glares at me; I sigh.

"You know, it wouldn't kill you to drop the tough-guy act for two days. You'll be rid of me soon."

I turn to leave but Diego grabs my arm gently. My breath catches.

"It's not an act," he says, jaw hard.

I wave him away nonchalantly, like his touch didn't just do all kinds of crazy things to my body—things that make me want to forget about the warning blaring in my mind.

I need to stay away from him.

I need to forget him.

Will you touch me again please?

I walk away. He watches me go.

"By the way," I say as I flick a look over my shoulder at his hardened face, "I see right through you."

4
diego

She sees right through me? What does that mean? I wonder for the twentieth time as I enter the cafeteria. I managed to avoid my peer helper after my first few classes, rushing out before she could meet me. Did she really think I couldn't get another class schedule? Maybe next time she won't underestimate me.

A sweet smell hits my nostrils as I pass the fruit section. It smells like my peer helper, and I'm reminded of my disgust for her. She thinks she knows me, but she knows nothing. She's a snob, trying to prove something. They're all the same.

Girls like her don't know what it's like to struggle, really struggle.

She's probably never gone so hungry her stomach knots. Never roamed the streets wondering if she'll have a safe place to sleep. With a face and body like hers, she's probably never had to work for anything in her life. The people she represents, the life she lives, it's all fake.

Javier, my cousin, warned me about her. She's one of the Big Five, the ones who think they rule this school. Even with her perfect boyfriend and flawless life, she isn't fooling me.

I hear Javier before I see him. "Diego, *aquí.*"

Through the crowd, I spot my cousin sitting with a group of Latinos. With his six-foot, two-hundred-pound frame, he's hard to miss. I approach him. One of his friends mumbles something in Spanish about how tall I am.

"Hey, what can I say? They make 'em big in *mi familia*," Javier says, laughing.

Truth backhands me. I realize now that I never actually thought I would see Javier again. After . . . after . . . no. I shove the thoughts away. Not here.

Not here.

"What's up, cuz?" Javier says.

"*Nada.*" I force a smile, though my relief is real. It's good to see family.

"*¡Siéntate!*" Javier says.

I sit. Sitting is usually an indulgence for those who can afford to relax. I pretend for a moment that I'm one of them. My cousin takes a minute to introduce his friends.

"Diego, this is Ramon, Esteban, Juan, Rodolfo, and Luis."

Ramon and Esteban, with their slight overbites and similar features, must be brothers. Juan has a large head for his small frame; he's covered in tattoos. Rodolfo has a smile full of white teeth and a dimple on the left side of his cheek. What happened to the other dimple? It's as though God had an asymmetrical look in mind when He created him. Next to my cousin, Luis is the biggest. He has lots of freckles, splattered on his face like paint, seeping into his skin.

"Welcome to *los Estados Unidos*," Juan says, biting into his burger.

"*Gracias,*" I reply.

My stomach growls, an animal hungry to live. Javier notices.

"Come with me." He motions for me to follow him through the crowd.

As we walk to the lunch line, I spot my peer helper at a table, surrounded by her friends. There's one of her kind at every school. The girl everyone hates to love and loves to hate. She's probably been stabbed in the back countless times. Not that she would know, since everyone acts fake to her face. Her friends remind me of worker bees, buzzing for the queen's attention. I wonder if she knows that the workers eventually kill the queen.

"When you get to the front, show them your student ID," Javier says.

The guidance counselor already explained that I get one free lunch a day because of our low income. As we pass the food selections, I cannot believe the prices.

"Are they for real?" I ask. "Six dollars for chicken and fries?"

I have an image of Faith Watters taking out her designer wallet and easily paying for one of the pretentious lunches.

"Yep. *Gringos*," Javier says, eyes hardening. He remembers what it was like in Cuba, the struggle.

Just by looking at the lunchroom crowd, it's clear who the haves and have-nots are. Surprisingly, though, there are more Latinos than I expected.

I grab a burger and make my way to the register. As I pull out my ID, football players in letterman jackets glance my way. Part of me wishes I had it easy like them: popular, at ease, able to pay for things.

I shouldn't want to be like them.

I don't want to be like them.

Yes, I do.

Some days.

The bigger part of me knows that a life like that will never happen for someone like me. It's just the way things are.

I grab a water bottle and head back to the table with Javier. Do people here know that most of the world doesn't get water from a bottle, but from a stream or river or muddy ground?

"So, you fittin' in well?" Javier asks.

"Yep." For the most part. No one has singled me out for being new.

"Latinos blend around here. One of the good things about Florida," he says.

We pass a beautiful girl on the way back to our seat. I take a moment to look. She smiles.

"That's Isabella," Javier explains. "Sexy, but taken."

"Too bad," I say.

I'm not looking for a girlfriend, but it would be nice to have a little fun. I'm almost at the table when someone steps in front of me.

"What's your problem?" my peer helper asks, one of her friends in tow.

Momentarily shocked by her boldness, I quickly regain my hard stance. Just like earlier, she doesn't seem fazed by me. She's either tougher than I thought, or she puts on a great front.

"I don't know what you mean," I reply. I try to feign confusion, but a smile creeps through.

"Oh, you think this is funny?" she asks, hands on her hips. For a second, she looks kind of beautiful, eyes hard and old. Wisps of hair fall out of her ponytail and around her face like angel feathers.

"A little." I grin.

She huffs. "You weren't there to meet me after your classes this morning. If I report you, you could lose your chance to attend this school."

Is she threatening me? "Like I said, I already have a *mamá*. I don't answer to you."

I hand my tray to Javier. He sets it on the table so I can deal with her.

"You're being difficult," she says.

"So are you."

What is your weakness? is what I want to ask.

She doesn't back down. "I'll be there *before* the end of your next class. Don't even think about ditching me again."

I have to, don't you see?

"I'm serious," she says.

This girl is asking for it. I glance at her blond friend, who's eyeing Javier, not paying us any attention. I wish my peer helper was as easily distracted.

Being tough does not scare Faith Watters. Time to change tactics. I relax and flash a grin.

"*Mami*, why don't I help you loosen up a little?"

She blinks, but doesn't show any outward evidence that my words have affected her. I move close, very close. When I look down at her, she doesn't look away.

Her eyes remind me of stained glass, bright and cutting.

"We could have a good time, you and me," I say, mischief punctuating my voice.

"I don't think so," she says coldly.

I will not let her upstage me. I give her a long, slow once-over. She dresses older than she is, like she doesn't belong in high school. I wonder what makes her so uptight.

What are you hiding, chica?

I usually don't have to try with girls. It's one of the very few advantages life has thrown my way.

"Oh, come on. You might like Latino if you tried it," I say, voice low. The guys behind me laugh, egging me on.

"When you're done with him, I'm available, *mamacita,*" Juan says. "I don't mind leftovers."

She sneers. Good. That's progress.

"Let me take you out," I say.

I'm not really going to take her anywhere. I just want to make a crack in her icy shield.

Why do you have a shield, anyway?

"Why?" she asks suspiciously.

Because I know it annoys you when someone else has control. "Because it would be fun," I say, bending close to her face. "And I can promise you one thing."

She looks cautious.

It's a look I know well.

"What?" she asks.

That one night with me will relax you.

Girls like her love bad boys, whether they admit it or not. I imagine it's similar to visiting a haunted mansion. Exciting, at first. One foot slips through the door, then the next. Heart hammers. Blood races. It's a rush. A fix. Never knowing what's around the next corner, through the closed door, beyond the shadows. Trying to find a way out. Not really wanting to leave. Wondering how close a person can come to danger before something bad happens. Looking for the moonlight at the end of the tunnel, an exit.

Sometimes there is no light at the end of the tunnel.

I can show her excitement like she'll never experience with that perfect boyfriend of hers.

But I don't say any of those things. Instead I let my lips brush her earlobe as I answer.

"That you will leave satisfied."

5

faith

As he pulls away, I can still feel the heat of Diego on my ear, fogging my mind. The tingle it leaves behind electrifies my body. It's only air, but it came from his lungs. *Stop sharing pieces of you*, I wish I could say.

"I have a boyfriend," I say instead. "But even if I didn't, I wouldn't give you the time of day."

He laughs. "Oh yeah. Why is that?"

"Because," I say, standing on tiptoes to reach his ear. "I don't date Mexicans," I whisper.

It's a total lie. I would date a Mexican if he treated me nicely. True, it might be a little hard to date someone outside of my culture because of the social pressures and expectations on me. But being Mexican is not a reason for me to turn someone down. I only say it to anger Diego, knowing he's Cuban, not Mexican.

"Lucky for you, *princesa*, I'm Cuban," he says smoothly, seductively.

"I know." I wink, one eye closing like the shutter of a camera.

A mental picture for later.

I don't know what's gotten into me. Something about this boy excites and aggravates me. Now he falters, realizing I'm not someone to push around. Two can play this game.

"Well, if you change your mind, let me know," he says, trying to save face.

I've embarrassed him in front of his *amigos*. Somehow I know I'll pay for it later, but for now I'm enjoying his reaction.

"Doubtful," I say, and walk away.

Even with my back to him, I know he's watching.

Melissa looks at me, wide-eyed. "What was that?"

"Nothing." I brush her off.

"That was not nothing!"

"Really, it's no big deal. Just some guy who thinks he can intimidate people with flirty arrogance," I explain.

A smile splits Melissa's face. "Wow," she says.

"What?"

Melissa looks directly at me, deep in my eyes, matching my every step.

"I'm winning," she says.

"Winning?" I ask.

" 'Flirty arrogance'?" Melissa repeats. "Do you hear yourself? I'm winning Prediction. You like him."

"Do not."

"Bye-bye, Jason," Melissa says in a singsong voice.

"Would you be quiet? Someone might hear you."

She giggles. "Come on, Faith. I *know* you. Better than you know yourself."

We're almost at the table. Jason's face is marred by concern.

"Admit it," Melissa says, finally turning around.

"Everything all right?" Jason asks.

"Yes," I answer.

"Was he giving you trouble? Faith, honestly, I don't see

why you even bother with the whole international-peer-helper thing. Half the kids end up dropping out anyway," Jason says.

"I bother," I say, trying to sound sweet, "because even if it only makes a difference in one person's life, it's worth it." And I hate it when someone is singled out because of race or ethnicity, but I don't say that to Jason.

Melissa moves closer so only I can hear her next words. "Or maybe it's because of the sexy new guy."

I blush, rose velvet caressing my skin. The color of shame.

The color of passion.

"Admit it," she whispers.

No way. I do not like Diego.

You can't fool yourself.

I can try.

To prove it, I bend over Jason and give him a long, intense kiss.

"Mmm," Jason says as we pull apart. "That's what I'm talking about."

He kisses me again. Our table watches. I never show this much PDA.

I lean back. Smile. Try to forget about Diego. Jason's brown eyes stare back at me. I wind my arms around his shoulders. Run a finger through his messy blond hair.

Sean, one of the guys at our table, clears his throat. "So, we're all thinking of going to Applebee's tonight. You game?" he asks us.

"Definitely," Jason says, and then turns to me. "If that's all right with you."

"Sure," I answer. Jason always runs stuff by me. I like that he's considerate.

Sean rubs a hand across his day's worth of blond stubble, which matches his short hair, waiting for Melissa's response. Everybody knows that Sean's been obsessed with Melissa since sophomore year. She agrees to come. So do two others.

While they carry on a conversation about dance practice tonight and our upcoming competition, I sneak a look across the lunchroom. I don't know what makes me do it. For some reason, I need to know that Diego sees me.

Maybe it's because I recognize a little of myself in him, or rather, I recognize who I would be if I didn't have to live up to other people's standards. His carelessness sparks something within me, stubborn embers that lately I've tried so hard to smother, to block out. Trying to forget the past.

But it's hard to be someone you're not.

From the other side of the room, Diego grins at me.

One hand is holding his water bottle.

The other is flipping me off.

6
diego

Faith Watters is looking at me from across the lunchroom, her stare like cold fingers trying to touch me, to freeze me in the moment, to curl around my heart. Perhaps even break it.

Keep your eyes to yourself, I mentally say.

Who does she think she is? Blowing me off. And then she has the nerve to walk back to her table and make out with her boyfriend like she's better than everyone else. Fine. She wants a reaction? Here.

I flip her off.

She turns back around. Her body speaks one language; her eyes another.

Can she translate for both?

"Come on, man," Javier says, diverting my attention. "Don't worry about her."

"I'm not worried. I just wish she'd mind her own business," I say.

"She makes this school and everyone in it her business," Javier replies. "That is never goin' to change. And what are you thinkin', asking her out? She'll sic her *novio* and the rest of the football team on you."

I cross my arms. "Let her."

I've been looking for an excuse to fight. I know I shouldn't, but I've had too much on my mind lately. I never expected to leave Cuba. Now I attend a school with overpriced food and girls who think the sun rises and sets on their perfect hair.

Javier changes the subject. "How's your dad?"

"Good," I say.

His eyes say he wants to ask more but he knows this isn't the place. There's a whisper of knowledge there, knowledge like a virus. If it were to get out, it would contaminate everything.

No one, besides Javier's family and *mi padre*, knows my secret, my days with the cartel. I'm not proud of it, but in Cuba a drug cartel means protection from the streets, protection you can't maintain on your own. A family of sorts, like a viper for a best friend.

I'm not sorry. I lived the life that kept me alive, however dangerous it would one day become. In my hometown, all it takes is one moment, one mistake, and the cost is your life.

Now I live in America, where people can dream about their futures like every day isn't a fight to stay alive.

"*Mi mamá* wants you guys to come over tonight," Javier says. "She's cookin'."

I miss Aunt Ria's cooking. My mouth awakens at the thought.

"Can't," I say. "Have to work." I eat my overdone burger, thinking it tastes a little like dirt.

"What about Wednesday?" Javier asks.

"Sure."

Someone drops a tray near me. I snap around, ready to fight. I can't help it. Side effect of years in a cartel. I'm in constant survival mode.

"Just a tray," Javier says, locking eyes with me.

I can never be too careful. I've had many enemies. Still do.

Luis laughs. "Jumpy 'cause it's your first day, huh?"

Javier and I know that's not why I'm jumpy. Not even close.

"Must be it," I reply.

I remain on guard until my meal is done. When lunch ends, I walk to fourth period. History. The class is beyond boring. From the first minute, I have a hard time concentrating, my thoughts wandering to someplace else. I'm used to being on the go, constantly on my toes. It's hard to sit still.

People were not meant to be boxed in.

The moment the bell rings, I'm out the door. And wouldn't you know it, Little Miss Faith Watters is waiting for me. I don't understand why she hasn't given up. Doesn't she see that she's not wanted? Her presence is irritating, jute against my skin.

"Still here?" I ask.

Maybe Faith Watters likes to make it known that she's in control at this school by having students follow her around; worse yet, maybe she actually thinks she can make a difference. She must not know that people like me will always be dealt the lesser hand.

I've tried living by the rules. It got me nowhere except dirt poor and starving, begging for work, a vulture happy for scraps.

Without a word, my peer helper turns and cuts through the crowded hallway, leaving a narrow path for me to follow in her wake.

I consider leaving, never coming back to this school, but *mi padre* would kill me. So I reluctantly follow her to my next class, and the one after that, and the one after that.

When school ends, I walk to the city bus stop and catch

a bus into town. The rough seat smells like sweat and metal, the threads stretched to the max, like my sanity.

It takes fifteen minutes and three dollars to get to work. In the restaurant, a girl with platinum hair, a green polo shirt, and khaki pants greets me with a huge smile.

"Welcome to—"

I cut her off. "I'm here to see Bennie."

Bennie is my new boss. He seems pretty cool. So far.

The girl walks away and returns with the manager. Bennie is a young guy, maybe thirty, with brown hair and a goatee.

"Hey, man," Bennie says with a smile. "Follow me."

I walk with him to the back of the restaurant, where he digs in his pockets and pulls out a key. Unlocks the office door, waves me in. It smells like dust, and is barely big enough to fit ten people shoulder to shoulder.

It's bigger than my room in Cuba. It's bigger than some people's houses in Cuba.

Bennie shuffles through a box on the ground. "What size do you wear?" he asks.

"Large," I answer.

He pulls out a shirt with the company logo on the left side.

"Here."

I put it on. Attached to one of Bennie's ears is an earpiece. He hands me one, as well.

Electronics are a luxury for most.

I can't help my way of thinking. My body abandoned my mind in Cuba. I can't get used to this place. I don't want to get used to this place.

"You'll be bussing tables today. Whenever you finish a table, you press this"—he points to a little red button—"and tell the hostess it's clean so she can seat more people."

We leave the office and Bennie shows me the proper way to sanitize tables and where things go, like the ketchup and salt and pepper. There's an order to everything.

Since learning how to clean a table doesn't take me long, Bennie leads me to the kitchen. He gives me a tour: the cooler, the break room, the cooking line, the place they call The Box, a small five-by-eight armed metal fence around the back door. It protects the place from being robbed, and the workers sit back there on their smoke breaks.

Next, we move to the prep line, where Bennie shows me how to cut veggies and portion side dishes. He has me work on that until six o'clock, when the restaurant fills with people. My boss hands me a small black tub for the dirty dishes, a towel, and a spray bottle. Tells me to go up front.

I feel ridiculous, and a little like someone's butler, as I clean tables in front of people eating around me.

Back home, I would make double the money and be subject to fewer curious eyes. But that was dirty money. It feels surprisingly good to know that my paycheck will come from honest work.

My eyes are pressed down by the weight of the bright lights that hang above every table, a sliver of electricity for their viewing pleasure.

In between cleaning tables, I go to the back for a drink. Attached to the soda fountain are tiny triangle paper cups that look like they belong on the bottom of an ice-cream cone. I reach for a glass mug but someone stops me.

"I wouldn't do that, if I were you," says the blond hostess. She smiles. Steps closer. Wafts me with her cherry perfume.

"Why not?" I ask.

She tilts her head toward Bennie. "Manager's rule. We're only allowed the small ones. They're refillable, though. Saves them money."

They're worried about mugs when there are a hundred lights, two fryers, two grills, two flattops? And zero consciousness.

I have a hundred emotions, two regrets, two eyes to see zero hope.

"Seriously?" I ask.

"Yep," she says, grabbing a paper cup for me. "Which one?"

"Coke," I say.

She fills the cone. Twirls the tip between her fingers. It's the same motion I use when rolling bullets before loading a gun.

"I'm Sabrina." She smiles. I think maybe she's flirting with me.

"Diego," I say, taking the cone. The thing holds about one sip.

"Your accent is nice. Where you from, Diego?" Sabrina asks.

"Cuba."

"Mmm," she says, smacking her glossed lips together. For a moment, I wonder what it would be like to kiss a white girl. I can see down her shirt, which she leaves unbuttoned at the top.

"Sabrina!" Bennie yells across the noise of the kitchen. "If you're in here, who's watching the front?"

"Later," Sabrina says, and walks away.

A guy in an apron approaches the soda fountain. "Be careful around that one," he says. He looks my age. Judging by the chef's hat, I guess he's a cook.

"Manuel," the guy says, sticking out his hand. I do not shake many hands. Mostly, I break them.

"Diego." I meet his grasp.

"Looks like Sabrina has her eye on you. She has a thing for Latinos, my friend," Manuel says.

"Familiarity talking?" I ask.

"No. I have a girl. But the other guys say she's fun."

Sabrina's pretty, but I'm not sure I'm interested.

"Thanks for the heads-up," I say.

When I hear Sabrina's voice in the earpiece, calling out another dirty table, I make my way to the front. *One restaurant, one job, one breath at a time.*

While I'm cleaning the table, someone walks behind me. Bumps me. I drop a dish. It shatters. Loudly.

Everyone is staring. So many eyes. Glued to me. I want to peel them away.

"Oops. I'm so sorry," someone says.

I turn to the sound of the voice.

No way.

It's Faith Watters.

7
faith

Diego curses at me and bends to pick up shards of glass.

A million shards of glass splintering, a thousand emotions.

I look at him, the broken dish, him again.

"Sorry," I mumble, and crouch down to help. I didn't mean to bump him. It was an accident.

"What are you doing?" Diego hisses.

I realize how close we are, only inches apart. People are staring.

"Helping," I answer. "What does it look like?"

"You've done enough already," he says.

I put on my game face, like I'm not bothered by the people staring, or by him. I carefully grab broken pieces and place them in the tub next to him.

"Please stop," Diego says.

Pause.

He said please. So. He actually has manners under that armor plating.

"Faith." Jason's voice, saying my name, the sound familiar, like a fuzzy blanket I might have outgrown. He holds out a hand. "Come on, babe. Let him finish cleaning."

I ignore my boyfriend and continue to help Diego. It was my fault the plate broke. Therefore, I will clean it up.

"You should listen to your little boyfriend," Diego says.

"Little?" Jason says, stepping up to Diego.

Diego stands. They're the same size. Big. Liable to cause a scene if anything gets out of hand.

"That's what I said," Diego fires back.

Suddenly, Sean and Rob, two of Jason's football buddies, are beside him. I stand and push a hand against Jason's chest.

"Lay off," I warn. He's mad. It doesn't look like he'll back down. "Please," I add, stepping closer to my boyfriend.

My leg brushes his. I press up against him and trail a finger down his neck. It distracts him.

"I'll meet you at the table in a sec," I say.

Jason leans down and kisses me. His mind is somewhere else now, content in the false reality I've created. I wait until he's seated to turn back to Diego.

Diego stares at me with angry eyes. "Figures," he says.

I ignore him and grab the last remaining broken pieces, contributing to an unfinished mosaic lining the dirty bottom of the tub.

"What's your problem, Faith?" Diego asks.

It feels weird to hear him say my name. I try not to like the way it sounds.

"I don't understand you," he says. "I try to get you to leave me alone, you don't listen. I ask nicely, you still don't listen. What's it gonna take?"

Tomorrow is my last day escorting Diego.

"One more day," I say. "That's all it's going to take."

I'm holding another broken piece when a guy with an earpiece approaches us.

"What's going on here?" he asks.

"Nothing, Bennie," Diego says. "Just a broken plate."

Bennie notices the glass I'm holding.

"Oh goodness. What are you doing?" Bennie asks.

"Helping," I say. What's the big deal?

"You can't do that," he says. "Please put that down. Have you been cut? Does anything hurt?"

"No," I reply.

He turns to Diego. "How could you make her help you?"

"He didn't make me. I offered," I say, putting down the glass.

"This is unacceptable," Bennie hisses to Diego. "Guests cannot help you clean. What were you thinking?"

"I offered," I say again. "He didn't make me do anything."

Bennie treats me as though I'm invisible. I almost wish I were.

"We'll talk about this later," he says to Diego and walks away.

The muscles in Diego's jaw are constricted, like guitar strings strung too tightly.

"Happy now?" he says. "My first day on the job and I am already in trouble."

The blond hostess walks up and trails a hand across Diego's arm, batting her eyelashes, a clump of dark spider legs reaching for her brows.

"Diego, sweetie, are you all right?" she asks.

Her hand moves up his shoulder, down his chest. I can't watch.

Someone make it stop.

"Looks like your first day on the job isn't going as bad as you say," I mumble.

Diego's eyes narrow but I don't wait for his response. I walk back to the table to join my friends.

"What the hell, Watters?" Sean says. "Are you trying to get us kicked out? I mean, don't get me wrong, we'll fight for you, but he doesn't seem worth it."

I don't correct him. Don't say it was actually Jason who stepped up to Diego.

Instead, I quickly glance behind me. Diego is gone.

"Want some *queso*?" Rachel offers, her hair red like smeared raspberries, her face crowded with freckles. Also on the dance team, she dates Rob, who's sitting beside her, his blue hat pulled tight around his fringe of black hair. When he smiles, you almost don't notice the bump in his nose, left over from a hard hit during a football game last year. Broken once, bent forever.

"Sure, I'll have some," I say, dipping a tortilla chip into the cheese, a gooey glob of melting wax. On second thought, I put the chip down. I'm not that hungry.

I glance at Melissa. She's looking right at me, grinning.

"So, anyway," Rachel says, "we were just talking about dance practice."

Rachel has a way of keeping conversation light, fun. I'm grateful for her presence.

"Can you believe how Tracy Ram challenged you?" Rachel says. "It's like she automatically vetoes everything you say just for the heck of it, no matter how great your suggestions are. Thank goodness Coach overruled her. That move was hot."

"You know what else is hot?" Melissa says, eyebrows dancing in mischief.

"Shut up," I warn under my breath. Melissa is sitting close enough to hear. Unfortunately, so is Jason. He gives me a weird look. Melissa ignores me.

"That new boy, Diego," Melissa says.

Sean cringes. Poor guy. He needs to let it go. It's never going to happen.

"You serious?" Jason asks. "The guy back there with the tattoos and scars?"

"Don't forget the hot bod and sexy grin," Melissa says. She's the only one in our group who could get away with something like this. People expect it from her—crazy, wild Melissa. If I said it? Watch out.

"You're weird, Lissa," Rachel says. "Is it just me who doesn't see it? Help me out here, Faith."

My tongue suddenly feels thick, an extra coating of syrupy spinelessness.

"What?" I say. She wants me to tell her whether I think Diego is hot?

"Sexy or not sexy?" Rachel clarifies.

"Come on," Sean complains. "No one wants to hear you girls talk about hot guys. Unless, of course, those hot guys happen to be us."

"Let her answer," Melissa says.

Sean backs off, a dog with his tail tucked between his legs.

All eyes are on me.

"I, um, we don't need to talk about this." I cannot possibly answer that question. If I lie, Melissa will know. I hate lying to my best friend. But if I tell the truth, Jason will get angry.

Melissa answers for me. "Of course Faith doesn't think Diego is cute. She's Faith Watters. Stays on the straight and narrow. Dates reputable guys—" She pauses to wink at Jason so he doesn't see the mockery in her statement.

"She'd never even think twice about someone of Diego's social standing."

I'm livid, my anger like hot lava, bubbling beneath the surface. And Melissa knows it.

"Fine," I say. "You want an answer?"

"Oh no, honey. We already know the answer. It's predictable," Melissa says sweetly, but I hear her I-dare-you-to-say-it undertone.

I don't notice that I am talking loudly. I'm too angry to care. "Diego Alvarez *is* hot!" I say.

Behind me, a spoon clanks to the floor. I automatically turn to look. Diego is cleaning a booth two spots away. He's reaching for the tumbled spoon.

My lungs tighten. Fear is a boa constrictor, squeezing, terminating my air supply.

Diego continues cleaning the table, acting oblivious. And I almost believe him.

If it weren't for his knowing grin.

When I get home that evening, my dad is waiting for me. Always waiting.

I wish he would stop.

I love him for caring.

I am two people living in one body. Constant turmoil. There's not enough space for both of us.

I wonder about rubber bands. Always stretching to fit situations. Always shrinking back down to size. Versatile, able to accommodate every need. Flexible. Wrapping around everything, holding it in place. Saving it from all falling to pieces.

I'm a rubber band, but I stretched too far. I broke.

I cannot save us anymore.

I cannot even save myself.

"I was about to call you," Dad says. It's almost seven o'clock. Time for Awana, a program at church where parents drop off their kids to learn Bible verses and songs. The children are split into groups and sorted by age. I'm a helper in Grace's room.

"Let's go," Dad says. "Can't be late."

My family piles into Dad's SUV. We only live five minutes from church, which can be good and bad. Good, because I can procrastinate until the last minute, like tonight, and not be late. Bad, because a lot of church people take that as an invitation to stop by unannounced. It's not that I don't like the church people—some of them go to my school and are really nice. It's just that I often feel out of place with them. Like a black sheep in a flock of white.

Certainly you see my stains.

Or are you truly blind?

Sure, I've read the Bible from beginning to end. And yeah, I know key verses. I even bow my head at the right moments for prayer. But on the inside, I'm different. I have secrets. A dark past.

Everyone sees me as they want to see me, the pastor's daughter who comes to church every week and says the right things. They miss who I really am.

I am a liar.

If any of them bothered to dig a little deeper, maybe they would uncover the truth.

Jason's parents go to our church, as do a few of my friends' parents. His mom loves me, wants me to be with her son. She's not the only one. It feels like an arranged marriage, as though it's already been determined that

Faith Watters will be with Jason Magg forever. It's what everyone expects, and they don't like to be disappointed.

Sometimes I wish Dad weren't a pastor. Maybe then things would be easier. Maybe then Mom wouldn't have felt so much pressure to be perfect. When she realized that she'd never live up to the church's impossible standards, she snapped like a twig under the weight of the church's body. Now I have to be everything she is not. Poor Faith. Can't turn out like her wayward mother. That would be a disgrace.

The church would look down on me if they knew the real reason I was gone last year. So they will never know. Just like so many other things in my life.

We pull up to the church and I enter Grace's room of five-year-olds. I inhale stale, dead oxygen. The same oxygen my mother breathed, once upon a time. I wish I had no memories.

But I need the memories.

They remind me.

Jason's mom, Trish, is already there. Of course she is. The woman has never been late to anything. Today she's dressed in a floral number, her graying hair pinned behind one ear.

"Hey, sweetheart," she says, "you ready?"

"Yes, Mrs. Magg," I reply.

Trish, the teacher, handles the Bible lesson; I play with the kids. This is my favorite part of church, seeing their smiling faces. They're innocent, accepting. They don't try to mold me into something I'm not. I don't have to be a rubber band, stretching to fit their needs. And since they're kids, they make mistakes without everyone pointing an accusatory finger. I love their freedom.

It's beautiful.

I sit quietly while Trish teaches the lesson. When she finishes, I practically jump out of my chair to play with the five girls and three boys. All around the room are props. In one corner is a kitchen; in another are blocks and trucks and cars. There's a bin of dress-up clothes, too.

The boys run to the trucks, but I go with the girls to the kitchen corner. I move around the room, making sure to play with everyone—first kitchen, then blocks, then dress-up. By the time the parents return for their kids, I've laughed and played so much that I've forgotten about my own problems.

Until Trish approaches me.

"How is everything, Faith?" she asks.

"Good, Mrs. Magg. And you?"

She's a talker. She prattles on about how the pool boy isn't doing a good job; she may need to fire him, and she wants to know if I know anyone who would be interested in the job. I don't. She moves on to another topic. Something about remodeling the house. Is this woman for real? Does she expect me to be sad that her biggest worries in life are the pool boy and how much larger she can make her home? I need to get out of here.

"So, tell me, Faith," Mrs. Magg says. "Have you thought about colleges yet?"

"Um, not really," I answer truthfully. I have enough to deal with.

Like life.

"You should look into UCF. That's where Jason will be." She smiles. "Wouldn't want you too far away. Long-distance relationships are so difficult."

I nod. The less I say, the better.

"UNF is another good school. Also close!" she says.

She really does not want Jason and me apart.

"Or maybe I'll just convince that son of mine to quit wasting time and ask you to marry him." Trish laughs like it's the funniest thing in the world. I feel like crying. Or running away. Marriage? Really?

"I know you'd love that," she says matter-of-factly.

She doesn't know me at all.

Just stop.

Just stop.

Just stop.

"Oh, think of it! Wouldn't it be grand?" she asks.

Who talks like this? I cannot deal with her another minute, much less a lifetime.

"I have to go," I blurt. "Sorry. I just have this thing tonight. Great talking with you!"

Outside, I take deep breaths.

In. And out. In. And out. In. And out. And in.

The air is sticky, coating my lungs like tar. The setting sun glows through the clouds, which puff like foam across the sky. What must it be like to have no problems, to be so light that you can float?

I want to join the clouds, to bounce on nothingness for one infinite second. I want to be airy and made of fluff. I want to be free to show my emotions. I want a release, an outlet, a vent. Because even clouds can cry.

I tell my dad that I want to walk home. I need time and space to think.

For some reason, my mind drifts to Diego. I smile. And with that, I no longer remember the weight of everybody's expectations. Or how I wish to be free. All I can think about is seeing Diego at the restaurant. Though I probably should, I don't regret my words.

I laugh to myself.

I can't believe I called him hot.

8
diego

Faith called me hot.

I didn't imagine it. I didn't imagine it. I didn't imagine it. I rest my head on the back of the seat as the bus drives me home. When I heard Faith's friend talking about me, I thought it would be bad. I was wrong.

Maybe it was a joke. Maybe they knew that I was behind them. Faith's friend sure knew. She glanced right at me as she said that last thing about how Faith was predictable.

Thing is, when Faith saw me, she looked shocked. And angry. So, I'm not sure it was a joke.

Forget it. I'm thinking about this *gringa* too much. Bennie gave me a warning for the broken dish. But the warning in my mind is worse. I shake my head, dislodge confusion. I glance around. I need a focus point. There are two other people on the bus. Both sitting up front. I am alone in the back. Good. I like being alone.

It's safer that way.

I peer out the window. Slow, steady traffic lines the road, pulsing like resin through the lungs of a smoker. On the street corner, thugs hassle a kid.

"It's a tough life," I mumble to myself.

The bus stops two blocks from my house, near the high school. Lampposts shine brightly every few feet. Cars pass. One slows down near me. It's a cop. Checking me out. He'll probably stop me and ask what I'm doing, walking near the school at eleven o'clock at night.

In America, it feels like being Latino is a strike against me. Having tattoos is another. And on top of it all, I have too many scars.

Too many scars.

Too many reminders.

I wish I didn't have the scars or tattoos, at least not the ones caused by my time with the cartel. Some of the other scars, though, are uniquely mine.

Like the one on my upper arm. I broke it when I was seven. The bone needed surgery to repair the break. And the small scar below my left eye, just under the lower lashes, where Javier accidentally hit me with a Frisbee. Those I don't mind.

Some of my tattoos are uniquely mine, as well. It's the cartel tattoos that bother me. The ones that mark me as a member. Those are the hardest.

Tattoos claim part of my skin. Shame claims the rest.

Surprisingly, the cop leaves me alone. But I don't get far before 67 steps out of the shadows.

"What's up?" he asks.

I keep walking, but I'm not sure it's a good idea. If I stop, I'm bound to run into trouble. But I can't lead him to my apartment, either. I decide to take a left, the opposite direction from my place. Maybe he'll leave.

"We just want to talk," he says.

I don't believe him.

I know better.

I am him, one heartbreak later.

I stop, turn toward the sound of his voice. I will not run. I'm not a coward.

Four guys approach from all directions, like dogs herding cattle.

I am prey.

"What's your name?" 67 asks.

"Rico," I lie with a hard voice. "What's yours?"

"Wink," he says, stopping in front of me. Obviously his gang, not birth, name.

I'm surrounded. Wink looks at the markings on my arms. His eyes settle on the tattoo on my left hand. *X*, skull, *X*. The *X*s represent links, like a chain. The skull represents death.

Linked to the cartel until death.

Once you are marked with that particular tattoo, you're in it for life.

The MS-13 members know all about what it means to be in it for life. In their gang, there is no leaving or being jumped out. You either live for them, or die.

Sometimes death is better.

It's considered an honor to reach a high enough level within the cartel to be branded with the particular mark tattooed on my skin. But it feels more like a burden.

"Where you from?" Wink asks.

"Not here," I answer.

Wink smirks. "And the ink?"

"Art," I say. It's not a complete lie. Some of them are art. Others were forced.

"Nice," Wink replies, crossing his arms over his chest. His shaved head reflects light like the flash of a Polaroid. "Why you locked up so tight? Protecting someone, or you got somethin' to hide?"

I get in his face without thinking twice about it. I'm not

about to take heat from this guy, no matter who he runs with.

"Listen, *cabrón*. Either tell me what you really came for, or leave. But do not expect me to tell you my life story. It's none of your business."

His friend pulls a gun. Aims it at me.

"From the way I see it," Wink says, pausing to look at the Glock, "you don't have much of a choice."

"Wrong," I say, right before I kick the gun out of his friend's hand. It sails through the air and lands in a bush. My fist connects with Wink's nose. It cracks. I hit him two more times in the same spot. Blood pours out. He goes down.

Red so red is the stain of our sins.

Someone punches me in the face.

Another guy charges. I send a powerful kick to his kneecap. He falls, tries to get up, can't.

I wish I didn't like the surge of adrenaline pounding through my veins like an uncontrolled current. My moves are flawless. I am a weapon. My fists are as dangerous as a double-edged sword.

I shouldn't like this.

I'm a monster.

A third guy is reaching for his gun. I rip his arm backward until it pops. He yells, a sound of pure anguish. Like waves when they hit jagged reefs and split with a roar. He hits me with his good fist. I taste blood. He tries to hit me again but I block him. Twist his good wrist at an unnatural angle. It breaks.

This is all I know.

The guy behind me punches me in the back of the head. I turn toward him in time to receive another punch to the face. It only takes one kick and one punch from me for him to go down.

I need to leave now, before they get up.

When a city falls to ruins, do you pick up the broken pieces and rebuild? Or do you leave it all behind?

Stay or run?

Live or die?

This feels like home. Fighting. Threats. Trouble to come.

Just like I told *mi padre.*

There is no such thing as a brighter future.

9

faith

The moment I get home, Grace plows into my legs, almost knocking me backward. Though her five-year-old body is tiny, she's mighty with her affection. As always, she creates moments of joy when I least expect them.

My parents had me young, barely into their twenties. When my dad married his new wife, he was thirty-three, Susan, thirty. They decided to have Grace. Despite the age gap between Grace and me, I don't know what I would do without her.

"Hi, Gracie," I say, smiling from ear to ear.

She looks like me—same hair, green eyes, high brow bones. It's nice to have someone who loves you so much that they tackle you at the door, begging for hugs and kisses. She can't wait for me to walk into the living room. She has to see me right then.

It's love like the sweetest chocolate. Only better.

"Hi, Faith," Grace says in her melodic soprano voice. "You didn't ride with us."

"No," I agree. "But I'm here now."

Grace smiles. "Missed you thisssss"—she pauses to stretch her arms as wide as they can go—"much!"

"Aw, I missed you, too."

"Want to play?" she asks.

Anything to make you happy. "Give me one second," I say and race to my room to kick off my shoes.

When I return, Grace is dressed in costume. A fluffy pink skirt with tons of ruffles at the hem, a sparkly purple shirt, and a pointy princess hat with pink tulle coming out of the top. She has a wand in her hand.

She is beautiful, so beautiful.

"Here," she says, handing me a flowery dress. One of Susan's castoffs. I think Susan purposely gave it to Grace so that I can dress up, too.

I pull the dress over my head. It's a little big.

"How do I look?" I ask with a spin.

"Like the most beautifulest sister in the whole world," Grace says. She puts one finger to her chin, taps her foot on the ground, looks up. It's her concentration look.

Billions and billions of people to love and you picked me.

"No. Wait," she says. "What's the word for more than beautiful?"

"Gorgeous?" I suggest.

"No," she says. "More than that."

I look down at her. "Not sure. Why?"

" 'Cause that is what you are," she says. "More than beautiful."

My heart *pitter-pats*. Grace is seriously my saving grace. I thought about her while I was away last year. She's one of the few reasons I stayed strong.

Now I pick her up and spin her the way she likes. She squeals. As I tickle her, her head tips back and laughter bubbles out of her mouth. I love her laugh. It's the kind that when you hear it, you can't help smiling, too.

When we're both laughing so hard that it feels like I've

run a marathon, we collapse on the ground and catch our breath.

One beat two beats three beats four.

I will always love you more.

"What are we playing tonight?" I ask.

Grace picks up the wand. "I am the magic angel. I will turn you into things," she explains.

"Okay," I agree.

First she turns me into a pony, and I give her a ride on my back. Then I am a sneaky fox who keeps hiding; she has to find me, like hide-and-seek. Then Grace shares her magic with me, and we set off together to battle pirates on a ship.

If only we could sail away.

It doesn't feel like we've been playing for two hours, but when I hear Susan call Grace to bed, I realize time has flown by.

"One more. One more. One more," Grace begs her mom.

Susan sighs. With a smile, she gives in. "Okay. But just one." She sits on the couch and waits for us to finish.

"For my last magic of the day, I will make everyone better," my little sister says.

And I believe with all of my heart that she thinks this is possible.

Grace instructs me to lie down on the floor, which, of course, is not any old floor but a special bed in a small town far, far away. I'm supposed to be a sick girl. There are a lot of us who are sick in this faraway town. We've caught a germ that Grace calls the Ick. Grace leans over me and peers into my eyes, ears, nose, and mouth. I almost laugh at her serious face. She really gets into her make-believe.

Then she trails her wand from my head to my toes and works her magic.

"Bye-bye, sickness in your vein. I take away all your pain," she says.

And just like that, I'm better. Grace jumps up and down and claps, and then gives me a kiss good night.

I blink back the tears as Grace walks away with Susan. I wish the flick of a wand could make everything better. I don't mean to get emotional, but Grace's magic makes me think about the real pain in my life.

It's an ache that started ten years ago.

The day she disappeared.

No, *disappeared* is too generous a word. What I mean is: left.

The day my mom left.

Abandoned me. Abandoned *us*.

Dad seems truly happy with Susan, but he was in pain once, too. There were dark years before he met his new wife.

Susan treats Dad well, and she's an awesome mom to Grace. She tried really hard in the beginning to be friends with me. She promised never to replace my mom. I remember her exact words: "Faith, I know that you already have a mom. I respect that. All I'm saying is that, if it's okay with you, I would like to marry your father. We've talked about it. He wants to be a family. Would that be okay with you?"

I couldn't say no to Susan. Not if she made Dad happy.

Anything was better than seeing him in pain.

Plus, Susan had the decency to ask me if it was okay. She didn't need my permission, but she had enough consideration to ask. I think maybe I could like her if I actually gave her a chance. But I don't give her a chance. I can't.

I don't let people in anymore. I never let them close

enough to have a shot at seeing the real me. Pain is a strong enough sealant to close my heart.

My mom left when I was eight.

For drugs.

Ever since she left, I've had a serious fear of abandonment. Once she was gone, it was like Dad had left, too. He went to work, preached the Bible, paid the bills. He sat at the dinner table with me to eat, but he wasn't really there. I'd catch him gazing at the wall, lost. A robot: pray, eat, go to bed. Repeat. He didn't talk to me anymore. He was hurting. He thought it was his fault that Mom left. She was a preacher's wife. Stuff like this wasn't supposed to happen.

But it did. Dad tried to get her professional help, checked her into several clinics. It didn't make a difference in the end. She still left. One thing remained: a ghost of a life, haunting.

I would hear Dad at night sometimes, crying. It broke my heart. I cried. Mom caused us so much pain. Her addiction broke her. And us, too.

Addiction is toxic, a drop of poison in pure water, tainting and infecting. It is awful how one tiny drop can ripple so far. The ripple is the worst. It reaches so much further than the original drop, and it lingers for a long time. Maybe forever. Dad and I are part of Mom's ripple. She thought that by leaving she did us a favor. She reasoned that if she was gone, we would move on, be happy.

Wrong.

I was not left with happiness. I was left with abandonment issues. Big ones.

According to the shrink, fear of abandonment is called autophobia. It's more specifically defined as a fear of loneliness. And it's awful. Like the plague, eating me from the inside out, rotting my soul. I do not trust. I cannot trust. I will not trust. Anyone.

Except Melissa. Melissa was there when my mom wasn't. She was two open arms, always constant, always welcoming. We carried each other. Her dad left her family at the same time. We've both experienced a heart tear. Together.

Melissa is sarcastic, edgy. But she has a true, loving heart. She accepts me. Flaws and all.

Melissa is safe.

Some people have places where they feel safe—a house, a car, maybe the park or the beach. Not me. My mind doesn't work like that. I look for safety not in the world, but in the people around me. It's a flaw, for sure. Because, honestly, most people are not safe. They seem good in the beginning, but they only hurt you in the end.

That's the problem with autophobia. It makes me skeptical of everyone. What it comes down to is this: I'm afraid to know someone, really know them, because what if I end up loving them? Will they be like my mom? Will they leave me, too?

There is always a chance.

I cannot take that chance.

Instead, I go about my life being who everyone expects. Happy, predictable Faith.

Sometimes I want to step out of my own skin, watch it fall to the ground like a discarded hide. I did that once, two years ago, but I went about it the wrong way.

I was a sophomore. Dad had already married Susan. He had moved on. I felt abandoned, by him, by Mom. They lived their own lives, oblivious to the fact that I was miserable, decaying inside. So I stepped out. I started secretly going to college parties that Melissa's older sister invited us to. At first it was about cute boys and dancing, but it turned into more. I started drinking. A lot.

Melissa drank, too, but not as much as me. My best friend assumed I'd be careful, that I'd know my limits because of what happened to my mom. She didn't know how much I pushed the boundaries.

Then came drugs. I'd always wondered what was so great about them. What could possibly be so wonderful that family and everything else took a far distant second?

I needed to know.

So I tried them. It wasn't what I expected. The drugs themselves were harsh. But their aftereffect drew me. Drugs made me numb. For once, I didn't feel the pain of abandonment. I didn't *feel* at all. Not anything.

I don't know exactly when it got out of hand. I was in too deep for Melissa to help, suctioned by a cyclone too powerful for her to fight. She had to tell my dad.

That's why I missed my junior year. I was in rehab.

Everyone except Melissa and my family thinks that I went on an international church mission. It sounds exciting. Travel the world; study in beautiful countries. Come back to a school where most people can only dream of doing something like that.

So many people envy me. If they only knew.

Green, green, green is our envy, volatile and vain.

Blue, blue, blue is my soul, withering and chained.

I kept up my relationship with Jason while I was in rehab. My dad gave me notes that Jason dropped off at the house. It was easier than explaining that there were no international addresses where he could send letters. Ink bled onto paper, sentiments too shallow to fill the envelope with anything of substance, anything worthwhile. The notes always talked about football or how the dance team wasn't any good without me.

Even today, when things with Jason aren't exactly exciting, I love that he stuck by me. True, he thought I was on a church retreat, but that's not what matters. Point is that he didn't leave me.

If I were strong, I would tell Jason the truth. But I'm a coward.

I should tell him about the parties. I should tell him that I cheated on him with college guys. I should admit that I got hooked on drugs, just like my mom. But I can't. Only Melissa knows the real reason why Mom left.

My parents' divorce was scandalous at first. Pastors are not supposed to divorce. But people got over it quickly.

I should tell Jason the truth. I should break up with him so he can be with someone more deserving. But I won't. People expect me to be with Jason. I must keep up the façade, keep living the lie. I'm not a good person; I know that. But I can't ruin my dad's life. I'm not sure if my dad's career, or heart, can take the hit of a divorce—and a wayward daughter. So I'm stuck, a pawn in a game I have no intention of winning.

Jason loves the fake me, anyway. He doesn't know the real one. Is it fair to take the fake me, the one he fell in love with, away? And then there's the piece of me that wants to keep Jason because he accepts my mask. It's easier that way.

I fold the pain, bending it at precise angles until it fits into my pocket, always carrying it with me where no one can see. I'm done with drugs and alcohol. I don't want them anymore. I don't even like cigarettes.

Today, tonight, in my room, it all seems like a fading dream. I can't believe I ever used drugs. Especially knowing so intimately the destruction they cause. I just wanted to forget the pain of Mom leaving. Terrible copout, I know. It will never happen again.

Melissa keeps my secret. She's the truest kind of friend. That's why I can't get mad at her for pushing me earlier, at the restaurant. She wants me to step out of my skin. The healthy way this time. Dress how I want to dress, date who I want to date. Melissa says that even though the drugs are gone, I'm still not free.

I don't know what free is.

I imagine a bird, soaring, screeching.

Flap, flap, flap go its wings, batting the air like a child smacking bubbles.

Melissa wants me to say things like I did earlier, when I admitted that Diego is hot. It's not that she loves the shock value; it's that she loves me. She wants me to be happy.

I wonder if such a thing exists.

10
diego

My face is jacked.

I realize the next morning that there's no way I can hide what happened. *Mi padre* is going to flip. Maybe if he hadn't hidden my gun, none of this would have happened.

Maybe if I didn't own a gun, life would be different.

Even after a shower, I still have dried blood on my lip, like a stain after eating cherries. I wet a washcloth with warm water and dab. It stings but I've had worse. The white washcloth comes away russet. Old blood. Soon it will be another old scar.

My bottom lip is split on the right side. Not bad enough for stitches, though. My left cheekbone is swollen and my right eye is turning purple, like a shadow hovers over it.

As if people don't stare enough already.

Time for school. People will notice. The suspicions they already have about me, confirmed. Screw it. I don't care.

As I leave the house, *mi padre* stops me.

"*Ay, ay, ay,* Diego. What happened?" he asks.

"Nothin'," I say, brushing him off.

"*No me mientas,*" he replies.

"Fine," I say. "I got in a fight. There, happy?"

I'm being sarcastic, obviously. But *mi padre* already knows what happened. What he's really asking is not what, but why. And by whom.

He stares at me with hard eyes, eyes that have seen unspeakable misery.

"*¿Por qué?*"

"Because some jerk thought he could push me around. No big deal."

"*No más peleas.*"

He wants me to stop fighting. Even though *mi padre* insists on speaking English in America, he slips up when he's angry.

"Fine," I say.

I hoist my bag on my shoulder and walk the back way to school. Javier told me about a new route last night when I filled him in on my fight with the MS-13 members. With any luck, they won't be prowling these streets, as well—and Wink got the message that I don't want to be a recruit.

I pull a cigarette from my pocket and light it. Relaxation washes over me like hot oil, all of my worries slipping away. It's a relief. I'm too wound up these days. Always watching my back. But that's to be expected. I take another drag and watch the smoke float lazily into the sky.

Won't you take me with you?

Cigarettes are my only addiction. Most people assume that I do drugs. Wrong. Even though I saw a lot in the business, I never touched the drugs. Literally. No dealing. No ingesting. No interest. I know a lot of people who got way too messed up. I've seen the damage drugs can do.

That's why I stick to cigarettes. Everybody has a poison, a vice. For some, it's caffeine. For others, the hard kind, cocaine, heroin. For me, nicotine.

In the cartel, it was my job to make sure people stayed in line. Which basically meant that I made sure no one was pinching more than their share, that cartel members had extra protection for drop-offs, that debts were collected. I roughed up a lot of people. Came with the territory. I never hurt anybody too bad, though. I was one of the boss's best fighters.

Some people are good with money, others with drugs. I'm good with my fists.

I am a weapon.

I am a monster.

It was hard at times. But I had to survive. On my street back home, the top killers weren't heart attacks and cancer, like you hear about in America, but starvation and violence. There are always people who will say that joining a gang or a cartel isn't the answer, but until they're lying on a street corner starving or dying of a bullet wound, how can they know?

Joining a cartel was my only option, if I wanted to live and have my family taken care of. I would've done anything for *mi familia*. The cartel offered protection and food in my stomach. Two things I would not have lived to see eighteen without.

Today I try not to think about it too much. It is what it is. Sure, I wish things were different. But they're not.

Inhaling the last drag of my cigarette, I stomp it out with my shoe. Oviedo High is a collection of large, multicolored brick buildings with lush green grass and a courtyard that looks more like a garden. The sparse clouds above are light gray charcoal caked onto a backdrop of sapphire. The sun shines brightly, swollen with arrogance, its rays like arms claiming all it can touch, blocking one whole side of the sky from being seen.

Javier calls me over to a picnic bench where he's sitting with some of his *amigos*. I rest on the dead wood, as well.

"You look terrible," Javier greets me.

"Thanks, man. You, too," I say, hassling him. "At least I have an excuse."

"You didn't get into it with Faith's *novio*, did you?" Luis asks.

For some reason, the thought of Faith makes me tense. I don't show it, though.

"Nah," I answer. "Just some *pandilleros*."

"That sucks," Luis replies. "At least with Faith, you would have a good reason to walk around lookin' like that."

"Good reason?" Rodolfo asks.

"Don't act like you wouldn't say yes if you had the chance," Luis replies.

Rodolfo laughs. "You're right. I probably would walk around with a banged-up face for her."

"Seriously?" I ask. " 'Cause I don't see it."

Faith's outside appearance is vague to me. It's the inside that holds the spark. I mean, yesterday, what was she wearing? Some fluffy blouse and a skirt that looked too big. Maybe she doesn't normally look like that.

"Watch the dance team. Then you'll see it," Javier says.

Ramon joins in. "Faith Watters is *muy caliente*. I bet she only dresses the way she does because of her father."

"What, he picks her clothes for her?" I ask.

"No, man. I mean 'cause he's the preacher."

I glance at my cousin for confirmation. "You're messin' with me," I say.

Luis busts up laughing.

"You should see your face, *ese*," Luis says.

A pastor's daughter?

"Why didn't you tell me?" I ask Javier.

"I didn't think you wanted to date her." Javier grins.

"You should have told me."

"Don't worry," Rodolfo says. "She will never say yes."

He's probably not trying to make me angry, but he does. Why do things have to be like that? Who says I can't get a girl like Faith Watters? Not that I want to.

"She might say yes," I counter.

"Oh no." Javier gives me a look. "Don't waste your time. The sky has a better chance of falling than of you dating Faith."

"You're probably right," I say. "It's just messed up."

And now thanks to Javier, I can't stop wondering what Faith looks like in her dance uniform. No amount of me telling myself she's a pastor's daughter makes it better.

"A pastor's daughter," I mumble, and shake my head. "Unbelievable."

"All the better," Rodolfo says. "A challenge. Like forbidden fruit."

Forbidden is not a good way to describe something to me. I love a good challenge. And I do not believe anything is forbidden. Locked up tight, maybe. But not forbidden.

"Forbidden is lookin' pretty good today," Luis says.

I look up in time to see Faith with her blond friend. My peer helper is wearing a red blouse and black shorts that are practically knee-length. It's not that her outfit is sexy or anything; it's just that red is definitely her color.

As she walks close, my heart breaks through my sternum and beats on my skin like a hammer.

Breathe.

My lungs refuse to cooperate, like a disobedient child.

Breathe.

And then she's gone.

11
faith

Diego's face is busted. Purples and browns and pinks and blues all blur into one another, creating a painting of abstract life—an image of anger, of survival in a bleak, hostile world.

One quick peek at him in the courtyard gave me one huge glimpse into Diego's life outside school. I'm not sure if I should ask if he's okay or ignore the bruises. Which is worse, acting like I care or acting like I don't?

Tough. I realize in that moment that I honestly want to know if he's all right.

I'm not sure what to expect from Diego today. He acted like I didn't exist when I sat near him in psychology yesterday, and then he gave me the cold shoulder the rest of the day. Now his face is a mess; plus I'm more than a little embarrassed about calling him hot. But at the same time, I'm not. It felt good to step out of my own skin. Even if it was only for a moment.

Ever-changing like a chameleon, blending in all the same.

I do, however, know exactly what to expect from Jason. My boyfriend is annoyed that I complimented another guy, especially in front of his friends. I don't understand the big deal. It's not like he doesn't find other girls attractive. I don't get bent out of shape.

People like me cannot allow the mask to slip. I won't let it happen again.

I wait for Diego in front of the guidance office, occasionally scanning the halls for his arrival. Then I see him. He's wearing jeans and a pale blue shirt that sets off his smoky-amber skin.

Simple.

Striking.

He is fluidity in every move. He is a boy with eyes like hope, with scars that tell stories, with muscles born of a hard life. It's plain to see, so long as you care to look.

I decide not to comment on his face. If he wants to talk about it, he'll tell me. Plus, I don't like the cocky expression he's sporting, like he knows that I think he's hot and now he's going to use it against me.

Maybe I should tell him that he's only hot on the outside, when he doesn't talk.

He stops in front of me, grinning. His eyes glint like the edge of a knife. For a moment, it feels as though they can cut right through me.

"How was your meal last night?" he asks.

I worried he would bring that up. Still, I can't help the heat that colors my cheeks, as though my traitorous blood wants Diego to know that his words hit their mark.

"It was great," I say casually and turn before he has a chance to see me blushing.

Diego is feeling brave today. He doesn't trail me like yesterday. Instead, he keeps pace beside me, smiling devilishly.

"And how's that boyfriend of yours?" he asks.

I stop. Shoot him a hardened glance. He's well aware that Jason heard my comment.

"He's fine, Diego. Why don't you ask what you really want to instead of beating around the bush?"

He laughs. "You surprise me sometimes, Faith."

There it is again. My name. He says it differently than most people. I don't know if it's his accent or the way my name tastes in his mouth; either way, it catches me off guard.

I don't want to ask why I surprise him. I turn around and continue walking.

"Red is a good color on you," he comments.

I'm not sure if he means my blouse or my face. I keep walking, wanting to be done with him for now.

And suddenly, I realize something.

I don't trust myself around him.

Not even my fake self. No, scratch that; *especially* my fake self. Fake Faith doesn't stand a chance around Diego. He's slowly unraveling the tight wire I use to secure the real me. He's trying to free her and he doesn't even know it.

Or does he?

Every time he speaks his mind, I want to do the same. And the dangerous part is that I just might. I wish I could dress how I want and date who I want. Why do some people have it so easy?

I glance at Diego's tattooed arms.

Then again, maybe some people have their own version of complicated.

On his lower bicep is an image of a girl on a motorcycle with something written in Spanish on the road beneath her. A five-inch gash on his arm makes her look as though she's been cut in half. The line of the scar is too clean to be an accident. Nothing but a purposeful slice makes a cut like that. I wonder what it was.

A piece of glass? A knife blade?

More tattoos and small scars snake down his arm—two by his elbow, three on his wrist, several on his knuckles. And that's just the left arm. Where the wounds have healed, the images appear slightly blurred, the original ink forever distorted.

And then there's his neck. I try not to look at it but I can't help myself. His lightweight shirt is made of thin stretched cotton. The slight outline of his muscles is clearly visible—especially where his neck meets his strong shoulders. Above the neckline of his shirt a scar sweeps across his skin like a smile. The mark on his esophagus is red and angry.

Raw.

New.

Someone did that to him.

Why?

Diego clears his throat. "Get a good enough look?" he asks.

I'm embarrassed. I shouldn't have stared at him.

"Sorry," I mumble. I blink several times, hoping that if I close my eyes hard enough, maybe the images of Diego will escape through my lashes into the swarm of bodies around us. My eyes are thieves, stealing glimpses, storing the evidence in my mind, making me guilty by association.

He grins. "There's more if you're interested."

I scowl. I cannot afford any more slip-ups. He has to stop provoking me. I need to get through the day. Then it's over.

"Go to class," I say, and turn to walk away.

Suddenly, Diego pulls me close. His body is pulsing, throbbing heat. I make a small whimpering noise. I don't mean to. It's just, God, why does he smell so good? Spicy almost.

His eyes are one thousand points of light blinding my caution.

He reaches around me. My chest presses against him. I'm so aware of my body, of how it's conspiring against me. My mind is urging me to step away, to snap out of it.

Abruptly, Diego releases me. In his fingers are stray hairs.

"Shedding," he says nonchalantly, letting my hair fall to the floor.

I try to sift through my confusion. Why did I not pull away from Diego when it seemed as if he was embracing me? But he wasn't embracing me. He was just ridding my shirt of hair.

Mistakes, mistakes. Too many mistakes.

"Didn't want to mess up your picture-perfect image."

Diego winks, and walks toward the classroom door.

I can't let him get away with that. If anyone saw . . . If Jason hears . . . I'll never live it down.

Witnesses, witnesses. Too many witnesses.

I part my lips to say something, anything, but embarrassment floods my mouth, chokes my words. The surge drowns any comeback I might've had.

And I'm left alone, standing in a hall full of snickering students.

12
diego

By the time I make it to lunch, even Javier has heard about my stunt.

"I heard you got close to a white chick," my cousin says.

Yes, too close.

"Something like that," I say, grinning, acting as though it didn't affect me, too.

"Face it. You'll never be good enough for that *princesa*," Ramon says.

You'll never be good enough.

I feel myself crack, a sliver of ice punched deep by the force of his words. He really should not have said that.

Ramon is holding a tray of food. I shove him. People stop eating to look.

"Hey, chill," he says.

I knock his food to the ground. Spaghetti splatters. People are whispering.

"Let me tell you something," I say. Might as well cut to the chase. "Nobody speaks to me like—"

Javier steps between us. "Relax, man."

I take a deep breath.

Exhale.

Yeah, I have anger issues. But for good reason.

Ramon bends to pick up his food. Without a word, he walks away. Javier's eyes narrow.

"Do you have to be such a jerk?" he asks.

"Me, the jerk?" I say, exasperated.

Javier doesn't say anything else. I make my way to the food line; I'm about to grab a tray when someone knocks into me.

Jason Magg.

He doesn't apologize. But that's probably because it's no accident. Jason is flanked by two of his football buddies.

My teeth clench. My muscles coil. Now is not the time to mess with me.

"You know what they call people like you who hit on another dude's girlfriend?" Jason asks, and then answers. "Dead meat."

I laugh. Because honestly, it's funny. The guy has no idea that his girlfriend likes it when I hit on her. I found that out today, when she didn't back away from me in the hall. Why not have a little fun with the pastor's daughter? And that little whimpering noise she made? *Ay.* I almost crumbled.

"You think it's funny to hit on girls who have boyfriends?" Jason asks.

"No. Just yours," I say, like the smart-ass I am.

His chest puffs out and falls, a balloon being blown up and deflated.

I smile.

"Stay away from Faith," he hisses.

"All right," I say. "But you should probably tell her that, because like you already know, it's Faith who comes on to me. Not the other way around."

Jason's fists tighten. His buddies move in.

"She's a peer helper," he says.

"Okay. Sure." I nod. "I wonder, though, when she's no longer my peer helper, and she's still coming 'round, what you'll say then? 'Cause let's face it, she won't be able to stay away."

I casually lean against the wall, like I have no worries when it comes to him. And I don't. I can easily take Jason and his friends. I can tell by the way they're fumbling around, looking nervous but trying not to, that they're inexperienced fighters.

Rule number one: Never show weakness.

Sure, a three-to-one ratio isn't ideal, but I'll manage. I might walk away with another black eye. But make no mistake: I will be the one walking away.

"My girlfriend is not interested in you," Jason practically growls.

"Oh yeah?" I say. "Then why did she agree to go out with me on Friday night?"

It's a lie, meant to anger him.

Mission accomplished.

Jason swings. I catch his fist before it hits my face.

Rookie.

Rule number two: Don't act in haste.

My knee connects with his gut while my fist hits his nose. I don't have time to deliver another blow before I'm yanked away by two teachers. They pin my arms behind my back like paper to a corkboard. I let them. Jason got my message loud and clear.

Rule number three: Don't mess with me.

Two more teachers place themselves in front of Jason

and his friends, a shield of sorts. Faith's boyfriend pulls himself off the floor, no doubt humiliated. He wipes a hand across his nose. Bloody. One of his buddies walks away, returns with a hand towel. Jason puts the cloth to his nose, tries to stop the bleeding.

I didn't break his nose. I could have. But I didn't. I purposely held back. I have broken enough bones to know what it feels like when they crack, and his are still intact.

Mostly, I wanted to scare him. I want him to know—whether I was out of line or not—that I am not someone to be taken lightly.

I am not your punching bag.

I will not ever be pushed around by some guy in a letterman jacket.

Just then, a wide-eyed Faith runs up to Jason. "What happened?"

One of Jason's buddies points to me.

Faith follows his direction. Her eyes land on me. Her face hardens, something like rose granite. Someone gets her attention. She looks away.

"What are you thinking?" a lady with big hair asks me. According to her name badge, she is Mrs. Slyder, science teacher.

I don't answer.

"There is no fighting on school property. You just earned two days' suspension. Are you aware of this school's policy about suspension for fighting?"

Is she aware that she just told me?

"Your suspension will start immediately."

Like I care.

"Who threw the first punch?" she asks.

I wonder if Jason is man enough to admit that he did. Probably not.

"I'll take your silence as guilt," she says.

Of course she will. Whatever happened to innocent until proven guilty? More like guilty for the rest of my life, simply because of who I am.

"Are you new here?" she huffs. "Why don't I recognize you?"

Because I don't like to be seen.

"What's your name?"

I still don't answer, mostly because no matter what I say, I know they'll believe a pretty boy over a troubled Latino.

"Now would be the time to explain."

Silence.

"Are you listening to me?" Mrs. Big Hair asks.

Unfortunately.

"To the office," says one of the teachers holding my arms.

I'm bigger than the puny teachers trying to haul me away. I push all my weight down, making it difficult for them to move me, a boulder of stubbornness. I will go with them when I'm ready. I want to make sure Jason sees me before I'm escorted out.

There. He looks at me. And in that moment, I plaster my face with the biggest smile I can muster and mouth the word, "look." A silent whisper meant only for him. I eye Faith. She is throwing the bloody towel away.

Jason looks at her.

I look at her.

Whatever punishment they decide to give me will be worth it.

It's all worth it because in the end, when her boyfriend

is bleeding down his face and ten other people are trying to get her attention and the lunchroom is in a shambles because of the fight, Faith notices none of it. She's not looking at any of them.

Because she's too busy staring at me.

And Jason knows it.

13
faith

My legs burn as though they've caught fire. One, two, three, four hundred steps on the school track before dance practice. My breaths come deep and quick. Sweat glides down my back.

When the whistle blows, I rest my hands on my knees until my heart slows its gallop.

Coach tells us to gather together. When she was younger, she also danced for our school team. I've seen pictures: long auburn hair, muscular build, dark Persian skin. She looks the same, just a few added wrinkles.

Melissa stands beside me, nudging my arm.

"Good run," she says.

"Thanks. You, too."

It's all about endurance. The more you have, the better dancer you are.

The music begins. The new routine, the one we'll perform at our next competition, unfolds with only a few hiccups. Being on the varsity team means many of us have practiced together for years. It doesn't take long to learn the new moves. The problem is perfecting them, making them ours. A twist at the end, a flip in the middle, attitude written all over our faces. It's the little things that add the most character.

"I don't like it," Tracy says, trying to veto my newest suggestion.

Coach huffs. "When do you ever?"

I bite back a smile. Our one-sided feud is long-standing. And everyone knows it.

Tracy glares at me.

"Do you have another suggestion?" Coach asks, trying to be fair.

It's a good thing Tracy is an incredible dancer, or we'd all have asked her to leave the squad by now.

"Of course," Tracy responds.

I watch as she demonstrates what she thinks is better. Truth: it's not bad.

Coach eyes me. I shrug, not wanting to start a fight.

"Okay," Coach replies. "Anyone object?"

Half the team raises their hands, which leaves the decision to the captain.

Me.

Everyone waits for my response. I look at Tracy. Her eyes dare me to object.

"Tracy's idea is fine," I say, backing down.

I don't offer any suggestions for the rest of practice. Guilt gnaws at me, hungry and relentless.

I should've stood up for my teammates who raised their hands. I should've stood up for myself. But I didn't.

I'm not sure I even know how.

After practice, I sort through pile upon pile of books.

The back half of the library is littered with spare books, crammed together like people in an overpopulated city.

My school is preparing for the annual book fair, and I'm on the organizing committee. Whenever big things happen—homecoming, book fairs, science fairs, plays, etc.—the committee organizes everything. I love it. Well, actually, I guess it's not so much the sorting through a million books that I enjoy, but the end result. I love knowing that I make a difference.

"Hey, sweets." Melissa plops down beside me. She's wearing a pink spaghetti-strap tank top with white shorts and flip-flops. A string of ginger jewels hangs from her neck, dressing up her outfit like tinsel on a tree.

"Hey." I smile.

Melissa is on the committee. So are three others. We don't actually have a president but most people come to me for final decisions.

"Bad news," Melissa says. "Sally has the pox."

"What?" I ask. "Small or chicken?"

"Chicken. It's serious, too," Melissa informs me. "She's being quarantined for three weeks. So is her sister, since they live in the same house. Molly hasn't caught it yet, but everyone thinks she will."

I groan. "Well, that stinks. For them and for us."

Sally and Molly, two members of our committee of five, will not be able to help us get ready for the book fair.

Another empty gap.

Another role to fill.

"You think we can get some of the dance team to step up?" I ask.

"Doubtful," Melissa says. "Remember what happened freshman year when we asked for their assistance? Total disaster. We're better off without them."

Right, as usual.

"Great," I mumble. "We'll have to stay later now."

"That just means more time with me," Melissa says, flipping her hair over her shoulder. She's forever finding the bright side of things, like flowers that bend and reach for sunlight no matter their environment. I smile.

"You're right. Let's do this, then."

Melissa begins sorting through books. We need to alphabetize and price them. Then set up tables and posters and flyers. We have four or five weeks' worth of work. The fair is in twenty days.

"Hey—" Melissa nudges me with her elbow as I try to rip open another box.

"Yeah?" I ask.

"What happened in the lunchroom?"

Freeze.

"Come on. You've heard," I say.

"Of course." Melissa nods. "I want your version. You know how stories get twisted around here."

"Weren't you there?" I ask.

It's hard to remember much about lunch today. My mind is distorted. I was handed parts of the story from different people, each contributing his or her piece of the puzzle. Trouble is, none of it makes a complete picture.

"I was late," Melissa answers. "My third-period teacher decided to give me a lecture about how important it is to be prompt. Which I find pretty ironic, considering that her lecture made me late for lunch."

Melissa reaches to the table beside us and grabs scissors. "Move," she instructs.

I scoot aside.

She cuts open the box that I've been struggling with.

"Thanks," I say.

"So," Melissa continues. "What's your version?"

I sigh. "I honestly don't know what happened. I was talking to Rachel and all of a sudden, I hear people chanting, 'Fight!' "

"Did you see it?" Melissa asks.

"No. I was on the other side of the lunchroom. By the time I made it over, Jason had a bloody nose and Diego was being detained."

Lori walks in. "Hey," she says, dropping her backpack on the ground. "Where is everybody?"

Lori's a bohemian. She wears bold black-framed glasses that point up at the corners in matching arcs. Her hair is almost always in braids and dyed different colors with natural products. And her clothes are made of strange things, like wheat and biodegradable materials. She makes them herself. I think it's cool.

"Sally and Molly have the pox," Melissa explains.

"Ugh," Lori says. "That sucks. When will they be back?"

"Not in time to help us move this mountain." Melissa motions to the messy pile of books and boxes. Lori sighs and sits down next to us. After a moment, she turns to me.

"Is Jason okay?" she asks.

If that question had come from anyone other than Lori or Melissa, I wouldn't answer. Anyone else would only be asking for the sake of gossip. But Lori is sincere.

"Yes," I answer. "He's mad, embarrassed."

"Clearly," Melissa interjects. "I would be, too."

"Diego didn't need to start trouble," I say. "Apparently he told Jason that I agreed to a date with him on Friday."

Melissa's eyes go big, bursting with unspoken surprise.

"Which I didn't," I clarify.

Melissa exhales. "Wow. Dude has guts, doesn't he?" She smiles.

I give her a look. "Don't even start."

On her face is the knowledge of something foreign to me. "Might as well come to grips. You have unfinished business with Diego," she says.

Lori looks confused. "Did I miss something?"

"No," I reply. "Melissa is just being, well, Melissa."

Lori shakes her head, understanding.

"I don't get why Diego has an issue with everyone," I say.

"Well, if he's anything like I think he is, it's probably because he's not fake," Melissa says.

"Fake?"

How could she bring that up? She knows I try hard to be what everyone wants me to be. It's not because I want to lie. I just wish I *were* that person. I don't know why it's so difficult.

"Yes. Fake," Melissa says. "Most people around here don't have a clue how fortunate they are. Their biggest worries are what time the football game starts and getting the newest whatever the day it comes out. Stuff like that."

Ah. Melissa means other people, not me.

Since the mission trip to Haiti our freshman year, Melissa hasn't been the same. We saw how some of those people lived. We viewed the world through someone else's eyes. One Haitian man had to walk ten miles every day to the nearest water hole. Ten miles, and the water there wasn't even clean. Many of the people we met looked disproportionate, arms and legs skin and bones, stomachs bloated. The volunteer doctors said that's what a body looks like when it's starving.

And their homes—if they were lucky enough to have a home, which most were not—were heartbreaking. Some were nothing more than four concrete walls measuring about five-by-seven, a block home in its truest form. Few had proper roofs. Instead of wooden doors, they'd hang a dirty sheet or palm fronds or sticks woven together. They had no shelter from the elements or from the violence outside. The spaces were large enough for a couple of people to sleep on dirt ground. Those who were really lucky had one or two cooking pots and a blanket.

Sometimes I wish I could fly to another country. Someplace where my problems would be things like finding clean water. Food. Things that matter.

"Maybe Diego knows how tough life can be. No offense, Faith, but I doubt Jason and his buddies have a clue. Did anyone stop to ask Diego his story?" Melissa says. "No. They just judge him because of his ethnicity. And because he's different. It's not right."

Lori nods. She's all about love and world peace. No doubt she wishes everyone could just get along.

"No wonder Diego's defensive," Melissa says.

"Maybe Jason's upset because he feels intimidated. Maybe he thinks Diego actually has a chance with Faith," Lori suggests.

I laugh. I can't help it. Because if I don't laugh, I might cry. I'll never be allowed such an indulgence, to choose to be with someone so freely, to choose my own destiny.

"Please," I say, "Diego only started the fight because he has a big ego."

Lori scrunches her eyebrows. "Faith, Diego didn't start the fight," she says. "Jason did."

What?

Jason lied to me. He told me Diego threw the first punch.

Don't believe everything you hear.

"How do you know?" I ask.

"I saw it," Lori says. "The whole thing."

"Ooh." Melissa's eyes light up as if a tiny town huddles under her lenses, a town of thoughts brightening at the prospect of Jason being at fault. "Tell us what happened."

"Jason cornered Diego and threatened him," Lori explains. "Then he tried to hit Diego."

Melissa's smile widens.

Lori turns to me. "I'm sorry to say it, Faith, but it looked like self-defense on Diego's part."

"Fantastic," I mumble.

Another link to a person I trusted, severed.

14
diego

Ordinarily I'd be removed from school grounds for a fight, but this isn't a normal suspension. One strike; not yet out. I get shoved in the library—where Faith and her friends are hanging out in the back, talking about me.

Faith is laughing so loud, she doesn't hear me approach. Then they get serious, and I can tell by Faith's tone that she's upset about something they said.

When did I start differentiating between her tones?

And now I'm standing here, wondering how I get myself into these messes.

Oh well. Might as well be the jerk she thinks I am. It's easier that way.

I sneak up behind her, lower myself to the ground, and whisper in her ear. "Did you miss me?"

All three of them jump and turn at the same time.

Her eyes. Her mouth. Her hands. Distracting.

Focus.

Faith looks too shocked for words. Her friend, I think Faith called her Melissa, stands up immediately. She grabs the other girl's arm and tells her there's something she needs to show her. They walk away.

I hate to admit it—because I definitely had the friend,

Melissa, pegged as the fake type—but I think she might actually be cool. From the bits and pieces of conversation I've overheard, she seems nicer than I gave her credit for. Makes me wonder what she's doing hanging out with predictable, uptight Faith.

But while I'm being honest, I have to say that Faith has also shown a feisty side. Clearly not often enough, but it's there nonetheless. Every time I see a glimpse of Feisty Faith, she locks herself back up as if she's securing an inner demon.

I know all about demons.

With my nearness, Faith's breath hitches. I can't help the small grin that pulls at my face. I move closer.

"So," I say again, "did you miss me?"

She blinks. Her breathing goes back to normal.

"Yeah," she answers. She stands. I stand, as well.

Did Faith just say that she missed me?

She leans against a bookshelf and reaches a hand to my shirt, pulls me to her, our bodies almost touching.

I look around to see if I'm being tricked, but there's no one in sight.

Faith presses one finger against my cheek and turns my head back to her. "Did you miss me, too?" she asks in a soft voice.

"What?"

"I think you did"—she pauses to lick her bottom lip—"Diego."

Those lips, ay, *those lips*.

Hearing my name come out of her mouth like that messes me all up. This was not part of the plan. And now I can't help myself. I can't look away. My will has dissolved.

"What's going on?" I ask, unable to keep my eyes off her rosebud mouth.

"I'm letting down my defenses," she answers. "That's what you want, right?"

I inch closer.

What is she doing to me?

Of its own accord, my hand reaches for the sensitive spot at the base of her neck above her collarbone. I trace a finger along the dip and my heart thrums faster. Her skin is so soft. I imagine what it would be like to kiss her there.

I drop my hand. I should not be thinking about kissing Faith.

She doesn't back away. Instead, she tilts her chin up, giving me a better view, almost like she wants me to touch her again. A small sigh escapes my lips.

"*Mami*, you should stop," I half-suggest, half-groan. But I'm not sure that I want her to stop.

"What if I don't want to?"

She's still clutching my shirt. I wrap my hand around her wrist and pull it down to her waist. Under my fingertips her blood pulses fast, a one-way train on a track bound for collision.

I should walk away. This has gone too far. And yet, not far enough. It's dangerous. I don't trust the feelings surging through my veins. I try to reason that it's no big deal, that she's just like any other girl. Too bad I'm immune to my own lies.

Do I really want to do this with Faith Watters?

Surprisingly, the answer is clear.

Yes.

"Diego?" she says.

"Yeah?"

"Will you do something for me?" Faith asks.

At this point? Anything.

"Maybe," I say.

"Tell me what you think of me," she requests.

One look into her eyes confirms that I'm losing control. I swallow, wait.

Faith sees my hesitance and moves on. "Is everything with me a game to you?" she asks.

I watch the way her lips move. Confident. In control. The way I used to be twenty seconds ago.

"No," I answer. Like this, right now. Not a game. I am truthfully coming undone.

"I know you heard what I said at the restaurant. Do you think I'm hot, too?"

Her shirt rises slightly, exposing a glimpse of hip bone. The bone juts out just a tad. I wonder how it would feel against me. Would it fit perfectly? Would it poke, prod?

"Yes," I answer.

"Last one," she says. "If I kiss you right now, will you pull away?"

"You'll have to find out," I reply.

Faith leans into me and I can smell her lip gloss. My head dips, waiting, wanting. She comes within an inch of my lips. My mouth parts.

I can't take it anymore. I have to close the gap, but right before I do, she whispers another word.

"Psych."

15
faith

I pulled it off. I beat Diego at his own game.

To say he's shocked would be an understatement. He's embarrassed. And angry. Really angry. I knew he would be. But there's something else there, too, and I'd be willing to bet money that the emotion I see in his eyes is excitement.

He mumbles something under his breath. It sounds like thunder rumbling before a storm. I don't speak Spanish so I can't say for sure what he just called me.

But I have an idea.

"Aw," I say with a triumphant grin. "Don't be mad."

Victory is a pile of happiness, and I'm rolling around in it.

For a second I think maybe he'll kiss me anyway, but he turns away as though nothing happened. His back muscles are taut beneath his thin shirt, each one dipping and curving like a road map to the unknown.

Leading Diego on was out of character for me, but I couldn't stand his cockiness any longer. Maybe besting Diego will knock his ego down a few notches.

We're lucky no one saw us—not that many people come to this part of the library anyhow. I can't deny my nervousness, but even though I'm out of my realm, I relish watching Diego squirm.

"So," Diego says nonchalantly. "What's with the boxes?"

He's obviously going to pretend nothing happened. That's fine—no matter how he acts on the outside, I know that I had an effect on him. He's not as tough and closed off as he seems.

"The boxes are filled with books for the—" I pause, realizing I have no idea why Diego is in the library in the first place. "Why are you here?"

He pulls out a yellow slip.

"You're kidding, right?" I ask.

"Nope." He smiles.

So many firecrackers go off inside me all at once. Because of one smile. He's stealing his way into me and I don't appreciate it. Not one bit.

"But the punishment for fighting is out-of-school suspension for two days," I say. "How did you—"

"Yeah, well, tell that to the guidance counselor who apparently thinks it's more of a punishment to make me work around the school during the day than sit at home."

Probably right, but still. Did she have to stick him with the book fair organizing committee? Of all the detention assignments she could've given him. Figures.

"Wonderful," I say sarcastically. "So how long do we have the honor of hanging out with Mr. Dauntless?"

He laughs. "Is that what I'll be known as? 'Cause I gotta admit, it has a nice ring."

I grimace. Here we go again.

"Or maybe it's something you want to keep private. Just between you and me," he says.

You and me. Me and you.

"Let's get one thing straight," I say. "There is no you and me. Never will be."

Diego is confusing me; right now he looks one part serious, one part mischievous. I can't tell if he actually thinks he has a chance with me, or if he seriously enjoys irritating me. Probably both.

"Haven't you heard the saying, 'never say never'?" he asks.

"Haven't you heard the saying, 'back off'?"

Diego isn't fazed. His shirt is still crinkled where I grabbed it. The thought makes me blush, red ink spilling over my skin, spreading to my chest, my shoulders. I don't want to admit how good he felt against me.

"I won't wait forever, Faith," he teases. "Plenty of willing *chicas* at this school."

"Great," I say. "Why don't you go out with them, then?" I mean to smirk but it feels more like a grimace.

He smiles. "Maybe I will."

Don't look into his eyes.

"How long is your detention?" I ask.

"Ten days," Diego answers. "And since your committee meets three times a week, it looks like I'll be around for a while. Though if anyone cares, I still vote for the two-day, out-of-school suspension. Seems like a better punishment."

A safer punishment, for sure.

Melissa and Lori turn the corner. I give my best friend a look that tells her I'm going to kill her later. She grins.

"Hey, Diego," Melissa says. "I don't think we've officially met."

He turns to her.

"I'm Melissa, and this is Lori."

"Nice to meet you both," he says.

Melissa takes a moment to check Diego out, a pleased look on her face. My stomach churns, some unnamed emotion clawing its way in, pinching, stabbing. Diego notices her appraisal. He's relaxed, used to the attention, it seems.

"So," Melissa says, "what's up?" She's looking at us like she's trying to figure out why Diego is in the library.

"Nothing much." Diego shoots me a mischievous look. "Just trying to get Faith to go out with me."

I make a choking noise.

Melissa laughs. "Oh yeah?"

"She has a boyfriend," Lori says.

"I know," Diego replies, then leans closer to them. "But between you and me, I don't think it will last. She's not really into him. It's just part of her image, you see."

I am absolutely aware that my mouth is hanging open.

Melissa is beaming, seven thousand rays of approval. It's almost blinding. "Good luck with that," she says.

I am finding a new best friend. Stat.

Lori clears her throat. "Well, as interesting as this is, we have to get back to work."

"Great." Diego smiles, knowing he's embarrassed me just as much as I embarrassed him a few moments ago. "Where should I start?" he asks.

"Start?" Melissa asks, and then notices the yellow slip in his hands. Understanding crosses her face. "Oh"—she laughs—"oh my God."

"The way I see it," Diego says, "I have ten days to help you ladies with your book fair. That gives me ten days to convince Faith to dump that boyfriend of hers and drop the mask."

I don't understand how Diego, of all people, sees through me. Why can't he buy the façade like the rest of Oviedo High School?

Because he doesn't wear blinders.

No, with him I'm on display. Like an X-ray, he sees through the clothes and pain and lies.

"But, honestly, I don't think it'll take that long." Diego smirks. "I give it a week, tops, before she's in my arms."

I plaster on a hard face, looking directly into his eyes as I answer him.

"I'll take that bet."

16

diego

After detention, *mi padre* and I make an appearance at Javier's house. This house is warmth and understanding and everything right. It feels good to be around *mi familia*. There is no shortage of relatives in *la casa de mi tía* Ria. Javier is one of twelve kids. Even though I'm an only child, I've never felt like one. I spent a lot of time at Aunt Ria's growing up. First in Cuba. Then in the States after they moved here five years ago. Technically, it's Uncle Dimitri's house, but everyone knows that Aunt Ria really runs the place.

"Diego! *¿Cómo estás?*" Aunt Ria asks. She's wearing an apron like always, as though it's an extension of her skin.

"I'm good. How are you?"

Aunt Ria is a short, petite woman with long black hair and crazy skills in the kitchen. Sometimes it amazes me that she could have given birth to so many kids. But what Aunt Ria lacks in size, she more than makes up for in personality. Her attitude reminds me of the poblano peppers she loves—spicy, sure to leave a lasting impression.

Aunt Ria wraps me in a hug, *tsk*ing when she pulls back and sees my purple bull's-eye shiner. She doesn't ask questions, though. Probably because she's seen a lot worse in the past.

"Come in, come in," she says, opening the door wider.

I say hello to my uncle next, an older version of Javier. While Uncle Dimitri and Aunt Ria say hello to *mi padre*, I make my way inside.

The house is small for all the people who live here. Of the twelve kids, nine are boys. One room belongs to Aunt Ria and Uncle Dimitri, one room to the girls, and the remaining three rooms are split among the boys. Each room has enough space for three twin-sized beds and shelves for clothes. It sure beats life in Cuba.

In the kitchen, I find the girls. They squeal when they see me. Their names are Maria, Tatiana, and Alejandra—fourteen, twelve, and nine years old. I greet them and offer to help with the cooking. They turn me away, telling me I have too many people to visit. I thank them and stick my hand inside a large brown bowl filled with tortilla chips, eating a few as I go.

The screen door is open and I find the boys outside. They range in age from twenty down to four, with two sets of twins. Javier sees me and runs over.

"*¿Que pasa?*" he asks.

"Not much," I answer.

The guys are playing soccer, which is hard for them to do in the small backyard, but they manage. I greet the rest of *mi familia* and join the game. Just like old times.

Images flash through my head. My mind is suddenly a fast-paced scrapbook of snapshots. Cuba. Home. Soccer. Finding my first soccer ball. The feeling of scoring the winning goal.

Florida is different. Grass instead of dirt, clothes instead of rags. But soccer all the same.

Uncle Dimitri moved his family here with nothing but the clothes on their backs and hope for a better life. His first job paid under the table. Immigration was difficult. They required Uncle Dimitri to memorize U.S. laws, pay court document fees, and take a bunch of tests. Once he passed, the U.S. government gave him a temporary visa. Fortunately his family didn't have to endure the same thing. As his wife and children, they were automatically added to his visa. Only then did he get a legal job, get promoted. Buy a house. After my cousins moved to the States, *mi padre, mi madre,* and I visited them every summer. That's how I learned English. Seventeen people in one small house was craziness, but I always looked forward to it the next year.

Sometimes I wonder why *mi padre* didn't get us out of Cuba sooner.

"Dinner's ready," Aunt Ria calls from the kitchen.

We go inside and wash up. Since the table isn't big enough to fit everyone, some of us take a seat on the couch, some on bar stools, and some on patio chairs. I sit outside with Javier and two of his brothers. Eduardo and Pedro are identical twins, two years older than Javier and me.

"What's happenin', Diego?" Eduardo asks.

He and Pedro look like Javier, but with shorter hair. I take a moment to soak in the subtle differences that time has given them: longer chins, darker freckles, more carefree smiles. Their features are sharper, mature. But also more relaxed, as though living in the States has rounded the edges. The line that used to constantly furrow their brows is not as defined. They seem happier.

I wonder what I would see in the mirror if I actually looked close enough.

"*Nada,*" I answer.

"Look at your face," Pedro says, laughing. "Already gettin' in trouble, I see."

"*Cállate la boca*," I reply. "It's tough gettin' used to America."

Aunt Ria brings plates, heavy with pork, white rice, black beans with finely chopped poblano peppers mixed in, and plantains. I take a bite of *maduros,* sweet fried plantains, and suddenly my mind is in Cuba again.

I am nine years old, laughing and playing, chasing a raggedy stray dog that took to me for some reason. I have a *maduro* in my hand, a rare occasion back then. It's not like I fed the dog; I barely had enough food to eat myself, but he liked me nonetheless. I pop the fried plantain in my mouth and the dog licks between my fingers, wanting a taste. I'm pretty sure he had mange and ticks, but I didn't care. He died after a few years, a life cut short by harsh conditions. Just like most of us.

It's strange how one bite of food brings me back home, as though no matter where I go, I will always be reminded.

I cannot escape.

"What's the deal with the big C?" Javier asks.

The big C means the cartel, but most of Javier's younger siblings don't know anything about that. I intend to keep it that way.

"They haven't come for me," I answer. "Yet."

"Do they think you're dead?" Pedro asks.

He takes a bite of food, almost finished with his dinner already. Another survival instinct. Eat quickly. Run fast. Hope to make it out alive.

"I don't know for sure," I answer. I can only hope that when they filleted my neck, they assumed it killed me. I don't like to think about the alternative scenario, the one where they find out I've left the country.

"You know what you need?" Eduardo asks.

"To meet some of the girls from our school," Pedro answers.

They're always doing that, finishing each other's sentences. Where one stops, the other picks up.

"What about Anita?" Eduardo suggests.

"*Sí*," Pedro says. "We should introduce you to Anita. She lives in the dorms."

The twins attend the University of Central Florida, better known as UCF. They have come a long way from our days in Cuba.

"Anita is Colombian and really chill," Eduardo says.

"Personal experience talkin'?" I ask.

I know what "really chill" means to them. And thanks, but no thanks. I have no interest in someone who has been with my cousins.

"No. It's not like that," Pedro answers. "She's just cool. You'd like her."

"What are you doing Friday night?" Eduardo asks.

I stiffen at the mention of Friday night. It makes me think of Faith. I wonder if I can actually get her to go out with me.

Javier laughs. "Diego already has a date. Isn't that right?" he says.

I take another bite of food and answer him coolly. "Maybe I do."

"Yeah, right," Javier responds. "Unless you plan on kidnappin' Faith, she will never go anywhere with you."

Eduardo and Pedro look confused.

"Who is Faith?" Pedro asks.

"This white girl from our school Diego has his eyes on." Javier laughs. "Give it up, man. Never happenin'."

"A *gringa*?" Eduardo says. "Diego, I'm surprised. But

hey, if that's what you're into, we know a lot of white chicks, too."

"I'll pass," I say.

I realize then that I don't want another white chick. I want Faith.

I think about her grabbing my shirt and pulling me to her. I want her to do it again, only this time without the "psych."

At the same time, I cannot want Faith. I have to stop. Now.

"I'll meet Anita, though," I say. I need to hang out with another girl. It's apparently been too long for me if I'm thinking about Faith like that. Maybe Anita can make me forget.

Here's to wishful thinking.

"Meet us here Friday," Pedro says. "We'll bring Anita and some of her friends."

Good. I need to get Faith off my mind once and for all.

17
faith

Jason has called seven times in three days. He is a big ugly lie that I can't ignore, a wreck I shouldn't gawk at but can't turn away from. I should feel bad. I should listen to his explanation. At the very least, I should answer one call. I'm being unfair, especially considering all the times I've lied to him. It's unlike me to avoid him at school, to eat in the library instead of with him.

With Jason.

Everyone knows that's where I belong.

Speaking of the library, Diego has been avoiding me, treating me like a disease he doesn't care to catch. I offered to explain the book fair process to him, tell him what we needed help with, but he said he'd rather talk to Melissa.

I'm thrown for a loop. And I find it strange that I've been thinking more about Diego than I have about my boyfriend.

"What do you want?" I answer my phone, irritated.

It takes Jason a moment to reply. I'm not sure if it's because he expected me to ignore the call, or because he can't believe I just spoke to him that way.

"Hi," he says.

"Hi," I reply sharply. "What do you want?"

"Come on, Faith. Tell me why you're mad."

"You know exactly why I'm mad."

Jason sighs. "It's about Diego, isn't it?"

Silence, my lips sutured shut.

"Faith, babe," Jason says. "I just wanted to make sure he stopped harassing you."

The seams burst.

"How do you even know he's harassing me?" I shoot back. "You weren't there for any of my conversations with him. Be honest; you're angry about what I said at the restaurant."

"Yeah, I'm angry," Jason says, a little too harshly. "When my girlfriend of nearly three years announces to the world that she thinks some tattooed thug is hot? Yeah, I get pissed!"

"What are you worried about?" I ask. "So what if he's hot! You think other girls are hot. I've seen you look at them. I'm not trying to beat people up over it."

I'm furious. My anger is a bubbling vat of acid.

"Who cares about that loser? Are you really going to let him come between us?" Jason asks.

He doesn't get it. "It's not him that I'm worried about. It's you, Jason. You're being insecure."

There. I said it.

Jason's silence speaks volumes. I've hit a nerve.

"I want a boyfriend who doesn't get bent out of shape like that. You could've gone about it differently. You could've smiled in his face, knowing I'm with you. You didn't have to corner him three-on-one like a bully."

What I really want to say is this: *Jason, you could've been a man.*

"What are you saying?" Jason asks.

"I'm saying that you acted like a fool. I'm saying that

you should know already that no matter what you do, my choices are mine and mine alone. If I want to leave you, there's nothing you can do to make me stay, so the least you can do is have some damn dignity!"

Even as the words leave my mouth, I can't believe I said them. I don't know that I've ever been this truthful with Jason. I'm suddenly nervous, anxiety pinching my stomach.

How will he react? Will he apologize for being out of line? Will he get upset with me but hold it inside? Will he act like nothing happened, the way we always do?

I'm sick of pretending.

"Are you there?" I ask.

"I think we need a break," Jason says.

Great. He's going to act like nothing happened—just like always, what he always says, what he always does. *Let's take a break somewhere to cool off. It's Friday night. Let's go to the park, or the beach, or the pier, just you and me.* And everyone will expect me to be a link on his arm, his shadow, there but ignored.

"I don't think we should ignore this," I say. "That's what we always do. Why don't we talk, really talk for once?"

I take a deep breath. Here goes.

"There are things you don't know about me, Jason."

Pause. Breathe.

"I'm not everything you think I am. Nights I should have been studying, I went out partying with Melissa. I did bad things. Tried stuff I shouldn't have. And then there's my mom . . ."

I choke up. Try to right my voice.

"When I said I never drank or tried drugs, Jason, I lied."

I'm opening up.

Do you see my insides displayed for you?

I've never exposed myself to Jason. I've never invited him into my world. My *real* world. But if we're going to be together—the image of his mother talking about marriage flashes through my mind, making my stomach knot even more—then I need to start showing him bits of the real me, the deep me, the treacherous me. I don't know how much longer I can be someone I'm not.

"So," I continue. "If you want to go somewhere, take a 'break', that's fine. But it should be spent talking about this."

I wait for him. Wondering. Will he be okay with all I have to say?

"No," Jason says. "I mean we need a break from *us*."

My heart drops. My innards spill. Is Jason breaking up with me?

I finally, finally let him in and his response is to tell me we need a break—*that* kind of break?

This is why I keep my lips locked up, so my words don't fall out. No one besides Melissa can handle the real me. Jason just proved that.

"Fine," I say and hang up the phone.

I'm trying not to cry. I refuse to cry. And I don't have time for this. I hear Melissa's horn. *Beep, beep,* pause, *beep*. It's time for school.

I rush out to my best friend's car. I don't bother to cover my emotions anymore.

"What's wrong?" Melissa asks, alarmed.

I practically fall into the passenger seat. "Will you call your sister?" I ask. "I want to go out tonight."

Melissa raises an eyebrow and takes a drag of her cigarette. "You sure you're ready for that?"

I am. I'm over the past. It's time to prove that I can have a good time without going overboard. I cannot show the real Faith to anyone at our school, but I can be myself around Melissa.

"Yes, I'm sure," I answer.

Melissa smiles, pulls out of my driveway. And with three words, I know she supports me.

"It's about time."

18
diego

When I get to Javier's house Friday night, I'm still having a hard time understanding Faith's attitude. I'm trying not to think about her, but it's hard. Earlier at school, she seemed different. She hasn't been coming to lunch anymore, and she didn't say a single word in the two hours that we spent sorting books today. Instead of her silence being a reprieve, it was unnerving, as though I had misplaced something but couldn't quite figure out what.

Maybe because she's stolen it, pieces of me, my thoughts . . .

"Diego!" Javier greets me at the door.

We go out back where Eduardo and Pedro have made a small bonfire; it blazes bright against the dark sky, like sunshine in the dead of night. Sitting with them around the fire are four girls. *Gracias a Dios.* I'll finally have a chance to stop thinking about the girl I shouldn't be thinking about in the first place.

It's too hard. Faith. All of it. I don't let people get close anymore. After *mi madre,* after what happened . . . I promised myself I wouldn't let anyone in. With Faith, I can feel the boundaries slipping, blurring, my guard coming down. In the library I came close to kissing her, to wanting something real. I can't let that happen.

Javier introduces me to the girls, the last of whom is Anita. She has long legs and dark eyes. Her hair curls, tumbles down her back like black ribbon.

You are exactly what I need right now.

"Hey," Anita says, "it's nice to meet you."

"You, too," I say. She has no idea.

"Want a beer?" she asks.

"You guys have beer?" I ask. "How did you pull that off with Aunt Ria here?"

Eduardo puts a finger to his lips, signaling me to be quiet. "She's sleeping. Keep it down," he answers.

"Was that a yes or a no?" Anita asks, then smiles.

"No," I say. "Thanks, though."

Some people might be surprised that I don't drink. This is how I see it: Drinking lowers inhibitions, and where I come from, that's not a good thing. I'm used to watching my back. I don't take the risk of being caught off guard. I like to know what's going on around me. Call it a control thing. Control is a remnant of my past life, one I want to maintain. It's the only way.

I take a seat next to Anita and listen as she tells me a little about herself. She's a sophomore at UCF. Met my cousins in one of her classes. She's two years older than me. In a subtle way, she makes it clear that she's just looking for fun, which is perfect. Fun, I can do. She mentions that she recently stopped seeing someone. By the way she says it, I think she probably really liked the guy. That's cool, because I have someone in the back of my mind that I need to forget about, too.

I stay outside for a while, enjoying the company. When

the fire dies out, I move into a shadowed section of the lawn where the moonlight is blocked by a tree's lush, far-reaching foliage. Anita joins me. I can just barely see her features. I lean up against the wooden fence and put my arm around her. She relaxes into me.

I pull out a cigarette and offer her one. She takes it. As I go to light it, Anita grabs the lighter from me and smiles.

"Let me do it," she offers.

I don't know how the girl makes lighting a cigarette look good, but she does.

"You know that's supposed to bring you luck, right?" she asks.

"Oh yeah?" I ask. I wonder if she means with her, tonight.

Anita lights her own cigarette. I exhale and watch as she blows rings around my smoke, like clouds around a jet stream.

"Want to go somewhere?" I ask her.

"Sure," she says. "I can try to sneak you into my dorm, if you want."

My thoughts exactly.

As we leave, Eduardo approaches. "Want to go to the club?" he asks.

I shoot him a look. My intentions are clear.

One of the girls runs up to Anita. "You have to come!" she says.

I learned earlier that Anita and this girl have been forever friends. Joined at the hip.

"All right," Anita agrees. "Want to come?" she asks me.

Eduardo gives me a look to say that he had nothing to do with it. Any dorm room plans are put on hold.

"Okay," I say.

That way if it doesn't work out with Anita, maybe I can

find someone else. As long as I'm not thinking about Faith.

We end up taking two cars. From the outside, the eighteen-and-up club doesn't look like much. The inside is a different story. Multicolored lights flash everywhere, their luminance bouncing off shiny surfaces in the dark. The DJ plays dope music. There's not much room to move. The place is packed. The best part is the dance floor.

"Want to dance?" I yell to Anita over the music.

"For sure," she answers.

We make our way to the dance floor. As soon as Anita sways her hips, I know she's a good dancer.

Perfecto.

For once, with Anita's body pressed against mine, I don't think of Faith.

19
faith

The hardest part about tonight will be telling Dad the truth.

It's probably easier to lie, to wedge falsehood into his mind like wood under a door, propping it open for my manipulation.

But.

Something has to give soon. Like a ticking time bomb, I feel ready to explode.

"Dad," I say, "I have something to tell you."

Cowardice is a nasty bug burrowing itself into my system, waging war within.

Dad is sitting in the living room with Susan, watching television. Grace is in bed. Sleep, a sweet reprieve. One day, maybe, she'll grow up. See the depth of my lies, understand that I'm damaged. On the inside.

"Hey, honey," Dad says, and glances at my clothes. He looks as though he's trying to swallow a boulder lodged in his throat. "Why are you dressed like that?"

I'm wearing black heels and a fitted dress the color of rubies. It falls to my knees and plunges down my back. For makeup I went with blush, gloss, and a smoky eye.

To hide the circles. To hide the evidence of tears.

I was hoping Dad wouldn't freak out about my clothes, but judging by his look, I'd say there's a good chance that he'll make me change. My clothes are merely different color frames that I slip in and out of. The picture stays the same. I never try another pose. I wouldn't dare.

Until tonight.

"Wow," Susan says. "You look great."

"Thanks." My cheeks instantly warm.

"I thought you were hanging out with Melissa," Dad says. "You're a little overdressed, don't you think?"

"That's the thing," I say, and take a deep breath. I falter. Try again. "We're going dancing, if that's okay with you."

"Dancing?" Dad repeats.

I feel the sudden urge to run. I don't care that I'm wearing heels. I pinch the soft inside of my arm hard enough to make my eyes water. Hard enough to bruise. Anything to anchor me in place.

"Yes. I've been back four months now and I think it's time I do something fun," I say, locking my knees, commanding my feet to stay still.

Dad pops his knuckles. *Crack, crack, crack*. I hold my breath. *Crack*. He's bound to say no. *Crack*. I shouldn't have asked. *Crack*. What was I thinking? *Cra—*

"Are you sure you're ready?" Dad asks.

His words send a pang to my heart, a pierce from a shiv of ice. I feel terrible about what I've put Dad through. But I can't take back the past. All I can do is make better decisions in the future.

"I'm sure," I answer. "I know it must be hard for you to trust me"—I swallow—"but I'm okay now. And I know I could've lied to you, but I want to be truthful."

"I appreciate that," Dad says. A few hairs fall across his eyes. He doesn't bother to swipe them away. He turns to

Susan, a silent plea for support. Dad is wavering. Susan's vote will probably sway him in the direction of his final answer.

That can't be good. I've never done anything to deserve her support.

"Well, Faith, can you promise us that you will not, under any circumstances, do drugs or drink alcohol?"

"Yes," I say. "You have my word."

I cross my fingers, uncross them, fidget.

"And if you feel overwhelmed at all, you'll call us?" Susan asks.

"Of course," I say.

She sighs. "Listen, Faith, I was a teenager once. I know the game. The music, the boys, the atmosphere. Just don't get carried away, okay? Remember who you are."

Her support weighs me down and lifts me up, both.

"All right," Susan says, and nods to my dad. "I think she deserves another chance, Carl."

In that moment, for the first time, I see that my stepmom is on my side. I smile. It feels forced. "Thank you," I say.

I give Dad a hug and run out the door as he's telling me to be home at one. Generous.

Melissa picks me up in the driveway. When she sees me, she drops a lit cigarette in her lap, curses, grabs it quickly. The loose embers float toward me like fireflies.

"Good gracious!" Melissa looks shocked. "I must be imagining things, 'cause for a second, I thought I saw Faith in a tight red number with *skin* showing."

Melissa is beautiful tonight in a dress that looks as though someone painted her with gold.

I laugh and crawl into the back. Melissa's older sister, Monica, is in the passenger seat. "Hey, Monica," I say.

"Hey, beautiful," she replies, turning to face me. She

has wavy blond hair and blue eyes as big as the sky. "Long time, no see."

I haven't gone out much, that's why. Nearly ruined myself. Another pang.

"Thanks for doing this for us," I say.

"No problem. Anytime."

When Melissa found out about my split with Jason, she called Monica. Monica arranged a night out.

I buckle my seat belt. Melissa is staring at me. She laughs.

"I cannot believe your father let you leave the house looking like that," she says.

"My outfit's not bad," I say defensively.

"You're right," Melissa agrees. "But for you, it's a huge jump."

I smack my best friend playfully on the arm. "Hurry up before I change my mind."

When we get to the club, it's packed. Really packed. The line is out the door, a million bodies trying to scramble inside.

"We're never going to get in," I groan.

I need this. I need to breathe. I need to live, if only for one night.

"No worries," Monica says. "I know the doorman."

Monica walks to the front of the line. I follow her as though I belong, evil stares like arrows piercing my back. Some of the people look like they've been waiting for a while; they've taken seats on the ground and propped themselves against the wall. They make me think of a string of puppets.

Monica smiles at the doorman and gives him a hug. She motions behind her to Melissa and me. The guy opens the door, waves us in.

The inside of the club is busier than the outside. Lights flash everywhere to the beat of the music. Plush white love seats and chairs line the back wall like marshmallows. The alcoholic bar sits at the front of the club, but you need a special wristband to access that area. A nonalcoholic bar waits parallel to it. On the second floor are more tables and chairs and couches. The DJ's booth is stuck above the dance floor.

For a moment, I zone in to the DJ. I watch as his hands move bullet-fast, spinning the records. Headphones cover one of his ears.

"Come on," Melissa yells.

It's hard to move. I'm sandwiched between sweating, gyrating bodies. Must be near capacity.

Melissa grabs one of my hands and Monica grabs the other so we don't separate. My best friend pushes through the crowd. It takes longer than it should to get to the dance floor, but when we do, it feels amazing.

Dancing is my thing, my release of life's frustrations. When I dance, the world fades until nothing is left but the music and me. I don't have to remember who I am, or who I try to be, or who I'm supposed to be. It's just me. And in that moment, when the world stops, I'm free.

At that moment, I'm ready to destroy the fake me, to tear her down until nothing but broken pieces remain. Later, when the night ends, I'll pick them up and rebuild.

Monica immediately finds a guy to dance with. I give my best friend a look, since it's too hard to hear over the music, and mouth "it's on" to her.

I'm not worried about running into anyone from school. Even though it's an eighteen-and-up club, it's nearly impossible for under-twenty-ones to get in without a connection. And honestly, I can't see many people from our school having connections to this place. If they did, they wouldn't recognize me, anyway.

Melissa and I dance. Within a few songs, I can no longer feel anything but the music thrumming in my veins. I'm in the zone. My body moves to the beat, pulsing, breathing the rhythm. Melissa is a good dancer; that's why I like to dance with her. There is nothing worse than being in the zone and having someone approach you who looks spastic. Melissa and I stay close, so that we can rescue each other if the need arises, a flotation device in a tempest of bodies.

Out of the corner of my eye, I see a guy watching me. He has a killer body, dark eyes, and dark hair. He looks like he's around our age, maybe a year or two older. He's dancing with a girl, not paying her much attention. When he sees me looking, he smiles.

Melissa yells in my ear. "You should dance with him!"

"I don't know," I say, unsure. I look away.

"He's good!" she says.

I glance at him again. Maybe this is what I need to forget Jason. Diego, too.

The guy approaches me, squeezing through the throbbing mass. He dips his head to my ear.

"Want to dance?" he asks. His voice rolls into my ear, inviting.

I should tell him no, but when I glance to Melissa for support, she attaches herself to another guy, dancing away.

"All right," I answer.

We dance. The guy is better than I first thought. I like that he isn't trying to talk to me the whole time. I know by the way his eyes close occasionally, by the way his body moves in harmony with the beat, that he enjoys the music.

"You're a great dancer," he says when the song ends.

"Thanks. You, too," I reply.

He smiles. "Another?"

I nod. It feels strange because I think maybe I should be upset that Jason dumped me. The loss of a boyfriend would be enough to make most girls ache. I don't ache. I don't feel bad. Which is crazy, right? I don't know what any of it means at this point. All I know is that I want to have fun, and this guy is fun.

A new song starts and we dance again, the music sucking me down in its undertow. I don't think about Jason anymore. I only feel the rhythm, thumping to the beat of my heart.

We dance for a long time. Sweat pearls glisten against my skin. I don't know how much time has passed. Hours, maybe.

"Want to grab a drink?" I yell to the guy.

"Sure," he says.

We make our way off the dance floor to the nonalcoholic bar. I order water. So does my dance partner. I take one of the ice cubes out of the drink and run it along my forehead and down my neck. When I look up, the guy's staring. I realize how I must look to him, and my cheeks redden.

"What's your name?" I ask, grateful that the ice cube has melted.

"Brad. Yours?"

"Faith." I realize once my name has left my lips that I didn't fake-name him. Melissa and I are notorious for fake-naming people. We make up random names to give to guys—that way they won't know the real us.

Very few people know the real me.

One day, if I try hard enough, maybe I'll erase her completely.

It's quieter in this part of the club, though I still have to raise my voice to be heard. The guy doesn't prod me for information, and that makes me want to know more about him.

"How old are you?" I ask.

"Nineteen," he answers. A drop of sweat falls from his left sideburn.

"Did you come here alone?" I ask.

Do you plan to leave alone?

"No. I came with one of my buddies."

I take several big sips from my glass. Water never tasted so good.

"I saw you with your friends," Brad says. "Looked exciting. Big occasion?"

You mean, like the fact that my boyfriend paused our relationship and I finally feel a little free?

"Nope," I say. "Just happy to dance. It's been a while since I've been to the club. I'm feeling rusty."

"Couldn't tell," Brad says. "You're a natural."

"Thanks," I reply.

There is something refreshing about dancing in the club. It's different from the team. Less organized. More from the heart.

Brad leans in to say something else just as one of my favorite songs starts up.

"We have to dance!" I set the glass back on the bar and grab his hand. I don't think about what I'm doing. I'm just enjoying being me, for once.

We hit the floor. Brad moves behind me, close, testing the waters.

"Is this okay?" he asks.

I nod, thinking it's perfect, like taking a warm bath in musical notes. I'm covered, drenched in the beat.

We're on a different part of the dance floor now. I have a better view of the crowd. With an eagle eye, I take inventory. I see a guy who looks like someone I know. Familiar. Too familiar.

And suddenly the atmosphere around me turns cold. Freezing.

I am paralyzed.

By fear.

20
diego

"What's wrong?"

Anita yells to me over the music. I can't answer her right away. My body has gone still in the middle of the dance floor. I'm dead weight. Seaweed in an ocean, anchored to the floor, swaying with the current.

"Are you okay?" Anita asks.

"What? Yeah. I just, um." I can't get my words right. I can't concentrate.

"You sure?" Anita asks. " 'Cause you don't look too hot."

What is Faith doing at the club? Should I go talk to her? And why is she dancing up on that guy?

I start dancing again. I hear the music, but I no longer feel it. I don't know when it happened exactly, but at some point Faith became more than a *gringa* to me.

"You're not as into it," Anita says.

That's because Faith is looking right at me. A challenge, almost. She moves smoothly, like she is the music.

Then she looks away. I don't know why, but it angers me. Maybe if I close my eyes, I can rid my brain of her.

Creamy skin. Stop. Coppery hair. Stop. Her.

No matter how hard I try, it doesn't work. I decide to dance nearer to Faith, bringing Anita with me.

The guy Faith is with momentarily blocks my view. I don't like how close he is to her. I thought she had a boyfriend. I also thought she was falling for me a little bit. When I leaned into her that day, she didn't pull away. And there was the library thing. No matter what she says, I felt the race of her pulse.

When Faith brushes hair off her shoulder and the guy leans further into her, I think I'm going to lose it.

I pull Anita into me. My hands are on her hips, my pelvis moving against her.

"That's what I'm talking about," Anita says.

Too bad I'm not doing it for her. This is strictly for Faith. She's going to act like she doesn't know me? We'll see about that.

Though the lines are once again blurring, I don't back down. I hate to lose. And more than that, I hate to see Faith with another guy.

Faith looks up and winces. I can't help grinning.

That's what I thought, mami.

She feels something.

Faith recovers from her slipup and tilts her head to one side, letting the guy place a kiss on her neck.

I'm thinking about punching him in his face. I know Faith is messing with me on purpose. She wants a reaction from me.

When I glance back at Anita, she regards me strangely. She peers at Faith, and then at me again.

"Oh," she says, "I get it."

"*Lo siento*," I say.

Surprisingly, Anita places a finger on my mouth. "Been there. No worries."

So it's like that? Competitive. Staking a claim.

"What do you say we give her a taste of her own poison?"

"You sure?" I ask.

Anita wraps her arms around my neck and dances up on me. Over her shoulder, Faith watches. One way or another, I'm going to make Faith come to me.

The song changes. The beat pounds faster. Faith smiles slyly and I think for a second that she might approach, but instead she presses the back of her body firmly against the front of the guy and wraps her arms behind his neck.

I'm trying not to lose it. That should be me behind her. When his palms start a slow crawl up Faith's stomach, I have to clench my hands on Anita's hips. It's the only way to control my fingers, which are itching to reach for her.

What's wrong with me?

I should not be playing this dangerous game, but I can't look away.

My hands cascade down Anita's body like a misting of rain. I make sure Faith sees.

Faith's eyes are hard, upset. Good, because I don't think I can keep this up much longer. I need to go to her, but I wish she would come to me. I hate giving up control. I know that's what Faith wants. And I'm pretty sure she knows I want her to do the same. So the question is: Who breaks first?

Me, apparently, because when she turns around and the guy leans down like he might kiss her, I get in his face.

"Mind if I cut in?" I say. It's not a question. I will be cutting in whether he likes it or not.

I don't have time to worry about Anita. She'll understand. Or not.

"We were kind of in the middle of something," the guy says.

"Yeah? Not anymore."

"Look, dude—"

I cut him off. "No, you look," I say. "This is not an option."

He looks from me to Faith. I don't have time for his indecision. I push him aside and pull Faith to me. He walks away. Smart move.

"Where's your boyfriend, *mami*?" I say into her ear. Now I'm behind her and she's pressed against me.

Like it should be.

She twists slightly to answer. A draft from the ceiling fan softly blows her hair.

"I don't have a boyfriend," she answers.

This stuns me. "Seriously?" I ask.

I'm almost yelling, trying to be heard over the pounding beat.

"Seriously," she says.

I grin. "Is that why you're letting that dude dance all over you and tryin' to make me angry?"

"Yes," she answers. "What about you with your hands all over that girl?"

She's admitting it. Out loud. Letting words become concrete evidence.

"What about it?" I shrug. She knows I'm jealous, though I can't admit it aloud.

Faith takes a step like she's going to leave, but I wrap an arm around her waist and pull her against me.

"Dance with me," I say into her ear.

She looks back and bites her lower lip, undecided.

I brush tresses of hair over her shoulder toward her face. Faith is dangerously close. I don't want her to leave. From behind, I take note of her bare back. Her skin is everywhere, intoxicating, alluring.

I place a kiss on the nape of her neck. She shivers. I kiss one shoulder, then the other. She goes loose in my arms.

"Dance with me, *mami*," I repeat.

This time she does. She moves slowly at first, like she's nervous.

"You can do better than that," I challenge.

She moves more to the beat, still holding back.

"You scared?" I ask, taunting.

Faith whips her head back and gives me a glance layered with seven hundred pounds of confidence.

"I am not scared," she replies.

"Then prove it," I say. "Give me all you've got."

21
faith

With Diego dancing behind me, I decide to let loose. I swear my soul shudders, mimicking the release of pressurized air, finally relaxing into its natural state.

He shouldn't have taunted me. Or more like, I shouldn't have let him. I could have walked away. I walk away from everything I want in life. Not this time. Because I know, as much as I've tried to deny it, that I want Diego tonight.

I don't want to think about tomorrow. I don't care about the world or its standards. I don't think about my past or what brought me to this moment. Tonight, I refuse to acknowledge anything but Diego and me moving together like we're one.

His fingers trailing up my arms incite goose bumps, though the club is hot and I'm sweating. Diego notices, and chuckles in my ear. He places a kiss on my neck and I groan. When he kisses my spine, my knees almost buckle.

I turn to face him. His lips are slightly parted, his breath on my forehead. I breathe him in, run my hand down his stomach, mold myself to him. My skin is steaming. His skin is steaming.

"*Mami,*" he groans. "You're drivin' me *loco*."

"Good," I say.

He grins, his hooded eyes like a partially drawn shade.

"You sure you want to do that?" he asks.

Tonight, yes.

I lean into his ear. "I thought you only wanted to get under my skin."

I say it because I know now, by the look in his eyes, by the way they are drinking me in, that he wants more.

"At first I did," he admits.

"And now?"

He pulls back and looks at me. With one hand, he cups my cheek. I don't back away. He moves his hand to my hair and leans down to my ear.

"If you're 'bout to say 'psych' again, I'll lose it."

I'm not messing with him. I really want to hear it. "Not this time," I reply.

With a brave finger, I trace the muscles in his shoulders, sinewy, taut, almost edible. "Tell me," I request.

The song ends. A new one begins.

"What do you want to hear?" he asks. "That I want you?"

"If that's the truth," I answer. I'm taking down my wall, one brick at a time. I don't dare take a break. I can't catch my breath. If I do, I'm afraid I'll change my mind.

"Faith, you know I want you," Diego says, moving against me. "It almost broke me to see you dancing with that *hombre.*"

It feels good to hear him say it. I let his hands roam my body as we dance. First my hips, then my stomach. Touching. Teasing. I skim his shoulders, the muscles of his back. Something inside me craves him. I shiver at his touch. Song after song, I stay pressed against him, hypersensitive with desire. I forget about my secrets. I don't think about Jason, about how I've hidden in the shadows for years. All I know is here and now.

"Faith!" Someone calls my name over the music. It's Melissa. She's smiling.

"What's up?" I yell back.

She points to her watch-free wrist. Almost curfew.

"I have to go," I say into Diego's ear.

I don't want to go.

He wraps his beautifully tattooed arms tighter around me.

"Stay with me," he says. A command.

I want to. Really, I do. If only time could stand still. An infinite mirror image of here and now.

"Can't," I say.

He stops dancing. His expression tells me he's disappointed. "Let me walk you to your car," he offers.

Diego keeps an arm around me as we approach the front of the club. On a couch near the door, I recognize someone from Diego's lunch table, from my psychology class, too. He stands when he sees us.

"Yo, Diego! You leavin'?" he asks.

"Just walking Faith out," Diego answers. "By the way, Faith, this is my cousin, Javier. Javier, this is Faith."

Javier is big like Diego. I see the resemblance. But unlike Diego, Javier looks clean-cut, except for a few scars. No visible tattoos.

"I'll catch up with you in a minute," Diego tells his cousin.

Near the couch, I spot the girl Diego was dancing with.

I continue out the door and into the parking lot. The sky is the color of a bruise. Stars punch tiny holes in the canopy above, try to squeeze into the small pits, just barely fit. I cast my eyes down. Melissa parked far away. I'm thankful for Diego's presence.

Up ahead, I make out the silhouettes of my best friend and her sister. Melissa's distance from me is no accident.

I can't stop thinking about the other girl. "Did you come with her?" I blurt.

Diego smiles. "*¿Por qué, mami?* You jealous?"

Absolutely. "Maybe."

"Don't worry about her," he says.

We stop walking. I lean into him. He's one concrete pillar of hope and I'm one melted puddle of desire. And jealousy. It shouldn't matter if he came with that girl, or if he leaves with her. But for some reason, it does. The thought is acidic, burning, bubbling.

"She likes you," I say.

Diego brushes a drop of sweat from my back. "I'm not goin' home with her," he says, like he read my mind, like he knows my thoughts. Perhaps he does. Perhaps they are merely flipped images of his own. In sync. On point.

I peek up. His face is just above mine. Though I have practically memorized his features, I'm caught off guard. As if I don't recognize him in this new light. I gaze at his lips and hear him chuckle.

I argue with myself. I should walk away. I should thank him for the most amazing dancing of my life and leave. I definitely should not be thinking about what his mouth tastes like.

But I'm losing the battle. I reach a finger to his lips and carefully trace them, hoping he won't notice the tremble, the longing rippling through my blood, through my fingertip.

He groans and my whole body reacts to the noise. Just the sound of his pleasure drives me crazy. A hundred million sparks ignite inside me. I cannot take it.

I kiss him.

There is nothing slow about it. His tongue flicks out and I meet it with mine. His hands wind through my hair and pull softly, bringing me closer to him. I gently bite his lower lip and tug. Our kiss is wild, unplanned. Nothing like my life.

I am wrecked inside. Totally and completely shattered. Lit on fire by his touch.

Diego kisses down my neck and back up to my mouth. I have never been kissed like this by anyone. I didn't know that a kiss could be powerful enough to reach deep inside and linger.

I kiss him harder, wanting more. My hand wraps around the back of his neck, pressing him into me.

"*Mami,*" Diego says against my parted lips. "Unless you plan on takin' me home with you, we have to stop."

I can tell it pains him to say it. I don't want to stop just yet. When he goes to pull away, I kiss him again.

"Do you know what you're doing to me?" he asks.

In the back of my mind, I know I need to leave. But I'm afraid that if I do, I may never be with Diego like this again.

I give him one last kiss before I pull away. He looks hungry for me. It brings a smile to my face, knowing I did that to him. I broke through the tough, impenetrable Diego.

I don't bother with words. I don't want anything to ruin the moment. I simply walk away.

With the taste of Diego on my lips.

22
diego

Faith leaves me standing in the parking lot. I take a moment to cool off, to calm myself after kissing her, like an engine powering down for the night.

I still feel her on my lips.

It takes a minute to realize that the sensation in my stomach is knots, nerves snaking around each other.

I don't know what happened to my resolve. I could've sworn that I was done with Faith when I came here tonight. Obviously, I'm not fooling anyone.

Especially myself.

"There you are," Javier says. "I thought maybe you had another run-in with MS-13s."

"No. Nothin' like that," I say. "I'm good."

I'm sitting on some sort of electrical box behind the club. Javier takes a seat next to me.

"Everythin' cool?" he asks.

I love Javier like a brother. He always has my back.

"It's cool," I reply.

He smiles. "Never thought I'd see what I saw tonight."

He means Faith, I'm sure.

"Me, neither."

"Are we goin' to have to fight her *novio*? 'Cause you

know I got you—just wonderin' what we're up against on Monday."

"Nope," I say. I cannot help grinning. "She doesn't have a boyfriend anymore."

"No?" He whistles. "Is that thanks to you? 'Cause we'll still have to deal with Jason, if that's the case."

I don't know why Faith and Jason split. I didn't think to ask.

"*No sé.*"

"So what happened tonight?" he asks.

"You have to be all nosy?"

"Yep," he says. No shame.

Usually a sleazy comment would slip my lips and knock Javier's curiosity away. But I think Faith deserves more. Something is going on under the surface with her. I intend to find out what.

"She kissed me," I admit.

I pull out a cigarette. Light it. Slow inhalation draws embers close to my face, sparks tangoing in my vision.

"*¡Dios mío, Diego!* How did you pull that off?"

I think about what happened right before the kiss. She traced my lips. Everything after was fair game.

"Don't know."

"She's a good dancer," Javier comments.

Yeah, she is. I'll be dreaming about the way she moved her hips against me for a long time.

"She was actin' like she wanted you, *primo*. How long do you think it'll take?" my cousin asks.

I check my temper, knowing Javier doesn't mean anything by it. And normally I would jump on the opportunity, tackle it with all I have, but Faith is different.

"It's not like that," I say.

Javier looks at me like I've lost it. He's never known a time when it wasn't like that for me.

"Less or more?" he asks, feeling out my train of thought.

Do I want nothing to do with her, or everything to do with her?

"More," I admit. I want to know what Faith is hiding. Why does she act *perfecta* for everyone else? Why did she let me see more tonight?

Why do I care, anyway?

Javier looks at me, the ground, the roof. He finds interest in the distant multicolored beams of light from some faraway building that probe the sky.

"You got it bad, huh?"

Is it that obvious?

"No," I answer. I don't need people to think I'm spun because of a girl. Even if it's true.

"It's cool," he says. "I won't say anything. Hey, if she's into you, maybe she isn't as bad as I thought."

I've never had a steady girlfriend. Javier is used to me going through girls like I go through Aunt Ria's homemade cookies.

"She's strange," I admit.

I think about the front Faith puts on for other people. How she let me in tonight. There was no front. Only the real, raw Faith Watters. I can never think of her in the same way again.

"It'll be tough," Javier says. "You better be ready for haters, 'cause you and I both know our kind don't mix with hers. It's like oil and water. Everybody will expect you two to be separate. And if I'm honest, I have to say it doesn't come from her side alone."

He's not lying. I don't think *mi padre* would care if I

date a white girl, but I know Aunt Ria cares if Javier does. It's not right, but that's the way things are.

"I don't care about them," I say. Let them hate if they want to. It's time someone broke the mold. I want to rip standards into a thousand pieces and watch them flutter away.

Javier laughs. "Your life is about to get a lot more interesting. Hope you're ready."

I *am* ready. I wonder if Faith will go on a date with me now that she's done with Jason. And suddenly, I remember the conversation I had with her ex earlier in the week.

I smirk.

Guess I got my Friday night date after all.

23
faith

Ten, eleven, twelve seconds I stare into the mirror, wondering at my reflection. Green eyes that used to be as soft as dew-moistened grass. Slightly tanned skin, roughened by the aftereffects of pain. Upturned lips that want to relax into their natural set, overworked for the benefit of others. I concentrate on a thin layer of eyeliner that clings between my lashes, holding on for dear life, begging to be remembered.

As if I could forget last night.

I'm not sure where to go from here. My options are few: give Diego a chance, or savor the memories with him as I reapply the mask. It has to be one or the other. I can't be fake with Diego close. I don't know why that is; I only know that he has a way of breaking down my defenses.

"Faith! It's time for church," Susan hollers.

I slip on a black dress and pull my hair into a ponytail. Like almost every other dress I own, this one has three-quarter-length sleeves, a high neckline, and falls below my knees. I look like a girl who wears confidence, who eats compliments for breakfast, who dishes out lies like candy.

When I get to the car, Susan and Grace are buckled in

and waiting. Dad is at church, always early on Sundays, preparing his sermon.

The usual crowd greets us in the parking lot, a swarm of mosquitos thirsty for a drink, just one sip before moving on to the next victim. Everyone smiles and asks how I'm doing. I tell them I'm well, my standard response. They never ask for more.

Church starts the same as every Sunday, with worship songs and Dad welcoming everyone. The sermon takes forty-five minutes. Typical. I try not to look for Jason. We usually sit together, but today I race to Susan's side. I muster my confidence and try for casual. My stepmom looks at me strangely, but thankfully doesn't ask questions.

People have probably noticed that I'm not in my regular spot. I'm glad Susan sits up front. That way I won't have to see all the curious gawking.

By the end of the sermon, I want to escape. I can't deal with Jason. I stand and turn. Suspicion confirmed; everyone is looking at me. Three hundred piranhas, six hundred eyes starving for a piece of me.

Mrs. Magg steps in front of me.

"Hello, Faith," she says.

Her face is pinched, unhappy.

"You've broken my son's heart, you know." Her voice is hushed, meant for me alone. "How can you be so selfish? Did you think at all about the pain this is causing Jason? I suppose you didn't think about Grace, either, about the example you set. You have obligations to the church body, to your family, to my son."

I open my mouth to speak, but she cuts me off.

"You are the daughter of a pastor, Faith. Don't forget where your commitments lie."

Before I can blink, Mrs. Magg is gone, moving through

the crowd to the door. A smile on her face as though nothing happened.

I fake not feeling well and tell Susan I need to visit the back bathroom—the one reserved for church employees. Less chance of bombardment.

I open the bathroom door. Stalls are clear. I walk to the sink and splash cold water on my face.

How did my life get so twisted? It's hard to tell when things went wrong. Or are they finally going right?

The bathroom door opens with a groan, its arthritic hinges protesting. A woman I recognize, but don't know well, walks in.

"Darling, are you okay?" she asks.

I must look awful. My face is wet from water that I haven't yet wiped off. Drops cling to my lashes, clouding my vision as though I'm looking through a kaleidoscope.

"Yes," I say, grabbing paper towels.

"Are you sure? You look a little pale," she says.

I wipe my face, bringing the woman into focus. Her image sharpens, exposing crinkles at the corners of her mouth. I ponder the lines. Maybe she's a smoker. Or a laugher. Or a person who smiles constantly to hide what's underneath. Just like me.

How little I know her, others like her.

How little they know me.

"Are you sure?" she repeats.

I want to tell someone. I need to tell someone. I'm desperate for a second opinion. But I have to be careful how I say it.

I throw away the towels. "No," I admit.

I cannot remember what department of the church this lady works in. A secretary, maybe?

"Go on," she encourages me.

I clear my throat. "If a girl likes a guy who's really different—I mean, nationality, appearance, race, past—but he's beautiful all the same, can it work?"

I want her to tell me that the past doesn't matter. That we all come from somewhere. That it's where we plan to go that makes a difference. I want her to water my seed of hope.

But I expect her to let me down.

The woman scrunches her eyebrows for a moment. "No," she finally says. "I don't believe it can work."

She pauses to smile at me. A sad smile. For my benefit, she pretends we aren't talking about me, and I'm grateful. I suppose small acts of kindness still exist.

"She's probably had a nice upbringing, like you," she continues. "Nice girls belong with nice, simple boys. There's nothing simple about a biracial relationship. Think about the social issues she'll face. And what about her parents? His? Can you imagine what her folks would think? Tell her to find a nice boyfriend like that Jason of yours. He's a keeper."

I swallow hard, fighting to appear calm. My mouth is a desert, dry, cracked.

"You're right. Thanks for the advice," I say.

I don't know why I thought this would be a good idea. The woman has confirmed everything I already knew. She's right, though. It would be tough to maintain a relationship with the world against you.

I cannot have Diego.

We do not belong together.

I could disregard her advice. But caution tells me to obey. The freedom I felt the previous night? It's gone. Freedom reminds me too much of drugs, of having a choice, too many choices, of spinning out of control. What if

Diego becomes my new drug? What if the feeling with him is too good? Too addictive? Suppose I let go too much?

And then he hurts me. What will be left?

The woman is still staring.

"I have to go," I say.

I find Susan in the lobby. I ask her if she can please take me home. Quickly. I tell her I need to rest. She picks up Grace and we leave. I try not to think about Jason. Or the curious eyes that follow me like the glare of a sharpshooter through a scope. I especially try not to think about what the woman in the bathroom said.

It's hard, though. All I want to do is see Diego. All I want is the pressure of his lips. My brain fights my heart, volleying shots back and forth, a war declared within. One will win. But somehow, I fear, as a whole I'll lose.

I have one day to hold on to him. One day to miss him. It's no time, really. When I get to school tomorrow, it's back to the old Faith.

The Faith who doesn't ruin people's lives with her selfishness.

24
diego

On the way to school, I think of Faith. Clouds move in and out of focus. The sun is too bright, but I stare at the sky anyhow. I remember her smile. Her fingers. Her freedom. Her words. All the things that served as windows into her world.

As I open the double doors and head to my locker, I keep a watchful eye. Her first class is near mine, but I don't see her yet. My hands reach for books. My elbow shuts my locker. My mind abandons me. I forget what I need to do, lose the task at hand, clutch the wrong books. Try again. Stare at too many numbers before I remember my combination. I grab the right books, but I can't grab my attention. It runs away, searching for Faith. Caring about nothing else.

I look down, double-checking; do I have everything I need? As I look up, Faith comes into view, wearing her usual one-size-too-big clothes. Her hair is in a braid. Not much makeup, not that she needs it. But what throws me off is the look on her face.

Wrong.

That is all I can think. She looks wrong. Like someone took her apart and put her back together incorrectly.

She doesn't smile when she sees me. She comes closer. I hold my breath. Pressure builds in my sternum, like I've dived too deep underwater. Her touch is the surface and I'm desperate for air. I push away from my locker. I open my mouth to speak.

Three steps, two, one, and she's within range. Doesn't matter, though, because she walks right by me without a word.

I hate how I want to make her smile, how I want to ask what's wrong. I should walk the other way. Instead, I cut through the hall after Faith, her current sweeping me up and carrying me along.

When I get close, I reach out a hand and grab her forearm. Her skin is warm and smooth and too perfect under my calloused palms. She turns.

"What?" she asks calmly.

I am fire and ice and fuel and water.

"Faith," I say, hating how her name feels so good rolling off my tongue. "What's wrong?"

"Nothing," she says.

Her face is blank. No anger, no passion, nothing. Void. Like the robot she's used to being. Not like the Faith at the club. Loose and free.

"Liar," I challenge.

She eyes me. Her head tilts slightly, a gun cocked, ready to fire.

She is fierce.

She is beautiful.

"Should something be wrong?" she asks.

Maybe she didn't see me. Maybe I'm overreacting. I try to relax.

"How are you?" I ask.

"Good." She smiles but it looks forced, like she's smiled

for too many people already today. Like she's saving the last remaining smiles for somebody worth her time.

I wonder if I should tell her that I've been thinking about her.

"Well, I need to get to class. Glad you're fitting in, Diego. See you around," she says, and begins to walk away.

This is not the same Faith that I danced with at the club.

"What's going on?" I ask, stepping in front of her. The bell rings. People shuffle into class. I'm officially late for first period, but I don't care.

Faith looks past me to the suddenly deserted hall. For the briefest second, I see a flash of panic in her eyes. Then she reins it in.

"I don't mean to be rude," she says, "but I need to get going."

I lean closer, just a little further over the edge, hoping my feet will stay solidly planted. "Not until you tell me what's going on," I say.

She laughs hoarsely, not like the sweet sound I heard the other night.

"What do you want me to say?" she asks. Her eyes are *fuerte*, unbreakable.

"I don't know, but say somethin'," I reply. "Give me some *sentimiento*."

Even though I'm angry, I still have an urge to kiss her.

She says nothing.

I think about biting my tongue, but at the last second, I let my words flow freely.

"Are you going to act like you weren't into me at the club, like that kiss never happened?" I say. "*Mami,* I didn't kiss you. You kissed me. So don't pretend there's nothing there."

Her eyes scan our surroundings. "Let's get this over with," she says sharply. "What happened the other night can never happen again. It was a stupid, irresponsible mistake. Are we done now?"

"No," I reply. "We're not done. Not even close." I thought we were just getting started. "What's the point of this?"

"Did you not hear me the first time?" Faith asks. Her lips are pressed into a thin line. "The dancing meant nothing. The kiss meant nothing."

She looks around, making sure the hall is still deserted. "You mean nothing."

Too far, Faith.

If she's going to have amnesia about how good our kisses were, then maybe I need to remind her. I move in. I'm teetering on the edge, close to falling. With or without her.

Her eyes are remote. I raise my fingers to brush her cheek. She steps back.

"What are you doing?" she asks.

"What do you think I'm doing?"

"Diego, please." Even though she uses nice words, her tone is rough. She's acting like I'm the scum of the earth, which, let's face it . . . next to her? I kind of am.

"What's the deal?" I say, exasperated. "You won't leave me alone when I want you to. Then you dance with me at the club and kiss me like it's your dyin' wish. Now you couldn't care less?"

"Yes. And if you're done, I'm late to class," Faith says. "Will you promise me you'll never bring this up again? That you'll let it go?" She looks unsure, like she expects me to expose our night.

"Don't worry, Miss *Máscara*. I'll take our little secret to the grave"—aside from Javier—"but I won't promise you anything about letting go. Because I don't think you want me to."

She smiles wickedly. "You obviously don't know me at all."

I wonder if I'm making a mistake. Even if I am, I can't deny that Faith intrigues me. Still. And I enjoy a good challenge.

"Give it up," she says, noticing the competitive glint in my eyes. "You and I will never be. It's unnatural. And you know it."

"All I know is that you won't let me close. I think it's 'cause you're scared." I smile. "Scared that the moment I get you in my arms, you'll never want to leave. And *you* know it."

Faith turns, walks away. No matter what she says, I'm not giving up that easily.

And one backward glance from her tells me that she doesn't truly want me to.

25

faith

"I don't understand. I saw you two kissing—"

"Give it a rest, Melissa. I can't deal with this right now."

"I'm just saying. That was not an accident, Faith," Melissa says, handing me a stack of books to price. "That was intense, it was real—"

"Seriously," I interrupt. "Can't. Deal. Please."

Talking about Diego is five hundred pencil points jabbing my skin, etching painful lines into vulnerable tissue with each word. My eyes water as though I've cut two dozen onions. The remembrance of the lies I told him is its own punishment, one that makes it hard to breathe.

He does mean something to me.

"You're pushing him away, aren't you?" Melissa says.

My eyes scurry across the library, hoping no one but me can hear. Two people—a guy and a girl—stand, twenty strides away. The guy places a hand on the girl's lower back. My fists clench.

"Yes. Now let it go," I warn.

Melissa doesn't back down. "Is this because of Jason?"

Honestly, no. What I feel for Diego scares me. I have to

think about other people. About Dad's reputation. We—Diego and I—do not belong together. Simple as that.

"No." I'm being short with her.

Melissa slams a book on the table. The force sends a gust of air over my arms and shoulders.

"So this is because of your dad? Faith, when are you going to start living for yourself?"

"Diego and I are not a good mix, Melissa," I whisper.

"What are you *talking* about?" she says.

I can hear our heartbeats in the silence between us.

"Diego and I . . . It's too intense. Too hot. I'm not getting burned." It's a cop-out, I know.

Melissa laughs, but she doesn't look amused. "Do you hear yourself? You could use some fire in your life."

"What's that supposed to mean?"

Melissa gives me a stern look. "It means that you need to lighten up. You *need* that fire, Faith. You haven't been passionate about anything in a long time. You're too worried about what everyone else will think, and you've created such a squeaky-clean image that you feel the need to constantly polish it. It's ridiculous. Let yourself enjoy Diego. If he burns you, so be it. At least then you'll feel some sort of emotion. You'll be *living*. Your life. Not theirs."

Her words hang heavy, an omnipresent cloud around me. Tears sting my eyes, and I jump up to leave.

"Wait," Melissa says.

"You're supposed to be the one who understands!" I realize I'm yelling, but I'm too hurt to care. "You of all people should get it!"

She knows why I can't let people in. Especially people who make me forget my name, who kiss me like there's no tomorrow and make me forget how to breathe. Who make my heart sing even though I've tried desperately to quiet it.

"I do understand, Faith. And I love you enough to tell you that you're fading. My best friend is disappearing before my eyes, and I want her back."

"You have me," I say. Lies.

"No, I don't. You know it. You feel it, don't you?" Melissa says.

Yes. "No."

"Don't lie to me, Faith. Not me. I *know.*"

She always has. It's one of the many things I love about her.

Diego and Lori approach. I quickly wipe my eyes. My hand is slick with tears. I radiate uncertainty and regret like a pheromone, marking myself as a target. I fear Diego's heightened senses will pinpoint my weakness.

"This conversation is not over," Melissa says quietly.

Diego's wearing ripped jeans and a plain green shirt.

He is breathtaking.

Diego stops one foot in front of me and sets down his backpack. He stares at me. I meet his stare, second for second.

"*Hola,*" he says.

"Hi," I say quickly. "I set the last of the boxes over there—" I pause to point to the mountainous pile. "If you wouldn't mind opening them and separating them according to category?"

I get down to business. It's better that way. My mask is flawless.

"Okay," he says.

No fight. I wasn't expecting that.

"Thanks," I say, businesslike. When I look back at Melissa, she's scowling. I pay no attention.

We're almost done unloading, categorizing, and pricing books. Posters, flyers, and advertising for the fair are next. I have nice handwriting, so I draw the signs. Melissa prefers to color them. We usually go to her house for that.

I like it at Melissa's. Her mom is sweetness and trust wrapped into one package. She lets Melissa make her own mistakes.

I wish my dad had opened up to me. I wish he'd tackled the pain with me after Mom left instead of being a locked box. I searched for the key for years, but I couldn't find it. I still haven't.

"Five," Melissa says, breaking through my thoughts. "That's how many times Diego will meet us before his detention is over."

"So?" I say, acting unconcerned. I fear my voice reflects the shallow breaths I take as my heart constricts.

Five more times, really? That's not much.

"Yes," Melissa says. "So, I wouldn't wait too long. He'll be gone before you know it. And I've seen the way girls look at him, girls who aren't afraid to take the risk."

I grimace. The thought of Diego with someone else is static, fuzzing my brain, making it hard to think.

I shouldn't care.

"Imagine some other girl dancing on him the way you did. Or him kissing another girl the way he kissed you," Melissa says.

"Okay!" I yell. "I get it!"

Diego turns, raises an eyebrow. He's far enough away not to hear me unless I raise my voice. I need control. I can't let him see me slip.

He turns back around. Lori helps him with books. If I had a spine, it would be me over there.

While Diego's not looking, I glance at him. I want to go to him. Questions skitter across the surface of my mind. Is Diego bad for me? Why do I care what others think? Was the woman at church right? I mean, what does it matter that his skin is different from mine? Why are tattoos considered art only by a select few? On and on and on. I have a hard time not being annoyed by it. I need to forget them, Diego, everything. But how?

Diego catches me looking. I glance back down, suddenly interested in my shoelaces. Melissa chuckles.

"What's so—"

But before I can finish, Diego is standing in front of me. "Can I talk to you for a second?" he asks.

I peer at him. "I already told you that—"

"Not you," he interrupts.

Melissa?

"Sure," my best friend says, walking off with him. Traitor.

Consumed by a sudden fit of anger, I want to put Melissa on stage and try her for treason, for conspiring with the enemy. Maybe I'm paranoid, and they're not talking about me? And Diego isn't really the enemy, anyway.

I want to believe that Diego means nothing. I want my best friend to quit bringing him into our conversations. I want to quit seeing him everywhere. The idea of him and me together brings me to the point of weakness.

Or is it strength?

If I am not extremely careful, I just might find out.

26
diego

Zero percent chance of rain, the Weather Channel predicts. The sun's rays coil around everything they touch—the trees, the asphalt, me. Pinned to a post is a flyer, curling around itself, flapping in the slight breeze. The letters are too bleached to be readable, the sun stealing the words with sticky fingers. Beads of sweat form on my upper lip.

It's been five days since I saw Faith in the library, since I pulled Melissa aside. Every moment outside of school I've spent at work, covering for someone on vacation, all the while looking forward to today. Part of me wonders if I should follow through with my plan. It's risky.

"You ready?" Javier asks, tossing a towel at me.

I wipe my face. "*Sí.*"

Ramon, Esteban, Juan, and Rodolfo are waiting in the Honda Civic parked in my cousin's driveway. Luis, Javier, and I pile into Uncle Dimitri's Explorer. He's letting us borrow it for the day. Though the car is big, there's only enough room for three; Uncle Dimitri's work things are the other passengers.

Rolling down the window, I let Florida's scorching heat bake my skin. It has to be near 100 degrees. I'm wearing board shorts and sandals. My scars and tattoos are visible, but I'm past the point of caring. I have other things on my mind.

Javier drives down the highway, Spanish music blaring. Wind whips through my already unruly hair. Stings my skin. Feels like a thousand tiny fangs biting me.

As we close in on our destination, we spot surfboards clinging to the tops of cars. As expected, the beach is busy. The sky is a crystalline blue. Cloudless.

It takes us fifteen minutes to find parking. The sand is off-white and burns my feet when I remove my sandals. Towels freckle the ground, the face of the beach a quilt of many colors. We stop to check out girls near us. I'm not as into it as I would like to be, which only confirms that Faith has taken root in me.

Mis amigos jump up to go after a group of girls walking down *la playa*, leaving Javier and me alone.

"What are the chances they'll get those *chicas* to come back with them?" Javier asks.

The girls seem out of their league, but maybe the guys can be smooth. I have no real way to know.

"Fifty-fifty," I say.

Javier pulls a loose string off the corner of his towel. "I'd give it more like thirty percent," he says.

Sure enough, the boys return a minute later, complaining about how the girls weren't feeling them. Doesn't matter, though. Day like today, beautiful people stretch as far as the horizon. The boys will move on as quickly as the tide turns.

A random thought intrudes, like an unexpected houseguest.

Make Faith jealous.

I never claimed to play fair.

"What time is she comin'?" Javier asks, voice low. The others don't hear.

"Should already be here," I answer.

I adjust my cheap sunglasses. They do little to block the light, which blares like a bullhorn.

"Ready?" my cousin asks.

No.

Yes.

Part of me wants to go to Faith. Explain. Have her drop the mask. Live in the States. Fit in. The other part wants to run home. Chance it. Stick with what I know.

It's like I belong to two different worlds.

Or neither.

"Yes," I answer. I'm not sure if it's a lie.

We get up, tell the others we'll be back soon. I double-check my cell. A text from Melissa.

Meet me at Jet Ski cabana. F's in water.

"This way," I tell Javier.

The Jet Ski rental cabana is easy to spot. Its old straw roof slouches like hunched shoulders. Melissa waits, one hand leaning against the makeshift cabana, the other on her hip; she's smoking a cigarette. Her pink bikini leaves little to the imagination.

But all I can think about is Faith.

My cousin almost stumbles, his steps stuttering.

"Why didn't you tell me, Diego?" he says. "Faith's friend is hot."

"You should talk to her," I suggest.

Melissa sees Javier watching and flashes a grin. A weapon of hers, I assume. Probably one of many in her arsenal.

"Hey, boys," she says. She pauses to check out Javier. I laugh. The girl oozes confidence. Javier looks nervous. I would be, too.

"I'm Melissa," she says, extending her hand to Javier.

"Javier," he says, meeting her grip. A moment too long, if you ask me.

"I assume you know what's going on," Melissa says to Javier before directing her attention to me. "So I'll get down to business. Faith is attempting to catch a wave, which isn't going to happen since the ocean is flatter than the surfboard she's on. I'd give it ten more minutes before she comes in. She knows nothing. Catching her off guard is your best bet. I'm sure you can understand why."

Melissa looks directly at me, and I understand then that there are some things she won't talk about. She thinks I know enough. I do. Faith is wearing her mask again. Becoming what everyone expects her to be.

But her best friend ultimately has her back and won't divulge too much. She's leaving it to me to crack Faith's mummified exterior. If I want answers, I have to peel away the layers myself.

I kind of admire Melissa. She loves Faith, but hates what she's doing to herself. Enough to invite us out here, but not enough to betray secrets. The perfect balance.

"Ten minutes, boys," Melissa says. She turns to Javier. Drags a fingertip down his arm, leaving grains of sand like a bread trail, marking a route. Perhaps to visit later. With a wink, she splays herself across a towel nearby.

Javier is speechless.

I grin. "Man, those best friends are trouble," I say, meaning every word.

Jealousy is an avenue that I hardly walk. Though it has

its advantages. It's quick. Cuts to the heart of things. But it's also messy. One wrong move, one wrong turn, and you accidentally sever an artery.

But if it goes smoothly, jealousy can be the fastest way to get what I want. Which is why I go for it today.

I can't seem to reach Faith at school. This is different territory. No watchful eyes. That was Melissa's reason for suggesting the beach; this is where Faith is free.

We walk back to our spots. The boys grab a football and ask us to join. We move closer to the water. Throw to each other. Girls take interest. Two of them, identical twins, are staring. One approaches me. She's fifty miles of legs and not much else.

"Hi," she says.

"Hi," I reply, grinning. I couldn't have asked for a better setup.

Her twin approaches Javier. In the background, *mis amigos* complain in Spanish about how Javier and I get all the girls. But that's not entirely true—a couple of the twins' friends are hanging back, waiting to be approached.

"I'm Allison," the girl says.

"Diego," I reply.

Not that names matter. I'll be forgetting you by tomorrow.

Javier, who's talking to the other twin, waves us over. He wants to take it to the water. I glance to where Faith should be, back on her towel. Empty.

As I approach the salt water, I see why. Faith is treading the current, heading toward the shore, a purple-and-white surfboard like a flower in bloom under her arm. A forest-green bikini hugs her skin. Tiny beads dangle from the triangle top. I have an urge to run my fingers across them, like a breeze through wind chimes. Her body is defined legs and stomach muscles—slim but sexy. Her hair tangles wetly over her shoulders.

Dios mío.

Tattoos? I ask myself. *Faith has tattoos?*

I squint. Try to make out the designs. Can't.

No idea she had it in her. She looks nothing like the Faith she pretends to be.

She's smiling, as if the water makes her happy. I wish I could make her happy.

Faith hasn't spotted me. I flirt with the twin. I purposely line myself up where Faith will see me as she exits the ocean. Caught in the crossfire.

Water laps between my toes, licking my feet. The girl next to me squeals.

"I hate the feel of the bottom of the ocean," she says, a smile on her face, one leg kicking back like she is posing for a postcard. I imagine it saying something like: "Welcome to Florida!" or "The Sunshine State! Where paradise is home!"

Home my—

The girl squeals again. Annoying. Piercing. Takes all I have not to let her tumble into the ocean and let the sloshing water quiet her.

But her squeal gets Faith's attention.

"Hop on," I say, winking at the *mujer*.

She jumps onto my back, holds on tight. Legs wrap around my waist. Arms pull me close.

Faith is seething.

She needs this, though. To be pushed. To make decisions that scare her. Just like she did at the club.

I don't bother to wipe the grin off my face. Faith accidentally drops her surfboard. Bends to pick it up. I nearly lose my resolve. She straightens, her board once again under her arm. Her mouth opens as if she's going to speak. I don't give her the chance.

I do exactly what she did to me. I brush past her.

Without a word.

27
faith

Diego is here. Three breaths. Two seconds. One shock.

"What's he doing here?" I ask Melissa.

My best friend is lying on her beach towel, sunglasses covering her eyes, a frozen virgin strawberry daiquiri next to her, melting faster than she can drink it in the heat.

"Probably the same thing we are," Melissa says. "Enjoying the beautiful weather isn't a crime, you know. Why so hostile?"

I sigh, frustrated. Diego swims in the ocean. Some girl on his back. She's borderline perfect. I hate that.

"I'm not hostile," I say.

Melissa laughs. "Sure."

"What? I'm not."

"Mmm-hmm."

I wring out my hair. Drops fall. Land in the sand, clumping it together.

"I don't care," I reply, knowing my lies are fooling no one.

"Then why are you staring like you want to kill that girl?"

I am staring, aren't I?

I can't look away.

"It's okay, Faith. It's me. You can talk to me."

I simmer. "It's hard to see him like that," I admit.

Melissa props herself up on one elbow. "So go to him. That's what he wants. To make you jealous."

I consider. But what if . . .

"Maybe not. Maybe he's actually having fun."

"Trust me. He's trying to make you jealous," Melissa replies.

My eyes slide over my friend. She very poorly hides a grin.

"How do you know?" I ask.

Melissa picks up her daiquiri and takes a sip. "I just know."

If he *is* trying to make me jealous, he's doing a good job.

"You should go to him quickly, though," Melissa suggests.

"Why?"

" 'Cause he may like you, Faith, but he's still a guy. See the way she's all over him? There's only so long that a guy can resist that stuff," Melissa says.

"He should be the one coming to me," I say.

Melissa shakes her head in what I can only guess is exasperation. "He did come to you," she says. "Several times. And if I remember correctly, you pushed him away, just like you will if he approaches you today."

She's right.

"No one knows we're here. It could be a secret, Faith, if that makes you feel better. Steal him away. It would drive him crazy."

Her suggestion makes me smile. Tempting. But I would have to remove my mask completely. In front of Diego—and his cousin, no less.

"I can't. You know that," I say. "Plus, he's having fun."

"Fine. How about this? Flaunt yourself in front of him. If he doesn't bite, I'll let it drop. Never say a word again," Melissa promises.

She is one hundred percent serious.

"Big gamble. Never is a long time," I say. "You seem confident."

"That's 'cause I am. You should've seen the way he looked at you when he first saw you in the water. I'm *so* not wrong."

I braid my hair to one side. Shake off the residual water that prunes my fingertips.

"And what would I do out there in front of him? I'd look ridiculous," I say.

Melissa smiles.

"What?"

"Nothing," she says.

"Liar." I scowl.

She tugs down her sunglasses, letting them rest on the tip of her nose. Humor graces her mouth and eyes. "I'm happy to see you admit that you're crazy about Diego."

"I never said those exact words."

"You didn't have to."

With the flick of a finger, reflective lenses cover Melissa's eyes once again. I reach into my bag, pull out ChapStick. My lips drink in the moisture.

"Why are you doing this?" I ask.

My best friend puts her hand on mine, her face sincere. " 'Cause I want to see you happy and I think Diego is a good start."

"I wish it were that easy."

"It could be," Melissa counters. "What better place to forget? Go to him."

I'm considering doing exactly that when Melissa says something that throws me off.

"Maybe then I can pull that girl off Javier."

"What?" I laugh. "Since when do you know Javier?"

"Since recently," Melissa replies. Something is off about her statement. I study her face. Like a childhood picture, I know each detail by heart.

"You like Javier." It's a statement. No question necessary.

"Not the way that you like Diego," she says. "I don't know Javier, but he's hot. Could be fun."

Might work better. I wouldn't have to face Diego alone.

"We should probably go in soon," Melissa says and points to the ocean.

My heart seizes. The girl is pressed against Diego's chest like a starfish.

"I can't take this," I say and stand up. Melissa follows.

By the time Diego looks at me, I'm up to my waist in water. I can't read his expression, but I'm sure he can read mine.

Melissa treads water behind me. The girl doesn't know I'm there yet.

"What the hell, Diego?" I say, angry.

Diego smiles lazily. "Oh, hey."

One hand slips down the girl's back, disappearing under the water. I want to dive deep, find that hand, and break it.

It lands somewhere that makes her giggle. She turns toward me.

"What's up?" Diego asks. The tips of his shaggy bangs

are wet, ink-like. Tattoos and scars are exposed in the area his shirt normally covers.

"What are you doing?" I ask through clenched teeth.

"Having fun," he says dismissively.

"Who's she?" the girl asks. Her arms rest loosely on his shoulders. Pale and silky. A rainbow aura surrounds the two of them where sunscreen has leapt from skin and landed on the water's surface, oil gleaming in the light.

I try to hold it together. She obviously isn't going to let him go easily. I don't blame her. If I were brave, I wouldn't, either.

"None of your business," I say.

Diego says nothing.

The girl grins, sensing my jealousy. Her arms tighten around Diego's neck. She leans into him.

"Why don't we go somewhere else?" she suggests, whispering into his ear, but making the words loud enough for me to hear. My fists ball. "We have a condo on the beach. I'd love to have you over."

I'm sure she would love to have him over. All over.

"Back off," I warn.

She scowls. "You back off." She turns to Diego. "Seriously, who is she?"

"His girlfriend. Who are you?" Melissa says, getting in the girl's face. She doesn't let anyone talk down to me. I do the same for her.

Javier clears his throat. "Girlfriend?" he says.

Not true. But this chick doesn't have to know that. Diego just looks smug. I tread closer. The girl lets go.

"Jerk," she mumbles to him, and swims away. The sister clings to Javier, refusing to give up her prize. One look from Melissa changes her mind.

With the twins gone, I turn my wrath on Diego.

"Have some respect," I say, angry.

Diego walks toward the shore. Mute.

Like I should learn to be.

Without thinking, I follow. His strides are giant scissors, cutting through the tide. I catch up as he hands money to a Jet Ski rental employee. The guy pushes the Jet Ski into the water.

"Diego," I say.

He doesn't stop to talk to me. Maybe Melissa's wrong. Maybe he did like that girl.

"Wait," I say.

He straps on a vest, moves into the water. Says something to the guy, who's handing him keys.

"Are you going to talk to me?" I ask.

Finally Diego looks at me. His eyes are dark, hard.

"What do you want from me, Faith?"

"I don't know," I admit.

What do I want? Him?

I make it clear that Diego cannot have me, but I'm obviously not okay with him having anyone else.

The Jet Ski attendant returns with a smaller life vest. Hands it to Diego. Diego looks at me. Extends the vest. "Hop on," he says.

The vest hangs in my hand like a limp rag doll. What if someone sees us?

"Now or never," he replies as he starts the engine. Water bubbles behind it.

I put the life vest on quickly. Stand, undecided.

Diego revs the throttle, ready to leave without me. At the last second, I jump on. My landing is wobbly, a dice unsure of which number to land on, teetering back and forth. A solid, tattooed hand steadies me.

I wrap my arms around his lower waist. Skin and muscle and warmth. I hold on tight. Diego speeds up. Jets out into the deep blue unknown. Wind whips stray hairs around my face, stinging me with each whack. No turning back. Diego drives farther away from shore.

Leaving behind all that complicates us.

28
diego

Faster, I think.

I want to feel Faith as close to me as possible. I push the throttle to the max. She tightens her grip to the point of pain, squeezing the life out of me. It's a good pain, though. The type that reminds me I'm alive, living in the moment.

Making sure the coast is clear, I close my eyes for a brief moment. I want to remember this: the sting of salt water, Faith's thighs squeezing me tight, her face nuzzled into my neck. When I cut the engine, the picture-perfect image will shatter like glass. Words will fly, hurling each broken piece in a different direction.

I'll never see them again.

But not now.

This moment is mine.

"Watch out," Faith says, fracturing my concentration.

I open my eyes. A piece of driftwood bobs ahead. I swerve. When I look back, the shore is miniscule. Buildings like tiny blocks. I slow. Faith loosens her grip. I cut the engine in the middle of the ocean.

I wait for Faith to let go of me before I withdraw the key and turn. It's more difficult than I thought to move on a Jet Ski without dumping us into the water, but I manage. Water sloshes on our lower legs, helping to lessen the scorch from the sun.

I take off my vest. Too bulky and awkward. Faith does the same. I hang them over the handlebars. Faith looks at my body. Her lips part slightly, her eyes skip from feature to feature. I watch her, too. Her ink, especially. It's beautiful. Images that wisp around her hips and up her ribs like smoke, stopping just beneath her underarms.

On the left, tattooed waves crash against the bone of her hip as if it's a protruding rock. Beneath the curl of a big wave is a surfer, riding the rogue. A sea mural—coral, seaweed, and neon-colored fish—drift in the current. Whoever inked her is a pro. Her work is amazing.

On the right, a skull and crossbones leaps out of bright red flames. Charcoal gray smoke seeps from the fire, carrying with it tiny images. Demons, if I had to guess. A message. Perhaps Faith has demons. Come to think of it, doesn't everyone?

Faith's body is near perfect. My eyes trace long legs, tiny freckles on her knees. Her hand cups saltwater, drips it along her arms and back.

"*¿Que pasa, mami?*" I ask.

She bites her lip. "Nothing," she replies.

"You didn't charge into the water back there for nothin'," I say.

The hard glint in her eyes suggests anger.

"Talk to me," I request, taking her hand in mine. I want to have a chance with this girl, a chance to know the real Faith.

She sighs. Looks at me. "You were flaunting her in front of me."

"True," I admit.

A small wave approaches. We grasp the seat until it passes.

"Is it real?" she asks. "With that girl, with any of them?"

I think about lying. Change my mind. "No."

"Then why do it?" she asks.

Gentle ripples in the water rock us slowly back and forth. I motion to our surroundings.

"It got you out here, didn't it?" I say. "You wouldn't have come if I asked nicely."

Faith bends, collects more water with her hand. Drips it down her legs. It puddles in places.

"Why be nice now?" she asks.

I lean against the handlebars. "I can be a nice guy. You haven't given me a chance."

I have her talking. I don't want her to stop. It's like the club, only better.

"Do you want a chance?" she asks, worrying at the strings on her suit.

"Of course," I reply. "But something holds you back. I know when people look at me they don't see someone who deserves you. And they're right. I don't. But I want you anyway."

She shakes her head. I'm losing her. She's fading.

I gently pull her toward me. She gasps when I place her hands on my chest. I take her pointer finger and lay it on a scar.

"That's from a knife," I say, holding her gaze. "Back home in Cuba—"

I pause, wondering if I should admit it. Only a few members of *mi familia* know the truth. If I tell Faith, she will be forever close, held to me by my secret.

No turning back.

"In Cuba, a deal went bad. Hospitalized me."

I watch her eyes. I expect her to want to leave, but she doesn't.

I continue. "This one," I say, moving her finger to my shoulder, "is where I was thrown into a metal fence. Twenty-seven stitches to close."

Faith breathes evenly, in and out. I move her finger again, this time to my arm.

"Bullet."

She gasps. I pause.

Neither of us speaks. I let it sink in.

When her face relaxes, I guide her fingertip to my other arm. "These five are from a broken bottle. Crazy how much damage a bottle can do."

She traces my scars. There is something insanely intimate about it. Her touch is soft. Her eyes are hope mixed with sunlight.

I move her hand to my scalp, where hair meets forehead. "Butt of a gun. Needed staples."

She moves to a four-inch slash on my stomach. "And this one?" she asks.

A gull screeches above, perhaps interested in the fish beneath us.

"Another knife," I answer.

Her fingers reach for my throat. I block her hand. Not that one. Not yet.

"Your turn," I say.

Faith stares at me. Debates answering. I don't want to push her, but I need something. Finally, she speaks.

"My scars are on the inside," she says.

I wait for more. She glances away, dips her feet in the warm water.

"My dad's a pastor," she says. "I live with him, my stepmom, and my baby sister, Grace. Grace is amazing." Her mouth curves up for a second. "Melissa is the only one I let get close. We've been friends forever. Our parents split at the same time. It was tough, you know? She was there for me."

She pauses. Blinks quickly. I'm not sure if she has salt in her eyes. Or tears. Or both.

"My dad's world is different. There's stuff we've had to compensate for. Past issues."

She hasn't said much, but it's something all the same. The possibility of her clamming up at any second is high. I rub circles on the back of her hand.

"At church, people expect everything from me. I have to be perfect. Have to date the star football player. Have to smile and nod and never make mistakes. They don't know the real me. None of them do."

She looks at me. Really looks at me.

"You being here with me, hearing me say that, is more time with the real Faith than any of them have ever experienced. Combined."

Baby steps for sure, but better than nothing.

"Thank you," I say. I want her to know I appreciate her trust. She has mine, too.

She doesn't say anything about her mom. That's fine. Neither do I.

"Why do you have to be *perfecta*?" I ask.

She squeezes my hand. Her body tenses.

"Because it's what's expected," she says. "I can't ruin my father's image. Someone . . . came really close to doing that once."

She winces as though she's said too much. I graze her cheek. This time, she doesn't pull away.

"I don't know what it's like to live up to other people's

standards," I say. "But I do know what it's like to want to run away. And you, *mami,* want to run away. I see it in your eyes. *¿Por qué tienes miedo?*"

"I've only had one class of Spanish, Diego. You're going to have to help me out," she says.

"What I'm askin' is, why are you scared? Why do it? Why do you care what they think? Stop goin' to church if you hate it."

She shakes her head. Thin strips of hair fall in her face like spun silk. Crazy beautiful.

"I don't want to stop going to church. I have never felt as calm as when I'm in that sanctuary alone," she says. "I've gone unaccompanied a handful of times. While my dad worked in the office on the other side of the church. There's nothing like it. I just don't get the same feeling when it's full of fake, pretentious people."

I understand now. It is not the church that drives her away. It's the people, their impossible standards.

"Do you know what happened when someone showed up at my church in board shorts and a tank top one day?" she asks.

"No," I answer.

"They turned him away. Told him to return when he was more appropriately dressed. Unreal." Faith scowls, frustrated. "What's wrong with showing up in board shorts? So what if he looked like he just stepped off the beach? At least he came."

"That's messed up, Faith. It really is," I say.

No wonder she dresses the way she does.

We drift, gazing at the horizon. Birds fly around us, occasionally diving headfirst for a fish. I stay quiet, listening to water babble with the wind. Old friends.

I'm dealing with a heart that I didn't break. Faith is a

wound that has been packed with gauze, but never actually closed. I want to explore her in full and then suture her injuries shut so no pain remains. I am fracturing rules that govern her life, and she is silently begging me to show her the way.

"Don't get me wrong, not all churches are like that," she says in a soft voice. "In fact, most aren't. But my father's is. He's the head pastor, but he can't change anything. A board of people makes the decisions. When the situation, the stupid shorts thing, was addressed at a meeting, my father and a few others voted against the dress standard that the church wanted to mandate. Majority ruled, said no to anything more lenient. They disregarded my father's wishes, and he still preaches there."

She reaches for a piece of lost seaweed. Bends it this way and that.

"Maybe my father's afraid of change," she says, almost a whisper. "So my fate's sealed. Because I will not abandon my family. Ever. No matter how bad it is."

I stare at her in disbelief. Words are not enough. I don't bother.

She is *trapped*.

In some people's worlds, reputations are everything. I would not have survived as long as I did in Cuba without mine.

When Faith looks at me, I feel the ice around my heart start to splinter. I have never let a girl in.

Until now.

Something changes between us. It's calming, freeing.

"Thanks for talking," she says. Leans toward me. For a second I think we might kiss. But then she pulls the vest out from behind my back and almost sends me toppling into the water.

She laughs.

Dios mío, it's good to hear her laugh. Even if it is at my expense.

"I need to get back," she says. A genuineness ropes through her voice that wasn't there before our excursion.

"Sure," I reply. Help her put on her vest. Then mine.

I turn around and start the engine. One more glance. A smile. I take us back to the shore. Faith holds on to me like she never wants to let go.

We're alike, Faith and I. And we are both messed up in different ways.

Different, but the same.

29
faith

When I get home that evening, my family is sitting down for dinner. Grace grins at me. Happiness floods my heart, filling every vessel with goodness. Grace does that to me. I want to hug her and make her smile and protect her forever.

"How was your day?" Grace asks, her voice low and sweet.

"Great," I say. "Yours?"

Tiny arms wrap around me. My eyes close. This is the best kind of happiness.

She lets go. "I finally memorized ABCs! Want to hear?"

"Of course."

She sings, pauses at one point, trying to remember which letter comes next. She gets it wrong, then remembers right and continues.

When she finishes, I clap like it's the best song I've ever heard. Which it kind of is. Grace can transform little things into something meaningful, because it's from her.

Dad tells Grace that her song was perfect. Susan agrees. They ask me to join them. A plate is waiting. Grilled chicken, veggie medley, and rosemary mashed potatoes.

I sit and eat. Susan picks up the conversation from

where she left off when I walked in. Something about work. Lawyers at the firm are sticking her with a case she doesn't want, but she has to represent it if she wants to stay on their good side.

While my stepmom talks, I tease Grace. I tickle her little leg underneath the table. She cracks up every time. Whenever Susan or Dad ask what's so funny, we act like nothing happened. We're a team, Grace and I.

When Susan finishes talking, everyone looks at me.

"So, what's going on in Faith's world?" Dad asks.

I try not to unload my problems on him. "Nothing," I say. Keep it simple.

Susan cocks her head. "Do you want to talk about last Sunday?"

My defenses go up. "No," I answer.

Susan chuckles. "Come on, Faith. You weren't sick. Are you and Jason fighting? Is that why you sat next to me?"

Years fade into oblivion, forgotten. Months pass with no intrusion from Dad or Susan. But now they choose to ask questions about my love life. My personal feelings misfire in every direction, confused, tentative.

Things with Jason are over. Word around school is that Jason wants to fix our relationship. I don't want that. When it's done, it's done.

Then there is Diego. Beautifully troubled Diego. He got me to talk, cracked my shell. It was the scars, I think. Seeing his weakness and recognizing it as strength.

Diego and I can't be together. But maybe we can be friends.

I trust him.

"Don't worry, Faith," Dad says. "I'm sure whatever it is, you two will resolve it."

I set my fork down, look, seriously look, at my dad. His

brown hair is thinning. Dark bags under his eyes collect stress like dirt in drainpipes.

When was the last time I was real with him?

"Actually, Dad, Jason and I broke up," I say. "For good."

I wait for his reaction. It's not what I expect.

"Are you happy with that decision?" he asks.

No yelling. He wants to know if I am happy. It feels strange, not like his usual demeanor when it comes to my personal life.

"I'm okay with it, yeah. I do care about Jason. I couldn't *not* care; I mean, we spent so long together. But it's not what I want anymore. And it was his decision—granted, I think it's a good one—so it's on him to explain to the people at church."

That way, it won't look bad on my dad.

"Honey, the only person I'm worried about is you. If you're happy, then we're happy," Dad says, though the pinched look on his face hints at something else.

My chest tightens. My eyes sting.

"Thanks," I say.

I eat the remainder of my meal, hope and sadness swelling within. I think Dad wants to be happy for me, but I know I'm not the daughter he expected. And change doesn't come easily.

In my room, I practice dance routines—readying myself for our next competition—until my arms and legs feel like rubber, until I sweat from head to toe. I take a shower and lie down to sleep. I replay everything from the beach. In my dreams, Diego is mine. And I love every minute of it.

At 8 A.M., Grace jumps on my bed like it's a trampoline. Time for church. My little sister wears a frilly yellow dress speckled with white flowers. Her hair is tied back with elastic bands. She looks angelic.

"Morning, Gracie," I say.

"Good morning, Faith," she says.

I wrap my arms around her and squeeze. She giggles and tries to squirm away.

My cell phone chirps. Text message. Probably Melissa. When I got back to the shore yesterday, I found her and Javier talking. As far as I know, they had a good time. Nothing serious. Diego's friends were there, too. They won't mention seeing me at the beach, Diego says. I believe him.

After we got off the Jet Ski, I wanted to touch Diego again. Of course I didn't. He kept a respectful distance. He understood that I couldn't go there, especially in front of so many people. I didn't miss the looks he snuck me, though—a smile here, a grin there.

I view the message. Don't recognize the number.

Good morning, bonita. *–D.*

Diego.

How'd he get my number?

Melissa. I should've known.

Diego's text makes me smile.

"Who is it?" Grace asks, reaching for my phone. Forever trying to be like me.

I lower my voice to a whisper. "Can you keep a secret?" I ask.

She can. Grace is the best secret keeper ever, even if she's only five years old.

"Yes," she says sweetly. Her eyes go big in anticipation.

"Okay," I say. "But you have to promise to never, ever tell."

"Bananas," she says, pretending to zip her mouth shut.

"Bananas" is Grace's equivalent to "Promise." I don't

know where she draws the similarity. I asked her once. It was disorienting, like getting turned around in an unknown city. Completely lost in her five-year-old logic.

"It's a boy," I say.

Grace isn't old enough to be grossed out by boys yet.

"Not Jason," she says, without missing a beat.

Have to be careful with words around her. She's a sponge, soaking everything up.

"Not Jason," I confirm.

She giggles. "Who?"

"D," I tell her. Just in case. I don't want her to accidentally say his real name too loudly.

"Come on," I say before she can ask more. "Time for church."

I quickly program Diego's number in my phone—under "D," of course. Grace leaves the room so I can shower and get ready.

Church is the same routine—say hello to everyone, *yes, I'm doing fine, thanks*, take a seat next to Susan. The sermon lasts forty-five minutes. At the end, Jason cuts through the crowd. I try to slip away. Too late.

"Faith," he says. "How are you?"

"Good, Jason. How are you?"

"Good," he answers. "You look nice."

I'm wearing the same thing I always wear—a dress that says nothing about my personality, except maybe that I follow the rules. I understand now how clothing can speak volumes, how it can tell a story. My dress feels like it's telling someone else's.

And Jason is wrong. I do not look nice. I look fake.

"Thanks," I say, being polite. People are watching.

Jason shifts from one foot to the other. "I've been wanting to talk to you. Do you think maybe we can go out tonight? Sunset on the beach?"

At the mention of the beach, my heart gallops. I think of Diego. Memories assault me.

"No," I say.

"No?" Jason asks.

He expected me to jump back into his arms.

"Don't be mad, Faith," Jason pleads. "I made a mistake. I hated thinking that you might be into Diego, or that he was into you."

Guilt crawls up my spine. He was right all along. I *am* into Diego.

"It would be better if we were just friends," I tell him.

Jason's eyes are exaggerated in their surprise. "Faith, babe, we have almost three years together. Don't throw that away."

Irritation makes its way into my tone. "You threw it away. Not me," I say quietly, sharply.

He shouldn't have let me go in the first place.

I turn away. Jason calls to me.

"Now is not the time," I say, referring to our audience.

I leave. Watching me go, he seems sad. Which is strange. Because he must have known.

I was already gone.

30
diego

My face is finally healed and looking normal again. Purple is definitely not my color. *Mi padre* comments on it at dinner.

"You look better," he says.

"Thanks," I say, taking a bite.

"How's school?"

I'm doing well. I tried to impress no one with my entry exams. In fact, I Christmas-treed most of the multiple-choice answers. Now I apply myself. Good grades are the reward.

"All Bs," I answer.

Mi padre looks up from his food, a smile on his face. "Proud of you."

I guess he thought I would find more trouble to get into when he brought me to the States.

"*Gracias,*" I say.

It's hard, really hard, to live a pure life after being dirty. My job doesn't pay much, but I keep remembering that it's clean money. If I want something now, I can't threaten or intimidate my way into it. I have to work.

And I haven't carried my gun, not once. I still feel naked

without it. Hopefully over time that will fade. Maybe one day I can stop looking over my shoulder.

Hope is a beautiful thing—dangerous, but beautiful.

On Monday, my first few classes are torture. I can't concentrate on anything but Faith. I reread my chemistry assignment three times before I take in the words on the page.

At lunch I search the cafeteria, looking for Faith. I don't see her. Both good and bad. At least she's not with Jason.

I wonder where she went.

"Lookin' for your girlfriend?" Javier asks, messing with me.

"Shut up," I reply.

"I've never seen Faith like she was at *la playa*. She's into you," Luis says.

I glance around quickly.

"Quiet," I say. "I don't need Luis's big mouth ruining things."

While the guys continue to mess with me, I think about what it was like to crack Faith's shield. I need to expose more of my past to deepen the crack. It's tough, though. I don't like to talk about the cartel or *mi madre*.

As complicated as it is, I still hope for a glimpse of Faith. It finally comes in seventh period. We've got the same class. While the teacher is quieting everybody down, I steal a peek at Faith, snatch it out of thin air, hold it close.

She's looking at me, too. Her cheeks redden. Her eyes go back to her desk. I want to tell her that I like it when she stares at me.

Javier grabs a chair next to me. He asks me something

about a paper that's due soon, but I can't concentrate on him because Faith is looking at me again. She grins, and I practically forget the whole room.

I don't get a chance to talk to Faith until we meet in the library after class. We're nearly done with book fair prep. My detention is over in one day.

Faith walks in wearing her dance uniform: short purple and black skirt, tight matching top. I have to work hard not to let my body betray how much I like it. Behind her are some of her dance team members. I recognize them from her lunch table—or at least, the table she used to sit at before she and Jason split.

Her followers are fake. Fake nails. Skin tanned by artificial sun. Colored contacts. Streaks of yellow woven through their hair like caution tape.

"Please. Not now," Faith says to them.

Melissa steps out from behind the Fakes. She waves to me. Faith sees me and winces.

They stop a few feet away. I pick up on part of the conversation, trying to figure out why Faith looks so uncomfortable.

"We're just saying, Faith. This is not normal," the first Fake says.

"Yeah," a second Fake chimes in. "You're, like, meant to be with Jason. You should totally give him another chance."

I tense.

"He wants you back," the third Fake says. "And as your friends, we think you should listen to us. I mean, who would've ever thought Jason and Faith would break up? No. You have to be with him or else, like, the world will stop."

Fake One takes control of the situation. "He broke up with you because he was having a stupid guy moment. You shouldn't hold it against him. He really is sorry."

I price the books, acting unfazed. Anger swarms inside me, a thousand wasps ready to sting.

They go on about reputations for what feels like forever. Finally, Melissa cuts in.

"That's ridiculous. Who cares what people think? If Faith doesn't want to be with Jason, whatever." She shakes her head, annoyed. "It's her decision. Not yours; not anyone else's."

The Fakes are stunned into silence. Faith glances gratefully at her best friend.

So do I.

Shrugging and flipping their hair, the Fakes walk away. Melissa asks Lori to follow her to another part of the library to get poster board and markers for signs.

Faith and I are alone.

Faith plays with the ends of her long hair. "I'm sorry you had to hear that," she says.

"It's okay," I say. I'm glad that she ignored her friends. I want her to myself.

"I'm not taking him back," she says.

I step closer. "You sure?"

You are incredible. So beautiful.

"Yes."

"Why not?" I want to hear her say that she wants me. That she can't stop thinking about me. Because I can't get her out of my mind, either.

"I don't want to be with anyone," she says.

My heart slams into my chest.

"No one?" I ask.

Faith looks at the floor as she answers. "Nope."

"I don't believe you," I say. "The club. The beach. You can't erase that."

"Can't we just be friends?" she asks.

"No," I answer. I want to be more than friends. A lot more.

"Well, that's all I have to offer. Take it or leave it."

I respect her. She tries to protect her father's image. But she doesn't want to let me go, either.

"Fine," I agree. I'll take it because something is better than nothing with this girl. I like her enough that I'll settle for "friends."

For now.

31
faith

Lying to Diego feels as though I am unraveling, coming loose at the ends, spinning out of control. I need a semblance of power, of having the upper hand. But I know in truth, I don't. I don't know when I lost it, exactly. Perhaps it was never mine in the first place.

I can't keep lying.

I do want to be with Diego.

Diego has spread through me, seeping into the cracks, infiltrating my mind. School was torture today. My eyes betrayed me, sliding to wherever he was in the room. Even now, I reach for my phone, thinking I'll tell him the truth.

I pull away at the last second.

"Will you be here for dinner?" Dad asks as I open the fridge, searching for a snack.

"No, sorry," I answer. "Working on book fair posters with Melissa. We're ordering pizza. I'll probably be home late, if that's okay with you."

I pull out a yogurt and cranberries. Should hold me over until dinner.

"All right," Dad replies.

As I eat my snack, Dad stands next to me, staring.

I pause. Look at him. "Is everything okay?" I ask.

He rubs the spot above his eyebrows. His allergies are awful this time of year. "I was about to ask you the same thing," Dad says.

He looks worn out. I worry about him.

"I'm fine, Dad," I say.

"Is there anything you want to talk about?"

Like what?

"No."

"You just seem, well, I don't know what," he says.

Dad can talk to a congregation of people, but when it comes to his daughter, he's tongue-tied. It's always been this way.

"I'm a little stressed," I admit. "But it's nothing I can't handle."

I'm not entirely sure that's true.

"Is it your grades?" he asks.

"No. Grades are fine."

"Dance?"

"No." Besides Tracy Ram's ever-present nasty attitude. Nothing new.

"Any relapses?"

"God, no. Dad, I don't want anything to do with that stuff."

He has to ask. Any good father would.

"I'm assuming that you and Melissa are fine since you're going over there tonight, right?"

"Yes. Melissa and I are okay." We have the occasional best friend fight. But we duke it out and everything is fine right after. I can't stay mad at her, and vice versa.

"Jason?" he asks.

What's with the twenty questions?

"There is no Jason anymore," I remind him.

"Another boy, then?"

My face burns. "Dad," I groan. "Boy talk? Seriously?"

"What?" he asks. "I just want to make sure that my girl is doing okay."

When he calls me his girl, I freeze. He hasn't done that since Mom left.

"I'm okay," I reply. "Just normal stress. No biggie."

"So you're not seeing another guy?"

I laugh. Bury my head in my arms.

"This is so embarrassing," I say. It comes out muffled.

"Ah, I see. There is another boy."

I look back up and try not to grimace. Dad is uncomfortable but persistent.

"It's okay for you to like a boy, Faith. It's bound to happen," he says. "You're eighteen now. I kind of expect it."

"I'm not seeing anyone."

Please make this stop.

"Yet," he amends. "But you clearly want to."

I don't know when my dad got so good at reading me. "Are you done?" I groan.

He laughs. "Yes, I suppose I am. Just be careful, okay?"

"Okay," I reply.

"And don't let anyone trick you into anything you're not ready for. I, of course, want you wait until you're married for, um, well, you know. But I'm also aware that things move a lot faster nowadays. Condoms do not protect against everything—"

Oh. My. God. I cut him off. "I have to go."

Forget the snack. I cannot take another moment of embarrassment. I put my food back in the fridge and race out of the house. I practically break down Melissa's door as I barrel through it.

Melissa is cleaning countertops.

"What's going on?" she asks, dropping the spray and towel.

"You will not believe what just happened!" I look around her house. "Is your mom home?"

"No, she's on call at the hospital all night," Melissa answers.

Good. I don't want anyone but my best friend to hear this. "My father, *my father*, decided to have a sex talk with me."

Dad is not the type to mention the word *sex*, much less talk in any detail about it.

"Sex?" Melissa asks. "Seriously?"

"Yes," I say. "It was mortifying."

"Oh Faith," she says. "That's good. I never thought the day would come."

"I wish it hadn't."

Melissa pats the bar stool next to her and we both sit.

"What made him want to talk to you about that?" she asks.

"Diego," I confess. "Only, I never actually admitted anything about Diego."

"What?" Melissa says. "Rewind. What do you mean?"

I grab chocolate chip cookies from Melissa's cupboard and pour a glass of milk.

"My dad thinks I have a crush on someone. But he doesn't know who," I say.

"Wow. Did he freak out?"

I swallow. Take a sip of milk. "Surprisingly, no. He said he expects me to like boys now that I'm older. It was so weird."

"Definitely," my best friend agrees, grabbing a cookie.

"He's been kind of different lately. He let me go to the

club. And he didn't freak when I told him about the breakup. Now he's talking to me about boys."

"Maybe the tides are turning," Melissa says.

"Maybe. But I'm not banking on it."

I eat the last cookie. Finish my milk. I raid Melissa's candy stash for a mint. "All right," I say, changing the subject. "You want to get started?"

"Sure," Melissa agrees.

I'm about to step on the bottom stair when Melissa stops me.

"Forgot that I have to pick up the pizza," she says.

I balance awkwardly, resting one foot on the stair, one on the ground.

"I would've paid for delivery," I offer.

Her mom does the best she can to afford everything. But occasionally Melissa picks up the pizza instead of paying delivery fees when funds are low.

"It's no prob. I'll be back soon," she says. "Relax in my room. I set out posters and markers. Maybe you can start on them?"

"Sure," I say.

When Melissa leaves, I lock the door and walk upstairs. Spy someone in Melissa's room.

My heart pounds against my sternum.

"Diego?" I say, confused.

What's Diego doing in Melissa's bedroom?

He flashes a lopsided grin. "Hey," he says.

"Why are you here?" I ask, suddenly realizing that I'm in casual home clothes, a tiny tank top and shorts.

"Helping," he says. He points to the markers and posters.

Bull. It hits me.

"Melissa's not going for pizza, is she?" I ask.

Diego grins wickedly. "No."

I am going to kill my best friend. "I can't do this," I say.

Diego steps toward me. He's wearing jeans and a black shirt. Simple. Sexy.

"Sure you can," he says. "Imagine we're in the ocean again."

I try hard not to reach for him.

"I really can't," I say.

He shuts the door and leans against it. "Melissa won't be back for a while. It's just you and me. Stay with me. No one knows we're here 'cept your best friend, and she won't tell."

His cocky stance—arms crossed over his chest, one leg bent so that the bottom of his foot rests on the door—makes me uneasy.

"Did you not understand when I said we could only be friends?" I ask sarcastically.

"Yeah. I understood." He smiles. "But I don't think you meant it."

"What do you want?" I cut to the chase.

He shrugs. "Just wonderin' when you're gonna quit living for everybody else."

Exhale. "Never. So drop it," I say. "I have to go."

Diego doesn't back away from the door. "So you don't like me?" he asks, then licks his lips.

Of course I do. Like crazy. I can't tell him, though. It would never work between us. There's too much stacked up against us: the church, Dad, people at school.

"No," I answer. "I don't like you. Not at all."

He moves away from the door. I turn, watching each step he takes. Diego positions himself in front of me. My back is to the exit. If I reach behind me, I can grab the handle and leave.

My body won't listen.

Diego shouldn't be looking at me with his mouth twisting upward.

How did he do that?

One minute I was in control, the next I'm pinned in place.

"Tell me again how you don't like me," Diego whispers.

I swallow. Fidget.

" 'Cause if you ask me, it's all a lie. Everything. Your clothes. Your standards."

He's right. On every count.

"Everything. Is. A. Lie," he whispers.

I try to find my voice. Finally locate it under a pile of nerves.

"I can't be with you, Diego." My words tumble out in one breath, barely audible.

"Fine," he says. "Kiss me one time, and if you don't feel anything, I'll back off. For good."

Kiss him?

"I'm not kissing you," I say.

He smiles. "That's what I thought. You do like me. Admit it. That's why you can't kiss me."

"It's not that," I say. There's so much more. Dad's reputation. My mask. The comfort of knowing that no one is close enough to ever hurt me like my mother did.

Then Diego says something that throws me off balance, an asteroid colliding with my world.

"I'm in a drug cartel."

32
diego

Faith's mouth drops open, hanging like a crooked picture. I back away from the door. Sit on the floor. I can't look at her. If she plans to leave, I don't want to see her go.

"You're in a cartel?" she asks.

I prop myself against Melissa's desk. The edge cuts into my back.

"*Sí*," I answer. "*El Cartel Habana*. Faith, they are evil like you have never known."

She'll leave now. The only girl that I've ever really cared about knows my deepest secret. And while I should be worrying about the repercussions of that, I can only think about how I do not want Faith to go.

"You deal drugs?" she asks, appalled.

"No. Never. I don't do, touch, or sell," I correct. "I'm more of a bodyguard."

"So you protect people who sell drugs?"

I wince. It sounds awful coming out of Faith's mouth, but I can't deny what I am. What I was.

"Yes," I answer.

"Why?"

I don't look up from the carpet. I don't want to see the disgust that laces her voice.

"To survive," I say. "The town I came from is different from Florida, Faith. It's touched by the finger of *el diablo,* I swear. On those streets, you'll be lucky not to die of starvation or violence. You have to pick a side. Live or die. I chose to live. The cartel offered *mi familia* protection in exchange for my services. It meant food on the table and a roof over our heads. But most importantly, it meant *mi madre* could stop livin' in fear every day. I'd do anything to protect her."

I still remember the times *mi padre* spent with me, teaching me how to fight. He's the one who told me about *El Cartel Habana. Mi padre* isn't a member, but he knew the cartel would offer a young, good fighter a position. He only survived the streets as long as he did because he's a good fighter himself, one of the few people who actually lived unprotected. He didn't think our family could be that lucky twice. It pained him to send me to them when I was fifteen, but the alternative was worse.

Today, we both regret the end result of his decision.

"So, it's like a gang?" Faith asks.

"Only worse," I answer. "It's on a bigger level. *El Cartel Habana* deals in massive amounts. They ship drugs all over the world. The transactions have to be flawless. People will double-cross them as fast as you can blink. That's where I came in."

"That's why you're always fighting," Faith says. "The scars came from the cartel."

I nod.

"Why are you here?" she asks.

I look at her then. Even after hearing about my demons, she hasn't left.

I have to tell her.

" 'Cause," I answer. "In the end, the cartel double-crossed me."

Faith says nothing. I close my eyes, remembering the worst night of my life.

"Four months ago the cartel told me they wanted me to move up in ranking. I was already in it for life. I didn't see why it mattered. But when they said they wanted me dealin' big transactions, I refused. That was always my condition. No drugs. I would do most things, but not that. It sounds odd since I was in a drug cartel, but it had been done before. Fighting was my skill, not drug slingin'."

Though the desk hurts my spine, I press further into it. I welcome any other pain but this memory.

"Apparently, I got too good with my hands. They wanted me on the forefront. When I said no, they told me I'd regret it. I figured I could talk to the boss the next day when everythin' cooled off. Maybe strike a deal. To be safe, I moved *mi familia* to another location that night."

I take a deep breath. This is the part that hurts the most. I feel tense. So tense. A billion invisible hands pull at my skin, stretching it tight, squeezing the air out of my lungs, strangling my heart till it hurts too bad to move another inch.

I haven't discussed that night with anyone. Not *mi padre*. Not Javier. No one.

"They found us, anyway. Five of them. Assassins. They stabbed *mi padre* first. He hit the floor. Dead, we thought. They tied me to the leg of the bed and made me watch—"

I pause. Swallow. Try to hold it together. "I watched as they killed *mi madre*."

Faith comes to me then, dropping to my side.

"They slit my throat. That's what the scar is from. It was meant to be my death."

Faith reaches for my neck; I jerk on instinct. Her hand falls away.

"They left us there, good as dead. With what I thought was my dyin' breath, I called a friend who owed me a favor. His father was a doctor. The next thing I remember was wakin' up a month later in someone's house hooked up to a machine. *Mi padre* told me everythin'. How the doctor kept us at his home so no one would know we survived. The doctor closed my father's wound, but mine took a lot of work. It was too late for *mi madre*. The doctor could only do so much outside a hospital. He drugged me for weeks so I wouldn't feel pain. We hid there, recuperating before coming to the States."

The memory is caustic. I am swallowing acid. I want to vomit.

"I'm sorry, Diego. I'm so sorry," Faith says.

It feels good to get it off my chest. But it hurts, too."

"My mom is gone," Faith suddenly says. "Not dead, but she might as well be."

I reach for Faith's hand. It's warm. Her fingers curl around mine and squeeze.

"She left when I was eight. For drugs."

Faith glances at me, unbearable pain in her eyes. No wonder she looked at me the way she did when I mentioned the cartel. Drugs were probably the last thing she wanted to hear about.

"She couldn't handle it. You know, life, the pressures of life. Everything was too much for her. Having a child young. The church's standards. Marriage. She never came back. Never called. Nothing. She abandoned us because drugs were everything to her."

I pull Faith close. Wrap an arm around her shoulders. She rests her head on my chest.

Maybe if we lean on one another hard enough, we can support each other.

"That's why I have to be this"—Faith motions to herself—"fake. It's the only option. Mom almost ruined Dad once. I can't do that to him, too."

"You won't," I say.

Faith looks defeated. "Yes, I will. If I slip up, I will. It's happened before, Diego."

She stands. I push myself up and go to her. She presses a hand to my chest.

"Don't," she says. "You have no idea. I'm sure you've heard wonderful stories about me going abroad last year, studying all over the world."

I have. What does that have to do with anything?

"I didn't go abroad. I went to rehab." Her eyes are like nails, sharp and piercing. "I needed to know what was so great about drugs, why my mom traded us for them. Before I knew it, I was in too deep. The numbness . . . I'm over it now, but I still have to be careful. That's why this thing with you will never work. You could hurt me like she did. I might slip up and want the numbness again. That would destroy my dad. And what would people think of you and me together? It's too much, Diego. That's why I can't kiss you. Not because I do or don't like you, but because I can't take the chance."

I don't judge her for the mistakes she made. Everyone has scars. If anything, I like her more because she's being real.

I push her hand away and draw her to me. Her only protest is a whimper.

"Trust me," I whisper, and lower my lips to hers.

33
faith

Diego's lips are better than a drug, subduing my pain, blurring the edges of my world. The kiss breaks me.

It's different from our first. Softer. Gentler. His hands wind through my hair. Mine explore his stomach. His muscles are rock-hard beneath the thin fabric. His kiss deepens. My blood thrums faster.

His tongue eases out, tempting mine to do the same. When his hands move to my hips, touching the exposed skin, I shudder. Diego lowers me to the floor so that I lie flat with him poised over me. My hair falls to the ground, fanning around me. I feel oddly exposed.

"Diego," I say.

"*Mami,*" he groans. "Please don't tell me you can't kiss me."

His mouth presses harder. His fingers lightly trace the spaghetti straps of my tank top, a pleasurable tickle. His lips find my neck. I arch my head back.

"Diego," I repeat.

He looks at me, his eyes heavy with pleasure.

"Wait," I say. I reach under my back, pull out markers. I laugh. He smiles. "Sorry," I say. "That was uncomfortable."

He kisses me again. "It's okay. Thought you were goin' to tell me to stop for good."

His lips are red against his dark skin.

"I don't want you to stop," I admit. "You're right. I do feel something. I have since the first day I saw you sitting in the office."

Diego grins. "*Yo sé.*"

"Confident much?"

Diego plays with my hair. Pieces fall through his fingers like thread.

"Maybe a little," he says.

I sigh. "I still can't be with you."

"Publicly," he says. "But no one has to know. You said so yourself, you feel something. So do I. I can't ignore it. Will you be mine, *mami*? I won't tell anyone. You can keep face. Not worry about your dad. I swear I won't hurt you. I only want to make you happy. And I'll keep fightin' for you until you say yes, so you might as well—"

I cut him off with a kiss. I lose myself in him, in the moment. I kiss his bottom lip, and then his top. When I part my mouth, he takes the invitation.

Diego's kisses are replaced with panting as he asks, "Is that a yes?"

I laugh. "Yes."

I can't deny him any longer.

"Finally," he says, smiling.

Diego is rightness and passion and pleasure. He is sharp edges that give way to softness.

"Kiss me again," I order.

He lowers his lips to mine, but right before we touch, he backs away. "Faith, I need to know that you'll never tell anyone about the cartel. No one. They don't know that I'm still alive. If they found out they'd—"

"I promise," I interrupt. I can't stand to hear him say the words.

Diego caresses my cheeks. I refuse to push him away any longer.

"How is this going to work?" I ask.

Diego's eyes are hungry. He doesn't push past kisses. "However you want it to," he replies.

I trail a finger over his lips. His breath is warm to the touch. "We can see each other in private?" I ask.

"As much as you want."

"What about school?"

Diego's hand moves from my hair to my hips, resting there.

"Your call."

"I can't see you at school. I'm not sure if that will work for you. And I understand if it doesn't. I'm sorry to ask you to do this," I say. "I'm not ashamed of you. Please don't ever think that. You're, well, you're amazing."

He smiles.

"You understand why I can't face that yet, right?" I ask.

"*Sí, mami.*"

"You're not mad?"

"Nope."

I sigh. "Maybe when I go off to college, I'll be free. I don't know where I'll go. I haven't started looking or applying but I definitely plan to go far away where no one can judge me."

Diego lies on his side next to me. I melt into him.

"People will always judge." He says it with such finality, with such certainty, that I know it to be true.

People will always judge.

I can't change them.

So maybe they shouldn't be allowed to change me.

"Are you sure you're cool with this?" I ask again. "Jason wants me back. Everyone expects us to get back together. You'll hear a lot of gossip."

"I can handle it," Diego says. "As long as you don't want him, I don't care what they say."

I look into his eyes. Confess the truth. "All I want is you."

His mouth curves up.

"Good," he says. " 'Cause now that you're mine, I don't plan on letting you go."

34
diego

Not an hour ago, my lips were on Faith. I replay her kisses, soft, rough, perfect.

Steaming water pounds into my back like a massage. I wash my hair, then my body. I stay in the shower until the water changes from hot to cool. A towel awaits me, crumpled on the counter. I fit it around my waist on the way to the kitchen.

I open the fridge to find apples, oranges, and two-day old pizza. Sometimes *mi padre* works on yards where people let him pick fruit from their trees. Free food is something he never passes up. I grab an apple and a slice of pizza.

Streetlights glare against the kitchen window like a flashlight in my eyes. I approach the window, taking a closer look at the nightlife below. One glance, and I jump out of view.

I run to my room and reach under my bed, pulling out the 9mm. *Mi padre* gave it back to me when I promised not to carry it around. I check the ammunition. Extra bullets. Just in case. I peek out of my bedroom blinds to get a better view. On the sidewalk stands Wink, like a curse dropped from the sky. At first I'm nervous that maybe the

MS-13s have found me, but I quickly realize they are only passing by. I haven't seen them since our street fight. And if I had it my way, I would never see them again.

I go back to my bed and sit. Put my gun down. Normally I wouldn't care, but these guys are different. They want to recruit me. I want nothing to do with them. I have Faith. I'll do anything to make it work with her.

I can't deny anymore that Faith drives me crazy in the best way. And she finally agreed to go out with me. I manage a shaky laugh.

Since when did I have to make girls agree to go out with me?

That's always been an easy point for me. Or many points, if you're keeping score.

Tonight, kissing Faith made me understand what it is to truly want. *More,* I kept thinking. I've never held back, but she's worth it. I don't want to rush her. I've heard rumors about how she wouldn't give it up to Jason, about how Faith has never given it up to anyone.

I glance at the clock. *Tick, tick, tick.* I dress quickly. Javier should be here any minute. Sure enough, he arrives like planned. He's got a smartphone, which works to my advantage since we can't afford Internet at home, and I need to research stuff for several classes. It's not easy to do on such a small screen but I manage, knowing that it's more than I could have hoped for in Cuba.

A tiny screen that connects you to endless information in seconds? A thing of dreams for most.

A way to educate yourself and rise above violence and poverty? Never an option before.

When I finish, we work on our psychology papers, which are due tomorrow. I procrastinated, spent time at the beach and at Melissa's instead of studying, and will most likely get my first C, but I don't care. Knowing Faith is officially mine is absolutely worth it.

My heart stutters in my chest when I spot Faith at school the next day. She sees me. Her cheeks are roses, blooming, bursting with color.

But she's surrounded by the Fakes. I'm close enough to hear their conversation, something about a dance routine. I'm also close enough to hear them mention me as I pass by. I open my locker and listen.

"Why do you think he left Cuba?" one of the Fakes asks.

"I don't know. The thug thing is kinda hot, though," another says.

A couple of girls shriek as though she's said something scandalous.

"Oh my God, no, come on. I'd never go for a guy like that," the girl amends. "He's not relationship material. Might be good for some fun, though."

"You did not just say that," a Fake says. "He's probably been with a million girls. You couldn't *pay* me to touch him."

Faith giggles. Playing the part. Though I know she won't, though I know we talked about this, I want her to say something in my defense.

Instead, it's Melissa who silences them.

"He couldn't have been with any more people than you, Zara."

The girls are shocked. The one Melissa called Zara storms off while the others mumble their good-byes and leave for class.

I lock eyes with Faith. She knows I heard.

We don't talk to each other. Not then. Not at lunch. Not

in psychology. But in the library, Faith waits for me, a big smile on her face.

"Hey," she says.

I brush off my annoyance at today's incident. She did warn me that something like that might happen.

"*Hola*," I reply.

She pulls the tie out of her hair and I am hit by the smell of strawberry shampoo. Hair falls down her shoulders, cascading.

Preciosa.

"I wasn't sure if you'd come now that your detention is over."

"Of course I came," I reply. I wouldn't miss time with her.

Melissa and Lori are late. I take the opportunity to pull Faith behind a bookshelf.

"*Mi cielo,* you look *hermosa.*"

She smiles, too much brightness in that one motion.

"What are you doing tonight?"

I wish I didn't have to work because I think maybe she's going to ask me to chill with her. "Working," I answer.

She bites her lower lip. Looks at the floor shyly. It takes all I have not to kiss her.

"I was thinking maybe I could pick you up from work," she whispers.

The air is electrified. Sparks ignite and pop along the invisible live wire that connects our bodies. I want to touch it, no matter the pain, just to feel her.

"Of course," I answer.

"What time?" Her lashes flutter.

"Ten."

"Okay," she says.

I stuff my hands in my pockets so that I don't grab her.

"No one will see you around back of the restaurant," I say. It's a given that Faith won't walk through the front door to pick me up. "There's a spot by the fence. I'll meet you there."

"Okay," she says again.

Faith looks around quickly like a crow about to steal an egg, and then walks back to our regular spot by the books. I wait a second before joining her. I wouldn't do this for anyone else. Pride is a serious thing. I have to bite mine back.

I want the world to know that she belongs to me.

Melissa and Lori eventually show up, and by the end of the day, we're ready for the fair. I kind of wish we weren't because I won't see Faith in the library after school anymore. Maybe she'll make picking me up from work a regular thing.

I feel like at any minute, it could all disappear. I want to do something special for Faith. On the way home, I detour through the school parking lot. Faith has dance practice, which means her car will be there. I pick wildflowers and make sure no one's looking as I slip the bouquet under her windshield wiper.

I only wish I could see her expression when she finds them.

35

faith

I pull up to Applebee's, my stomach churning like I've swallowed snakes. I'm nervous. And excited. I try not to look at the back entrance a hundred times.

I reach for the door handle, and spot Diego. He can't see me in the dark, but I smile in his direction anyway.

Diego is beautiful under the light that shines on the back door. He pauses. Pulls out a cigarette. Lights it. I try not to cringe. I know he smokes. I've smelled it on him. I've seen him light up before. It bothers me, but I'll never ask him to stop. It's not my place.

I fidget with my skirt. In my hair is one of the wildflowers he left on my car. My sandals, the straps winding up my lower legs like vines, match my top. The skirt cuts off above the knee. The tank top is a V-neck, but not too low. Definitely not what I would normally be seen wearing but I want to be the real me with Diego.

A metal fence guards the back door. Security reasons, I'm guessing. Diego has one hand on the door when a blond girl walks up behind him. Her arms wrap around his waist. Every one of my muscles clenches.

It's not hard to see Diego's reaction. He's surprised. His

hands fly to hers, unwrapping her arms from his body like a bow from a present. He says something. She frowns. Then smiles, not giving up.

I'm out of the car before I realize I've stepped into the night, and I'm almost at the door when I hear Diego tell the girl that it's not going to happen. I can just imagine what it is she wants.

Diego looks up at me and smiles. "*Hola, princesa.*"

The girl says nothing as Diego opens the metal door. I turn to her. Extend my hand. "Hi. I'm Faith."

Kill her with kindness.

"Sabrina," she says, clearly thrown off guard.

"Nice to meet you," I reply. Shake her hand.

Diego is skeptical.

I stand on my tiptoes. My arms reach around Diego's broad shoulders. My fingers clutch his hair as I bring his face down to mine for a deep kiss. The kiss goes on for a while, yet it's still not long enough.

I break away gently, and am rewarded by a small grunt from Diego. He wants more.

"Oh, and by the way," I say pleasantly, turning to Sabrina. "Don't ever touch my boyfriend again."

Diego laughs. Sabrina is a hurricane, storming back inside.

"Well played," he says in my ear.

I grin.

"Do it again," he orders.

"Do what again?" I ask, though I know what he wants.

"Don't play with me," he replies hoarsely.

"Don't know what you're talking about," I say, holding back a smile.

He pulls me to him. His heart jackhammers against my skin. Both of our pulses are thick with yearning.

"You know what I want to hear," Diego says against my lips. "*Mami,* you called me your boyfriend."

"That's because you are."

He kisses me then. His tongue is thunder, rolling against mine, muting all else around me. His hands weave under the back of my shirt and up my spine. His lips are soft, plump. I bite them gently. He bites me back.

His fingers trace my ribs, strumming them like a violin. I want to make music for him. I forget about everything. My brain shuts down. My heart takes over.

Diego is right for me. A missing link. I kiss along the stubby hair on his jaw, reach his mouth.

"*Mi novio,*" I say, liking the way Spanish feels on my lips. "Only mine."

"*Siempre,*" he replies.

He presses me against the metal gate and cups my face, kissing me again.

The click of a lighter catches my attention. We have an audience.

When did they come outside?

Probably when I lost myself in Diego. Two Latinos in chef hats light cigarettes. I pull away. The desire in his eyes is matched in mine.

Diego says something in Spanish. The guys laugh. Diego's cigarette burns on the ground where he dropped it when I kissed him. I press it out with my foot and grab his hand. We walk to my car.

Inside my car, Diego gives me another kiss. I start the engine. It purrs like the pleasure in me.

"You know, for someone who wants to keep this on the down low, you're pretty open so far," he teases.

I look away from him when I answer. "Couldn't stand her on you."

Somehow I know his eyes are still on me, resting, burning, consuming.

"I would never jeopardize what I have with you. In the past, I admit, I saw two girls at once, but I'd never do that to you," he says.

"I know," I reply, flashing a grin.

When we pull up to Diego's apartment, I wait for him to invite me in. He leans over the center console and kisses me. I'm a little hurt when he reaches for the door handle, not asking me up.

"No invitation?" I throw the question out casually. My insides say something entirely different.

"You sure you want one?" he says.

My eyes scan the dilapidated building, copying it to memory. Sun has aged it. Yellow paint flakes like peeling skin from the sides. The concrete is covered in graffiti.

It doesn't look too bad.

"Why wouldn't I want to go inside?" I ask.

"Seriously?" he says, and then laughs. "Look at it. The outside is better than the inside."

"What are you trying to say?"

Diego realizes that I'm not smiling.

"I'm teasin'," he says. "It's just that my apartment is a lot different from what you're used to."

"How do you know what I'm used to?" I ask sharply.

" 'Cause I've seen Melissa's house. Yours is only a few spots down. Where I live is nothin' like that."

"You say it like I live in some mansion," I retort. "I live in a regular house. We don't have a lot, Diego."

"I'm not sayin' you do," he replies. "Come inside. You're always welcome here. Just, you know, be prepared for less than average."

I rap my fingers on the wheel. Each pound is a release.

"It's not what you have that matters to me. You know I don't care about that kind of stuff," I say. "As a matter of fact, I despise it."

"*Perdón, mami.* I didn't mean to be rude."

I try to relax. "It's okay."

I cut the engine and follow him to the door. There's no number on the outside.

Inside, the walls are white and plain. No decorations besides a worn-out couch and a small kitchen table with two chairs. One wicker. One wood. None of it matches. I'm guessing they took whatever they could to get by when they arrived in the States. More proof that Diego left Cuba with nothing but his life.

He's lucky to have that.

His place is minimal and tiny and a little dirty and unimpressive and perfect.

Diego studies me. I grin. I don't care what conditions he lives in. It's a clean life. Away from the cartel. That's all that matters.

He leads me to two doors within earshot of each other. The one on the left has a small mattress on the floor and a dresser. Diego stops in front of the closed door.

His room, says the smirk on his face.

"Have to tell you, I never thought you'd be comin' in here," he remarks. "Don't get me wrong, I'm loving it. Just didn't think it would happen for someone like me."

"Likewise," I reply.

I never thought someone could know my secrets and not run away. Look at the way Jason handled things. I invite him to see a slice of the real me, and he breaks things off? Says a lot. But Diego doesn't.

Inside his room, the scent of Diego is strong, curling around my body. The space is small but comfortable. A light wood dresser leans against one wall. A bed sits opposite. Diego's books and homework litter one corner of the room. There's nowhere for us to sit except on the mattress.

"So, what do you think?"

"It's perfect," I say. I mean it.

He laughs humorlessly. "Hardly."

"It is," I argue. "It's simple. Sometimes having more than the basics complicates things. I wish I could live in a place like this. Not that we have a lot; it's just that I think it could be less. I'd prefer less."

"You're crazy," Diego says. "Do you know how many people would love to have a place like yours? And you would trade it all for this?"

"In a heartbeat."

"You're strange, Faith," Diego says, winding his arms around my waist. "You could have anything you want. Anyone you want."

"I definitely don't get everything I want. But," I say an inch away from his lips, "if I could pick anything in this world to hold on to, it would be you."

36
diego

My lips are on fire with warmth and desire. They practically jump off my face in their eagerness to taste Faith. She would pick me over everything else. She said it. Her words hang between us. I break them with a kiss.

Our lips crush the breath out of us. Our tongues dance. I thought I could control myself, but it's instantly clear that I'm wrong. From the moment our lips meet, I want more. All of her. Everything.

It's too hard to have my girl on my bed and still take it slow. I break away from her. I need to grab kitchen chairs. Maybe if I bring them into my room, I won't be as tempted.

"What are you doing?" Faith asks before I reach the door.

"Thought maybe you would be more comfortable in a chair."

She laughs. "I won't bite, you know." She moistens her lips. "Unless you want me to."

She's probably joking, but the look on her face makes it hard to concentrate.

"Come here," she says.

I am back by her side in a second. She lowers herself

onto my bed. We lean against pillows on the headboard. Her fingers roam my face, outlining my eyes and nose.

"What are you thinking?" she whispers.

"That you look incredible," I say.

I play with the hem of her shirt. It hitches slightly. The tips of her tattoos show.

She notices my stare. "Did my tats surprise you?"

"Definitely."

"Took me two summers' worth of part-time jobs to pay for them," she says.

My tattoos were free. But I would've gladly paid for ones I wanted, rather than be branded with ones I despise.

She points to some of mine, asking the meaning. I explain. Ask about hers. As I suspected, the haunting images in the smoke are demons. Now I understand why.

"You're brave to get tats there," I say, thinking of the pain.

"No one can see them unless I want them to. I like it that way," she says.

I wonder if maybe people wouldn't look at me like I'm a no one who will never amount to anything had I chosen more discreet locations for mine. Then again, I didn't really have a choice when it came to the cartel tats. They chose where to brand me—the more obvious, the better. That way everyone knew whom I belonged to.

I am not theirs to take.

I draw circles around Faith's pierced belly button. A charm hangs from the loop. Broken wings, I think. I touch the silver. It's warm from her skin.

"I went to the zoo once. They had a beautiful bird sanctuary," Faith says. "There was an eagle. Regal. Strong. Sun glinted off its white head . . . it was almost blinding.

"The zookeeper said that one of the eagle's wings was misshapen. Broken beyond repair. He'd never fly again. It broke my heart that a creature so beautiful would never reach the sky. The zookeeper said nothing can fly with broken wings. Injuries have to heal first, he said."

Faith twists the charm and peers deep in my eyes. Like fingers touching my soul.

"But, sometimes—like this eagle—injuries never heal right. So, what then?" Faith glances at the charm and smiles. "I'll never forget that eagle's look, Diego. He watched the sky like he trusted that one day he'd soar again. I think if you're persistent enough, you can fly on broken wings." Faith drops the charm. Truth fits her face like a glove. "I'm going to be proof of that."

She thrives despite the scars, despite the past. I feel an intense connection to Faith. When we're together, we're the rawest, truest forms of ourselves and both of us accept one another. Even with flaws. Especially with flaws.

I bring my hands to her face. Brush the hollows under her cheekbones. Her big eyes watch me intently. Her hands draw patterns on my back. She reaches under my shirt. Touches me softly. My control is fading.

"I don't know if—"

Faith cuts me off with a kiss. I forget to warn her that I'm losing control.

My hands reach up her stomach. I lay Faith flat and lean over her. Strawberry shampoo intoxicates me. I hope the scent lingers on my sheets. A part of her with me even after she leaves.

My room is heat and humidity joining hands. I think about opening the window. Then decide not to. I don't want Faith to hear what goes on in the streets below.

I softly brush over her breasts as my hands go to her arm. When she leans into me, I touch them again. I feel the outline of her bra. *Dios mío*, I want to take it off.

Faith's hands wander underneath my shirt. Over my chest. Down my stomach. She stops above my belt. I groan.

Faith surprises me when she sits up and presses down on my shoulders, flattening me. She lifts my shirt. Kisses my neck. Her mouth trails down my body to my waistband. She comes back up. Kisses my lips.

"What are you doin' to me?" I ask. My voice is gruff.

"Driving you *loco*," she replies. "Is it working?"

I love it when she speaks Spanish. Maybe I can teach her more.

"Yeah, it's workin'," I answer, pressing my pelvis into her. "Too good."

I lift her top a little, enough to expose her ribs, and kiss her sides. Her breaths are heavy. Her hands weave through my hair, pressing my head down harder, wanting more.

I lick a trail from her belly button around her hips. I move to her legs. Her shoes are sexy, and like everything else, I want to take them off, see every inch of her. I kiss her knees. Move back to her lips.

"Diego," she moans.

She shouldn't do that. It's too much, my name coming out of her mouth between heavy breaths. I care nothing about control at this point. I've gladly lost it. The heat of the moment burns away every thought but Faith. She is fireproof.

"Diego," *mi padre* says from the other side of the door.

Faith jumps back. Straightens her shirt and hair. I'm momentarily stunned. It takes me a minute to snap out of it. I clear my throat.

"*Un minuto,*" I say as I stand. Faith sits up.

"I'm sorry," I whisper to her.

"Shh. It's okay," she says.

I search her face. Her hair is perfect, but nothing can disguise her puffy lips.

"Are you okay?"

"I'm fine," she replies. "Are you okay?"

"Yeah."

I open the door. *Mi padre* tells me about one of the landscape clients today. They gave him herbs, fruits, and vegetables from their garden. He stopped by the store and bought a package of chicken and rice. He wants to cook dinner together tomorrow.

Mi padre doesn't notice Faith at first. But when he does, he goes completely still. He looks from me to her like he doesn't know what to say. Faith stands and smiles.

"*Lo siento, lo siento,*" *mi padre* says. He goes off in Spanish about how he didn't realize I had someone over.

"It's cool," I tell him.

I motion for Faith to come to me.

"Faith, this is my dad," I say. "Dad, this is Faith. *Mi novia.*"

"*¿Tu novia?*" he asks.

I've never had a girlfriend.

"*Sí,*" I answer.

Faith sticks her manicured hand out to shake *mi padre*'s. "It's nice to meet you," she says.

"Yes, yes. You, too," *mi padre* says eagerly. "I was just telling Diego about dinner tomorrow night. Like to join us?"

Though *mi padre* speaks in a heavily accented voice, Faith has no problem understanding him.

"I'd love to," Faith answers.

"What time can you come over?" I ask.

"Um, after school. After dance rehearsal. I don't have anything else going on."

"Great," *mi padre* chimes in. "See you then." He closes the door as he leaves.

Faith smiles from ear to ear. "Your dad invited me back over," she says. "It's like he doesn't care that we're different."

My mind flips at the thought. "Does that mean you'll come over more often?"

She laughs. "Yeah. I think so." She bites her lip. "I hate to do this, but I have to go."

I look at the clock. It's late. And a school night.

"Okay," I say, leaning in for a kiss.

I walk her to the car, thinking about change. I don't want to admit it, but I think maybe I'm wrong. Maybe change is possible.

Maybe there is such a thing as a brighter future.

37
faith

"I don't get how it's going to work, Faith."

Melissa is sitting on her bedroom floor painting my toenails purple, the color of the sky when it's swollen with rain.

"It's pretty simple," I reply. "We're not going to tell anyone that we're together. Well, except you and a few of Diego's buddies."

I finish painting her nails a pumpkin orange, the color of the harvest that Florida never has.

Melissa's eyebrows scrunch together. "But don't you want everyone to know he's yours?"

Yes.

"In an ideal world," I say.

"Okay, yeah, your dad will freak and gossip will fly at school, but so what?" Melissa says. "Forget them. I mean, I'm happy for you and Diego and I, of course, won't say anything, but I think it's a mistake to hide your relationship."

I wish I had another option. Now that Jason and I are through, it's easier to push prying eyes out of my mind. The place where I need to keep up my image is church, though. If Diego and I were together at school, it would eventually get back to the church community. Last thing I need is to hear about it from Jason's mom. Volunteering with Mrs. Magg makes me susceptible to her constant meddling.

"It's not that big a deal," I say. "Diego knows people want me and Jason to reconcile. He can handle it. And his dad has no problem with us being together. We can spend a lot of time at his place."

Melissa snorts. "That's stupid, Faith. You're a teenager. You should be having fun. Going on dates. If you only meet at his house, it's like you're forty years old or something." She stops painting my nails. "Look at me, Faith."

I look at her. She places a hand on my knee.

"I love you, girl. I've seen you through a lot. You. Need. To. Have. Fun. I think it's great that Diego's your boyfriend. Really, I'm your biggest fan, but this secrecy stuff is not going to work. Trust me."

She's probably right, but I have to try.

"I can't break things off with him."

"Who said anything about breaking things off?" Melissa asks, exasperated. "Like those are your only options? Meet in secret or break up? I have half a mind to call your dad myself and let it out."

The look I give my best friend is scathing.

"Chill. You know I'd never do it." She rolls her eyes. "But someone should."

She's daring me.

I can't.

She finishes my toes. I walk like a duck, trying not to ruin them. We head outside. I stretch out in a lounge chair on her back porch. We're both wearing bathing suits. Melissa's is solid red. Mine is pink-and-silver polka dots. Melissa had the idea to sunbathe after school in hopes that

I would catch a tan for my date with Diego tonight. The day is relentlessly hot. Within five minutes, I've perspired enough to fill an ocean.

Next to me, Melissa lights a cigarette. I have no idea how she can smoke when the air alone is hot enough to singe my lungs.

"Enjoy that," I say, adjusting my shades. Even with glasses on, the sun is blinding. " 'Cause as soon as I win Prediction, you'll have to quit."

Melissa laughs. "Not a chance."

"I'm gonna win, Melissa."

"Please. You and Jason are over. You've replaced him with a hot boy. Just as I predicted. And you bought new clothes. That's two out of three," she replies.

I swat the air with my hand, brushing her smoke away from my face.

"Well, you never did stop bugging me about Jason. Plus you have a C in senior calculus. So, ha."

"Fine," she says. "We're tied. But I'll win eventually."

"We'll see."

An hour later, I say good-bye to Melissa and head home. A few days ago, I agreed to let Melissa take me to the mall for new clothes. She persuaded me to pick what I would wear if I could choose freely, like what I'd pick out if I were heading off to college tomorrow.

I take a quick shower. Throw on a new outfit. I don't know what to expect from Dad when he sees my clothes.

I walk like the ground is covered in broken glass, each step careful, wary, scared that I might tumble into the wrath of Dad, cut up my insides worse than they already are. I hate lying to him, but I have to make something up about hanging out with Melissa tonight. No way he'll let me out of the house if I admit my real plans. I almost choke on the bulk of the lie.

"I'm hanging out with friends," I say. "I'll be home by ten."

His mouth doesn't say anything, but his look does.

"Okay," he says, eyeing my clothes.

"Thanks, Dad." I kiss him on the cheek and head out the door.

Misleading him is easier than I thought. Experimenting with drugs made me a natural deceiver. It's how I got away with lying before Melissa's intervention. I'm not proud of it. But like everything else that's too hard to chew, I swallow it whole.

Even outside Diego's apartment, the aroma of food hangs in the air, savory and mouthwatering. I knock on the front door. Nothing. I try again. Nothing. I turn the knob. Diego and his father are already cooking. Paper plates, napkins, and plastic silverware decorate the table. Music plays in the background.

Diego spots me immediately. He sets down a large mixing spoon and wraps his arms around my waist.

His dad smiles and waves. It feels strange to show affection in front of Mr. Alvarez, but Diego assures me that his father is happy for us.

Mr. Alvarez excuses himself to go to the bathroom. Diego and I take over the kitchen. I pick up tongs. Shuffle food around in a skillet.

"*Mami,* you look amazing," Diego says.

His eyes rake my outfit: shorts and a black top held up by one shoulder strap, leaving the other shoulder bare.

I try not to blush and fail miserably.

"You, too," I say.

Jeans and a button-down, checkered blue-and-black. I've never seen him wear anything but plain shirts.

Diego presses me up against the counter and tucks his hands in my back pockets. He kisses me softly, sweetly.

A buzzer goes off. Diego takes something out of the oven.

We cook, cramped all together, but it feels nice. Like I imagine home should feel. We fill the table with *pollo asado en salsa* (roasted chicken with sauce), *frijoles y arroz* (black beans and rice), and homemade tortillas.

When we dig in, Mr. Alvarez tells me about himself, pausing to ask questions about my life. He insists that I call him by his first name, Adolfo. His mannerisms, his features, are Diego twenty years from now.

As we talk, a warm feeling spreads through me, and it's a lot like love. This little pocket of an apartment is rich because of the people in it. Somehow Diego's place feels more like home than my own. I talk and smile and listen and eat and simply enjoy the little things. Diego makes me laugh harder than I have in a long time. Hard enough to decimate my problems like an F5 tornado. Nothing left.

Time to rebuild.

38
diego

When Faith says she's going to the car for something, I don't expect her to come back holding two giant beanbags.

"What are you doing?" I ask, amused.

"Getting our new chairs." She smiles.

Yes, chairs are definitely good. Faith plus my bed equals trouble for me. Still, did she have to pick a purple one with pink flowers?

"You're not bringin' that into my room," I say.

"Aw, come on. Yours is blue," she says, trying to justify the flowery stuff.

"No way," I say.

Truthfully, I'll probably let her get away with it.

"What's wrong with regular chairs?" I ask. We even bought a new one for Faith.

"These are more comfy since we'll be watching a movie," she explains.

"We will?" I don't know how she expects that to happen with no television.

Faith pulls out a miniature DVD player.

"Want to?"

I can't help thinking how different this is from my cartel days. It's a good thought.

"Only you could get away with this," I mumble.

She laughs at the look on my face. Throws her arms around me. "You know you love me."

She meant it as a joke, but I tense anyway. All of my muscles violently collide with each other.

"Oh no. Sorry. I didn't mean it like, um, just forget I said—" Faith breaks off nervously.

It is not that she said something wrong; it's that she's right. I'm falling for her. I don't know what to do with that yet. It's scary. Big. Enough to make me consider staying distant. Because if the cartel finds me alive, Faith will suffer.

I walk to my room. Pretend she never said anything. Faith starts the movie with shaky fingers. I should comfort her, but I focus on the film instead.

If I try hard enough, my past weakens to a dim pinpoint. Like a dying star in the vast universe of my mind. There, but fading.

I search the auditorium for Faith, replaying our movie night in my mind. Replaying the beach. All of it. Anything to picture her face. The book fair is in full swing. Everywhere I look, books, books, books. Some new. Some old. Some filled with messages from people long gone, who speak to us still. Letters on papers so powerful that those in the grave can rest, knowing their voices are forever heard.

The walls are covered in posters. This is our work, mine and Faith's. We put this together.

I spot Lori and make my way toward her. "What's up?"

"Hi, Diego. Everything looks great! Couldn't have pulled

this off without you. You worked so hard. Did I get a chance to thank you yet?" Lori talks fast, excited. It's hard to keep up.

"I think you just did," I reply.

She gives me a hug. "Anyhow, you're the best. Got to run. Catch you later, okay?"

Lori is gone before she finishes the sentence. I never got to ask if she's seen Faith. I make my way through the crowd. My eyes snag on something. Jason in a corner, folded between two walls like the edge of a blanket. I catch a flash of the person in front of him.

No words. No words. No words.

I push my way through people to get to them. Apparently I push someone too hard because they shove me back and say something. I don't hear them over the roar in my ears.

Jason's hands are on Faith. One hand touches her arm. The other strokes her cheek.

Closer. Closer. Not close enough. Too many people.

"Can't, Jason. I'm done," Faith says.

I pause. Try to hold it together. Any second now she'll walk away from him.

"But we had years together, Faith. I miss you. I love you," Jason replies.

The last thing I need is a school suspension. The last thing I care about is repercussions.

"I know," Faith says. "But I'm done. I can't turn back."

Faith doesn't see me. I wish she would look my way. I remember our conversation: Faith warning me about the rumors, the gossip, about Jason wanting her back. I also remember her not defending me, her laughing as her fake girlfriends talked shit and called me names.

"Come on. Don't throw this away. We're good together."

Faith doesn't reply. But she doesn't walk away, either.

"I waited a long time for you, Faith, while you were studying around the world." A flash of pain cuts across Faith's face like lightning in the black of night. She covers it up. "And then, I don't know, I just lost it. I'm sorry."

Faith tries unsuccessfully to wiggle away, to slip the knot of memories Jason is hanging her from.

"I forgive you," she responds. "Can't we just be friends?"

Friends? Why would she want to be friends with him?

Jason runs a hand through his hair, looking miserable. "I guess. I just, God, how are we supposed to do that? I want to kiss you all the time. I can't stop thinking about you."

My fists ball.

"Don't you miss me?" he asks.

Faith looks down. Her voice is soft. "Yes. Sometimes."

Faith's words are a sucker punch to my diaphragm.

"Is it Diego?" her ex asks.

Faith's answer comes without hesitation. "No. Like I'd have anything to do with him."

It shouldn't bother me. But it does. I knew she'd deny it, but did she have to sound so repulsed?

A group of students walks in front of me. I lose sight of Faith. When they clear away, Jason is kissing her. She tries to push him away, but he has her backed against a wall.

My hands are on Jason's shoulders, ripping him away like torn paper. Effortlessly.

"*¿Qué crees que estás haciendo?*"

"Back off, man," Jason says.

He tries to shove me. I'm stronger. I slam him against a table. People stare.

Too many eyes.

"Don't you ever touch her again," I growl.

Faith wipes her lips and shakes her hand as though she can dislodge the kiss from her skin.

"Diego, stop," she says.

A crowd has gathered, half-circled around us like a horseshoe.

"No means no, dickhead," I continue. "If I ever see you anywhere near her—"

"I'm serious, Diego," Faith says. "Stop. Now."

I turn to the sound of her voice. Her eyes are volcanoes, ready to erupt.

"How could you let him—"

"I didn't let him do anything," Faith says, voice full of poison. "As you probably saw, I didn't initiate anything. Not that it's any of your business."

"None of my business?" I hiss.

Secrecy isn't working. If it's not Jason, it'll be another guy. They'll step on each other to get to her now that she's single.

"That's right," Faith says. "None of your business. And I've had enough of this, so if you're done—" Her words linger. Their meaning is clear.

Faith dismisses me as though I'm not worth her time. My anger bubbles over. Burning everything. Everything. I release Jason.

She isn't the only one who's had enough.

39

faith

Night bleeds into day, and day into night, until neither is distinguishable. I'm a clot of deadly emotions. Fear. Hesitation. Eagerness. Guilt. Love.

Diego hasn't talked to me in five days. With dance competition less than an hour away, I shouldn't be thinking of him. Everything we worked for, every shared moment, broken by one wrong move. I'm left alone, buried in an avalanche of jagged pieces.

I wish I could've stood up to Jason. The pain on Diego's face was serrated, sawing through me.

He won't return my calls. He missed two days of school. I don't know how to fix anything. I'm nothing more than a busted heart.

I ease into a split, my legs scissoring on the mat. Backstage, girls stretch around me. My dance team is present, preparing like everyone else. Competition starts soon. We're one of the last to go.

Forty minutes to get Diego out of my mind. I reach for my toes. They're a thousand miles away. Everything is tense. I rise up. Lay myself flat on my stomach and arch back, grabbing my ankles.

"Smile, babe," Melissa says, stretching next to me.

"Can't," I grumble.

Only Melissa knows how much pain I'm in.

"I feel horrible. I lost one of the best things that's ever happened to me, didn't I?"

I blink back tears. One slips away. I wipe it quickly.

Melissa doesn't reply. Her silence confirms my worst fears.

"Oh, Lissa. He's going to break up with me, isn't he? What do I do?"

"I don't know," she says. "I think he's pretty crazy about you, and you treated him like he meant nothing. It's hard to come back from that."

We have to come back from it.

I can't lose him.

"Don't think about it now. Concentrate," Melissa says. "Come on. We'll work on flips."

I stand. Stretch my arms. Roll my neck. Tell my muscles to relax. I approach the mat. People practice tumbling. I wait in line for my turn. Tracy Ram is in front of me. You'd think that after years on the same team, she'd get over whatever it is that makes her hate me. Guess not. She sneers and whips her head around. Her blond hair whacks me in the face. An undeserved lashing. The team knows that she despises me. We try to work around it, ignore the tension hanging heavy like an impenetrable fog.

Melissa says Tracy is jealous of me, that Tracy wants everybody's attention. But with such a foul attitude, she pushes people away. The smell of her envy is putrid.

Tracy's up. She's confidence and hunger, eating yards of mat with each landing. My turn. I blink. Try to remove the embedded image of Diego.

Don't think about him.

My first run is good. Three backhand springs followed

by a twisted pike. I nail it. Melissa doesn't tumble. She cheers. I tell her to practice the routine, but she refuses to leave me.

Tears threaten.

"Stay strong," Melissa says in my ear. She notices the tears, of course.

My turn again. Seven backhand springs in a row. The final landing is wobbly, like a fawn on unsteady legs, but I pull it off. Competitors gasp. I'm a good tumbler. Better than most.

I wait for my turn again. My mind disobeys me, reaches for Diego. Remembers so much so much so much. His spicy smell. The way pieces of hair fall into his eyes, determined to stand out from the rest. Much like him. I allow myself a small smile. I picture his plump lips. I want to kiss them.

My turn now. I inhale a shaky breath and take off. I land my last backhand spring on my knees. Pain shoots through my legs. Melissa runs to my side. Emergency workers, too.

"I'm fine," I tell them.

By regulation they have to momentarily massage my knees and apply a cream. The one in charge gives me the okay to continue.

Melissa pulls me to the side. "Faith, you're not going to make it through this if you don't stop thinking about him."

She's right.

"I'll try," I say.

When my team finally takes the stage, the crowd goes silent. We almost always win. That's another thing. Last year during my absence, Tracy was the captain. And our team lost the competition. I think she hates me for that, though it's not my fault.

We begin our routine. Music echoes through speakers.

My heart thuds, adrenaline pumping it faster and faster. I smile, just like my teammates, keeping up with the beat. Everything goes off without a hitch until the end. I think about Diego again.

Raw pain in his eyes. Staring at me as though I've broken what we have. I want to say sorry. I want to go to him. I stand my ground instead, watching him leave. Farther and farther.

All my strength is not enough to push Diego out of my mind.

As I land a triple flip, the grand finale, my foot twists the wrong way and I fall hard.

Pain shoots through my leg like a rocket taking off. I can't catch my breath. Spots take over my vision, a hundred flashing lights. I look down. The spots dim to a pinprick. My foot is the wrong way. My toes reach behind me. I can't stomach the image.

We've lost the competition, I'm sure. No one can fall like that and win.

The pain is too much. I close my eyes and think of Diego. My only relief.

Something beeps in my right ear, waking me from a deep sleep that feels like hibernation.

Where am I?

I blink. Bright lights sting my eyes, making them water. I pull a hand to my face to block the glare. My arm snags on something. Pain lacerates my veins like a hot poker.

Eleven seconds until my eyes adjust. And even then, everything blurs slightly as though I'm looking through a distorted lens. I look down. I'm wearing a hideous yellow gown, the color of mustard. The beeping to my right is a heart monitor and my leg is in a sling of some sort, connected to the ceiling by narrow chains.

What the—

"Faith! Are you okay?" Melissa runs to my side. "I only leave the room for what, five minutes? And you wake up. Go figure."

Her voice is too loud.

"Shh," I try to tell her but my throat is sandpaper that's been left in the sun for days. I'm not sure that I actually make a sound.

"I only went to grab a muffin. I didn't think you'd wake up. The nurses said it could be hours," Melissa says. "How are you feeling?"

I can't talk. I try to lift my arm again, and realize why it's so difficult. A bracelet of IV tubing is wrapped around me. I untangle myself—careful not to move my hand too much—and reach my fingers to my throat.

Melissa understands. "Here," she says, putting a cup to my lips. I lift my head and swallow. The effort is painful. Like a fork grating the inside of my throat.

"What happened?" I ask. My voice is hoarse.

Melissa winces. "You fell, sweetie. At the competition. You landed wrong and, well . . . Faith, you really messed up your foot. Then you passed out. Probably better that way."

Memories attack me.

"How serious?" I whisper. It's easier to whisper.

Melissa takes my hand. "I'm not a doctor, but from what I understand, it's not that great."

I put my right hand, the one with the IV, to my head and rub circles on my temple. My brain hurts. My left hand is sore, too. A cast molds around my pinky and ring finger.

"When you fell, you gave yourself a concussion. The

doctors had to stabilize you before they could take you into surgery," Melissa says.

"Surgery?" I ask.

Melissa points to my leg. "You broke a bone in your foot and ruptured your Achilles tendon. They had to surgically repair it." She points to my hand next. "And you broke your fingers when you landed. One of the fractured bones popped through the skin. They repaired that surgically, as well."

My God. "I don't remember anything after the fall," I say.

"I wouldn't, either, if I had the amount of medicine you have pumping through you."

Well, that explains it.

I look around my hospital room. Everything is focused now. The walls are off-white with pictures of palm trees and oceans. One window. Blinds closed. A television hangs from the ceiling. Flowers decorate the nightstand and windowsill. Balloons float around the room like multicolored bubbles. I spot a card with Jason's name on it.

I wonder if any of them are from Diego.

"Then you decided you wanted to be combative," Melissa continues. "They had to give you a medicine that knocked you out for a few days so you wouldn't injure yourself further. You are the most stubborn person I—"

I interrupt. "A few days?"

"Yes," Melissa says. "It's Monday. Four o'clock in the afternoon. I came straight from school. You were supposed to be taken off of sedatives today. I wanted to be by your side when you woke up. Susan is working on some big case that she can't get out of and your dad is home with Grace. They didn't want to expose her to all the germs here, so I came instead. I promised your dad I'd call as soon as you woke up."

A nurse walks in and takes my vitals. She asks me no fewer than a million questions. Then explains the reason my throat hurts. Breathing tube during surgery. She tells me it will take eight weeks for my hand to heal, and six months of physical therapy for my foot, though I'll be able to walk on it much sooner than that. I should be able to dance again, too, as long as therapy goes well.

It will be too late.

Dance season will be over by then, which means Tracy Ram will be captain once again.

My days on the squad are over.

40
diego

"Are you going to call her back, or what?"

Javier holds my phone out to me. Faith's ring tone plays for the second time today, like an eerie echo of what once was.

"She keeps callin' you, man. You gonna stay mad forever?" Javier asks.

That's the plan, but with each day, my strength fades.

"It's been what, a week since her surgery?" my cousin asks, situating himself on the couch next to me.

"Nine days," I say. Nine agonizing days.

"And you still haven't talked to her?"

"Nope."

My eyes make me remember. Everywhere I look is somewhere she's been. The couch. My room. Even the carpet. I want to ball my fists and squeeze my eyes shut and forget, forget, forget.

"You gonna let her think you don't care?" he asks.

"Yep."

Javier shakes his head. Pity emanating. "You need to call her. I'm sick of seeing you mope around. You're playin' the game with the wrong girl. Because whether you admit it or not, you have it bad."

Javier puts the phone in my hand. Faith's call goes to voice mail.

"Call her," he says again, and gives me a serious look.

Javier leaves the couch. Grabs a drink from the fridge. The phone is still in my hand when he returns. I'm staring at a blank screen.

"Give me the phone. I'll call her."

"No," I reply, and shove my cell in my pocket. It chimes. One new voice mail.

"You gonna listen to it?" he asks.

"Nope."

"Have you listened to the others?"

"Nope," I say.

Faith has left several messages. I listened to the first one. It'll be the last. Her voice is too much.

I can't let her treat me like that. Sneaking around is one thing. Treating me like garbage in an auditorium full of people is another.

"Does she know you sent flowers?" Javier asks.

"No. I didn't leave a name," I answer.

"And the visits to the hospital?"

I rub my tired eyes. "She was unconscious. I doubt she remembers."

"You still angry about the way her dad looked at you?"

"No," I say. "I expected it. But as far as her dad knew, I was there as Melissa's friend, not Faith's."

I remember the hospital. *Walking in with Melissa. Faith's father bent over in a chair, his head in his hands. He doesn't hear us at first. I can't take my eyes off her: her leg in a sling, a million wires, her face like she's taking a nap, eyes closed, lost in a coma. I want to run to Faith. I want to rip out the wires and carry her home. I dare anyone to stop me. My fingers form fists.*

Mr. Watters looks up, spots me. His eyes linger.

Melissa introduces me as her friend. I shake his hand, but I can't stop looking at Faith.

I blink. Back to the present.

I hated the way Faith looked, hooked up to machines. So many snaking tubes biting at her skin.

I want to take her pain away.

"She's miserable at school," Javier says.

"So am I. Am I supposed to feel bad for her?"

Even though I say the words, and even though I don't want to care, I do feel bad. Faith is no longer actively on the dance squad, though she still holds her position from the sidelines, but Melissa is. So Faith's been alone a lot.

"She has a broken foot and hand. Probably a broken heart, too," Javier says. "She calls you every day. She can't catch up to you on her crutches at school. She even stopped me in the hall the other day to tell me she's sorry for what she did."

I close my eyes. Memories haunt me. Jason's lips on her. Her hands on him. Faith is supposed to be mine. I don't share.

"She chose this," I say. My tone is sharp. Pain's fingers wrap around my neck. Choke me. Deepen my voice.

Javier leans into the cushions and takes a sip of soda. "You should at least hear her side of the story before you call it quits. I've seen you with other *chicas*. You're different with her. You love her."

He shouldn't have gone there. I get in his face. "*Cállate.* You know nothing."

Javier shoves me away. "I'm not the enemy, Diego. You're falling apart. You won't talk about *tu madre*. You're having run-ins with MS-13s. You're pushing Faith away now, too. You need to get it together. That girl is good for you. I'm not sayin' what she did was right, but come on. She made a mistake. You act like you never have."

I try to control myself by walking away, even though it's my apartment. Javier follows and backs me up to a wall.

"What do you care?" I yell. "Who cares if I fall apart?"

"I do!" he yells back. "I care! *Somos una familia.* I won't let you do this to yourself. Not a second time. And you're not going to kill off another person you love."

That's it.

Too far.

I punch him in the face. "I did not kill *mi madre*!" I yell.

He punches me back. The force of it slams my shoulder against the wall.

"No, but your actions did!" he shouts.

Mi padre races into the room. Rips the two of us apart. He yells in Spanish. It takes a minute, but I finally cool off. Javier wipes blood from his mouth with the back of his hand. Blood trickles down my face, as well. The skin at the corner of my eye is cut.

"If you're not careful," Javier says in a low tone, "your actions will kill off Faith, as well."

41
faith

Two weeks since I've spoken to Diego. The distance creates a canopy of cobwebs in my mind. Blocking colors, blocking light, blocking the promise of anything hopeful. I can't handle the separation any longer. If Diego won't speak to me, I'll go to his place. He may not have good news for me, but I need to hear him say it. I need the finality, if that's what this is. My injury, being away from him, has brought everything into perspective.

My right foot is uninjured, so I'm able to drive. Still, it's difficult to get in and out of the car. Getting up Diego's steps on crutches is so much effort that I have to take a minute to sit on the concrete halfway up. The pain is intense, but worth it if I can finally talk to him.

I make it up the rest of the steps and take a deep breath before knocking. The pit of my stomach coils like a spring. I remind myself to stay calm.

When I knock, no one comes. I worry that he's not here. I knock harder. Wait. Knock again. Finally the door swings open. Diego says something in Spanish, annoyed with the intrusion.

Air whooshes out of me at once, like I've taken a kick to the gut. It's hard to breathe. Diego's hair is dripping wet.

Beads of water fall down his shoulders and bare chest, only to be absorbed by the waistband of his jeans, the elastic of his boxers.

His face falls slack. He lets go of the door. His arms drop to his sides, deadened. His expression softens, a mixture of pleasure and pain.

"Diego," I say.

The door is wide open. I want to walk in, but don't know if I should. He looks tired.

"Am I interrupting something?" I ask.

"Just my shower," he answers. "What are you doing here, *mujer*?"

My stare lingers on his tattooed chest. I want to touch him.

"I needed to see you," I reply.

Hope holds me with a tight grip, refusing to let go.

"For what?" he asks, not gently.

"Don't do this."

"I didn't do anything. You did." I flinch at the sharpness in his tone.

"Melissa told me," I blurt. I wasn't supposed to say that last part but it slipped out. "I know about the flowers, and your visits."

He shakes his head slightly. "So what?"

"So I know you care, that's what."

I take a step toward him and almost fall, wobbly on my broken foot. He reaches out, automatically steadying me.

His touch is everything, everything to me.

"I miss you," I say. I should give him space but I need to feel him against me.

Diego winces.

"I miss *us*," I say, reaching for his face.

"Don't."

My fingers stop midair. My hand drops.

"*¿Estas bien?*"

"No. I feel like my heart is breaking, if that's possible."

"Your foot, I mean," he amends.

My emotions are a scale ready to tip either way. Unsure of where I'll end up. Happy, maybe. Or perhaps more devastated.

"My foot's not really better," I answer. "Not yet. It hurts. I don't take the pain pills because they make my mind fuzzy. I'm unsteady, as you can tell, but I manage."

He lets go of me then.

"You shouldn't be here," he says, businesslike, looking at the wall as he speaks.

"But what about us?" I ask.

"What about us?"

I wish he would look at me.

"You won't return my phone calls."

"And you show up anyway."

I swallow the lump of rot in my throat. "You don't have to be rude, Diego."

He's pushing me away. I can't say I don't deserve it.

Diego looks at me then. "And you didn't have to treat me like garbage in front of the entire school."

"So this is how it's going to be?" I ask, voice rising. "You don't care anymore? What we had means nothing?"

"*No sé*. You tell me," he snaps back. "You let Jason kiss your lips. Lips that are supposed to be mine."

My face burns with shame. "I didn't let him. He pushed himself on me."

"I heard you ask him if you could be friends, Faith," Diego says. "Why would you want to be his friend?"

I uncurl my fists and blink back tears.

"I don't. I was just trying to be nice," I say. "Look. You're mad. You have every right to be." I pause, trying to decide if I should go on. Then, with a deep breath, I let everything out. "I know I don't deserve you. You've been good to me, helping me talk through all that stuff with my mom, even. And I hid you like a secret, yet you still stuck by me. I never should have done that to you. I'm sorry. I want to make things right."

I don't know what to expect when I look back up at him.

He steps toward me. Waits. Battles himself. I reach for him, grasping air, hoping he will accept me, forgive me. Another step. I hold my breath.

"You sure?" he asks.

"Absolutely," I say, nervous.

There's a difference between *want* and *need*. I need him. Diego knows it.

"I don't want to be played. *¿Me oyes?*" he says. "'Cause what you did at school was wrong. I need to know that you're mine, *mujer*. Only mine. The guys will keep coming as long as they think you're free."

"You want me to announce that we're together?" I ask. At this point, I'll do it. I love Dad, but I need to know happiness. The accident showed me that. I have to try. This thing between us feels more real than anything in my life.

"*Sí*," Diego says.

"Okay," I reply.

His eyebrows arch. "For real?"

"For real."

I hobble closer. He lets me this time.

"And I want one more thing if this is going to work between us," he says.

I am skeptical of the sly flash in his eyes. His stare traces my body: pink halter top, jean shorts, vulnerability on display.

"Let's hear it," I say.

Diego trails a finger down my bare shoulder. I shiver. Chills erupt, though his touch is searing. "*Prométeme* you'll dress like this every day."

I laugh as he scoops me into his arms and kicks the front door shut. He locks the dead bolt and carries me to his room, laying me on the bed.

"Done," I agree, smiling. "Can I have a little time to think about how to break it to everyone? I promise I'll do it; I just have to figure out a plan."

"Deal," he says.

Diego climbs next to me and pulls a pillow under his head. "*Te extraño*," he whispers.

Heat pulses off his bare skin. I place my palms on his chest. "I miss you, too," I reply, my eyes on his lips. "So much. Too much."

"You want to kiss me?" he asks, smiling.

"Bad," I admit.

"How bad?" he whispers. Quick as a wink, he brushes his lips against mine. It's not a kiss, more of an enticement. He laughs, but it's gravelly.

"Kiss me, Diego," I order. I need to know that I still have an effect on him.

His breathing slows. He licks his mouth. His thumb grazes my bottom lip.

"Diego," I say, my voice barely a whisper.

That's all it takes. He kisses me with pent-up passion. His lips work out his emotions.

Hard at first, angry.

Then fierce, missing me.

Then finally softer, happy. One hand cups the back of my neck. The other plays with my shirt.

It's dark in Diego's room. He must think the same thing because he reaches for matches on his nightstand to light a candle. Diego in the candlelight is breathtaking. My hands slide over muscles in his lower back. His fingers sweep over my breasts. My body reacts to his touch. His hands slide up my legs to my inner thighs.

I'm losing control again. And this time I don't want to stop.

42
diego

Faith's legs are soft under my fingertips. One of her knees is bent, propping her good leg up while the other foot rests comfortably on my sheets, swathed in a cast that looks more like a pink boot.

"*Eres tan bella. Preciosa. Perfecta*," I say.

She kisses me again.

"Diego," she says.

"Yeah," I say between kisses.

"I need to tell you something."

I pull back an inch. I'm spinning in a vortex of happiness. Faith is everywhere. On my lips. In my mind. Building a shelter within my heart.

"I'm not a virgin," she says.

I'm not expecting that.

"*¿Qué?*" I ask.

"I'm not a virgin," she repeats.

This shouldn't matter. I'm not, either.

"But I thought—" I break off because I realize she never actually told me she was a virgin. I heard rumors that she hadn't been with Jason. I assumed she hadn't been with anyone.

"I cheated on Jason," she explains.

I sit back on the bed. Thrown for a loop.

"When you first met me, you insinuated that maybe . . . I was. I felt like you deserved the truth," Faith says. "I couldn't think of a good time to bring it up. I don't know that there is one. But it needed to be said."

I don't move. Don't know what to say.

"Are you mad?" she asks.

"Not mad," I answer. "Surprised, maybe."

"Sorry," she says again.

" 'S okay," I say. I play with a piece of her hair that has fallen down her shoulder.

She sighs. We're quiet for a minute. I want to fill the silence with my questions but I know I don't have any right. I'm definitely no angel.

Faith watches my face. Answers the question I didn't have to ask.

"It was during the drug time," she says.

"You don't have to explain," I say. I wouldn't want to replay my past.

"I know. But I want to. I don't want you to think I would ever cheat on you, because I wouldn't," she continues.

I believe her. We are starting fresh. She is laying everything out. Honest.

"I never slept with Jason. That's why the school thinks I'm so untouched. But parties with Melissa's older sister introduced me to a world that didn't know the Faith I was pretending to be," she explains. "I wanted to get lost in something, anything, to ease the pain of my mom's betrayal. I didn't think about who the guy was. He didn't matter. What mattered was that for those moments, I forgot her. I forgot everything."

I say nothing, sensing she's not done.

Faith looks up at me then, pain etched in every crevice of her face. "The guy meant nothing, though, and it wasn't worth it. I got checked afterward. I'm clean. I wish I'd waited until it meant something. It's too late now. That's the problem with doing things for the wrong reasons. Once they're done, they can't be undone."

I know all about that. "I'm clean, too." I want her to know. "I had a physical when I arrived in the States."

She nods. Twirls a silver band on her pinkie finger.

"And you don't have to be sorry. Neither of us is perfect," I say.

She curls into me. It feels good, right. Nothing more needs to be said. Some bridges are meant to be burned.

I grab a cigarette from the nightstand and light it. Faith's nose scrunches up.

"You don't like when I smoke?" I ask.

She bites her lower lip. "No."

"Why didn't you tell me to stop?" I don't want her to be uncomfortable.

"Because," she says. "People have controlled my life forever. I would never try to control someone else's."

Faith could not be more different than I imagined. She's not trying to control anything. But knowing she doesn't like it makes me put the cigarette out.

"You don't have to do that," she says.

"I know."

Faith reaches into her pocket and pulls out a piece of gum. Folds it onto her tongue but doesn't chew. She leans toward me. I meet her lips, not expecting her to kiss the gum into my mouth. It's perfect, the way she rolls it off her tongue onto mine.

She grabs another piece for herself.

"Maybe I'll smoke if it means you'll do that every time," I say.

She smiles. We stay like that for a while. I don't know how much time exactly. It doesn't matter anyhow. My arms hold her tight. I want her near me always.

This time, I won't let her go.

43
faith

Four weeks. Three almost-healed bones. Two hearts. One love.

Four seconds. Three breaths. Two joined hands. One Diego.

Four moments. Three kisses. Two joined mouths. One million fears.

Overcome.

Because of Diego. He destroyed all that I hated, all that held me down, every choreographed routine that sucked the life out of me like an engorged tick, taking all I have.

I refuse to be drained of what I love.

"Where to?" Diego asks.

He's driving my Jeep to make it as much like a real date as possible. With my crutches gone, I can finally move around better though the walking boot remains.

"Movies?" I suggest.

We have been going on a lot of dates recently. It feels good, like we're a real couple, doing real things, not hiding from the world.

"Sure," he replies as we leave his apartment building.

Darkness plays with night, coloring it varying shades of gray and blue. Headlights illuminate the street like one giant glow stick. The windows are at half-mast, inviting a warm breeze.

Latinos with bandannas hang on the street corner. A regular fixture, like multicolored artwork in a museum: look, but don't touch. Diego glances at them. His eyes widen, shooting daggers and warnings.

He curses loudly. Jams the brake at a red light.

"What?" I ask.

"Get down," he orders.

"Why?" I ask, avoiding his command, regretting it immediately.

His only answer is a hand pushing my body down so my head is near the center console. "Don't move," he says through tight lips.

The seat belt buckle crams into my side. Spanish words are flung at our car, threats.

Diego guns it, a bronco in a rodeo. I wrap my arms around my waist as though I can stop my stomach from lurching into my throat. The Jeep shakes from cars whizzing past. Horns blare.

"What are you doing?" I yell, scared to open my eyes.

Diego ignores me, speeding farther away.

I don't know where we are. I don't know what's happening.

Diego drives another minute before letting out the biggest breath.

"You can sit up now."

Diego slows the car. I sit up, dizzy, the world tilting at an unnatural angle.

"Did you run a red light?" I ask.

"Yes," he replies.

Diego glances repeatedly in the rearview mirror. His face is ashen, like he's seen a ghost.

"Why?" I question.

His lips press tightly together.

"Why?" I repeat.

"Don't ask questions you don't want to know the answers to," he replies. Slowly. Like each word needs to pack its own punch.

"We could've been pulled over. What if we got a ticket? You're not on my insurance to drive this car, Diego. Why would you do something like that?" I ask.

"Trust me, *mi reyna*. A lot worse would've happened if I didn't run that light."

Diego rubs the back of his neck. His tension is contagious. "Now, can we talk about something else?"

"No," I answer. "You're hiding something from me. I trusted you. Why would you hide something from me?"

Silence.

"Please tell me you're not involved with that gang."

More silence.

"Say something!"

We stop at another light.

"This is nothing you need to be concerned with," he says roughly.

I have to work to keep my voice steady. "It involves you. And those guys didn't sound like friends."

"That's 'cause they're not," he replies.

I take his hand in mine. It is tense. It is hesitant. It is warm.

"Please tell me."

The light turns green. Diego looks back at the road.

"They want to recruit me," he says.

Please, please, please, no. Diego just got out of that back in Cuba. "You can't—"

He cuts me off. "I'm not. That's the problem. I said no. I fought them, Faith. That's why my face was busted at the beginning of school. They don't take rejection well."

I run a finger down his profile. Bruises and stains and pain and blood and fear. Me and him and chances and possibilities and hope.

"I'm sorry," I say.

"Don't be," he says, confident, somehow knowing that it will be okay. Or maybe that it won't. But assured either way that it will be what it's meant to be. "Forget about them. This is our night."

They're hard to forget, but I try for Diego's sake. I stare, stare, stare, at his face until I can see nothing but him on all sides. Consuming my thoughts in the best way. We pull up to the theater. Diego opens the door for me like a gentleman. We walk hand in hand to the ticket booth. Connected in a thousand ways. Touching in only one.

Some kids laugh off to the side. My ears are pierced by their mockery. My eyes are shot through with their stares.

They go to my school.

"Ignore them, *mami*," Diego says.

I have not gone public. We've been on dates but I've told no one. I decided to deal with my healing injuries before I invited everyone's criticism. Once the word gets out, it'll spread like wildfire.

I've been lucky to not run into anyone I know.

Until now.

I'm not ready to tell everyone. But then again, I don't know that I'll ever be.

Diego rubs my tense shoulders. One, two, three, four, five fingers form a fist.

"It's okay," he says into my ear.

I know his words to be truth. It'll be okay as long as I have Diego. He leans down to my lips, kisses me softly.

"Mmm," he says with a grin.

I straighten my spine and square my shoulders and walk right past the gawking crowd. It seems as though the worst of my worries are over.

Then the person in front of me turns from the concession stand.

"Tracy," I say. "Hi."

I'm holding Diego's hand. I want to hold it tighter. I want to drop it. I want to run. I need to stay.

Tracy Ram looks from me to Diego, and back to me.

"Oh my God." She laughs.

She's been heaving smiles at me lately. They're not genuine. They're condescending. She's taken my position as the dance captain. She's elated to see me fail. I wish the patronizing smiles would boomerang back and hit her between the eyes.

The moment is incredibly uncomfortable. I have nothing to say.

"Forget the popcorn," Diego says and pulls me in the direction of the theater.

I don't look back at Tracy.

"What's her deal?" Diego asks.

"I don't know," I reply. "She hates me, which makes no sense because she got what she wanted. She's the dance captain. Why waste energy on me?"

"Ah," Diego says. "I get it. She's probably the type of girl I thought you were."

"Hey, what's that supposed to mean?" I feign anger but my grin gives me away.

Diego smiles. "There are always people like that, ones

who want what everybody else has. Nothing will ever be good enough. She'll always be jealous. You could give her the world and she would still hate you, still want more."

I welcome Diego's arms as he winds them around me. "Is it always going to be like this for us?" I ask.

"What?" he asks. "You mean movie dates with no popcorn? 'Cause if it means that much to you, I'll go back and get some."

I smile. "No. You know what I mean."

He sighs. "Probably. People from your side of town will always look at you and wonder what a beautiful *chica* like you is doing with a Latino like me."

"And people from your side of town will always look at you and wonder what a beautiful *Cubano* like you is doin' with a *gringa* like me," I say.

Diego raises an eyebrow, grinning. "Touché."

"Do you think things will change in the future?" I ask. The possibility is as dark as the theater we walk into.

"Hopefully. One day," Diego says.

That's all we really have, isn't it?

Hope.

Hope that this world will stop seeing people in terms of the color of their skin and the size of their paychecks, and start seeing them in the size of their hearts and the love they offer.

We slip into back row seats. I rest my head on Diego's shoulder. My bones ache with a yearning for something out of reach, something obscured by hate and ignorance. As the movie begins, I block out the rest of the world, people like Tracy Ram included, and concentrate on the here and now.

* * *

I don't see Tracy Ram again until the next day at school. She's leaning against Diego's locker, flirting with him. I am too far away to hear her actual words, but I recognize her actions from a mile away.

Stop.

Stop.

Stop.

Blood pounds, roars, in my ears. I'm holding my breath and my body is a pillar of ice.

Diego looks uninterested. Maybe a little angry. He cannot stand girls like her. Tracy runs a finger down Diego's arm. He pulls away quickly, as though she burned him. His friends are standing nearby. It looks like one of them would love to be in Diego's shoes. Ramon tries to talk to Tracy but she pays no attention. She is there for one reason. To anger me. She never cared about Diego before she saw us at the movies together.

Thief.

Backstabber.

Liar.

I've almost reached them, my walking boot slowing me down. The crowd parts quickly. I am Moses and they are the Red Sea and I will get to the other side and she will regret ever touching him.

Today is the day I decided to wear what I want to school. I promised Diego that I would eventually do this. Today seemed like as good a day as any. Especially since I knew everyone would have heard about my secret relationship from Tracy anyhow. Pull off the Band-Aid quickly. Get it over with all at once.

People stare. I am a picture of transformation. Before: conservative knee-length skirts and loose blouses. After: teal shorts and a white shirt with a pink tank underneath.

It's refreshing, like a tall glass of tea on the hottest day of my life.

I don't bother with everyone else. I don't even look at them as I pass. The whispers have no effect. I am deaf and blind to anything but Tracy and Diego. This is my life. My choice. And my boyfriend.

I step in front of Tracy, ignoring that she's saying something to Diego. I wrap my arms around his neck and kiss him. Doesn't matter who's looking.

"*Hola, mami*," Diego says.

I smile against his lips.

His friends hoot behind us, saying things in Spanish. One of them slaps him on the back. "Teacher's comin'. Heads-up," he says.

The crowd disperses, Tracy included. Our school has a no-PDA rule. No touching. No kissing. No grasp on reality. Diego and I pull apart before they catch us.

"What's going on here?" a teacher asks. I recognize him. He teaches junior math. Nice guy. Rule stickler.

"*Nada*," Diego says with a cocky grin. "What's goin' on with you?"

His buddies laugh. The crowd watches us like we're a scandal in motion.

The teacher looks at me. "Get to class," he says.

Diego gives my hand a squeeze as we part ways. I smile to myself.

That felt good, like running a marathon and winning first place.

Here's to hope.

44
diego

"That was awesome!"

Mis amigos keep doing that, telling me how cool it is to finally see one of our kind hooking up with one of Faith's kind. Though, to be real, I'm not just hooking up with her. They treat it like it's a huge infiltration. Which, I guess, it kind of is.

"Faith Watters! Unbelievable!" Ramon continues.

"Yeah, yeah," I say, brushing him off as I take a bite of my chicken.

There are a lot of eyes on me today. Watching, watching, always watching.

I expect Javier to be mad about our fight. He's not. My eyes tell him all he needs to know: I'm sorry.

"She looks good today," Javier says, and points over my shoulder.

Faith and Melissa head our way. Faith is agility and beauty and love, love, love.

"Hey," she says, stopping in front of me. My hands automatically go for her.

"Hey," I reply. I look at Ramon, sitting next to me. He moves down a spot to make room for Faith. Luis tries to stand to make room for Melissa but she stops him.

"I'm good," she says with a smile and takes an empty seat next to Javier instead. My cousin grins at her. Then realizes the rest of the table is staring. Blood stains the underside of his cheeks, turning them red.

"What's up, boys?" Melissa says, breaking the ice.

I introduce everyone.

"Mind if we join you?" Melissa asks. Faith and Melissa brought bag lunches.

"Of course not," Javier says, a little too eagerly. Faith raises an eyebrow at me, catching on. Javier has never dared to date a Caucasian, knowing his mom doesn't approve. She doesn't see the beauty in diversity.

"You sure your people won't mind?" Luis asks. " 'Cause it looks to me that some of them are *enojados.*"

Back at Faith's old table, Jason looks especially angry. His disgust is palpable.

"Who cares about them," Melissa says, no question intended. "But it does look like we may not be welcome there anymore. You sure you don't mind being stuck with us from now on?"

"*Mujer,* I'd love to be stuck with you," Ramon says, all sleazy.

I laugh. Javier punches him in the arm.

"*¡Ten algo de respeto!*" Javier warns.

Melissa smiles, though I'd guess that she doesn't understand a word he said. His actions are clear enough.

"So what are you guys up to tonight?" Melissa asks.

I have no plans. My friends mumble a chorus of "Nothing."

"There's a *reggaeton* concert going on. Twenty bucks at the door, but my sister knows the guy running it, so I can probably get us in for free. You game?" Melissa asks.

"Definitely," a few of us answer at the same time.

"You got a sister?" Ramon says. He looks excited. Hopeful.

Melissa grins. "I have three."

"*Si ella se parece a tí—*"

With one look from Javier, Ramon shuts up midsentence.

"You like *reggaeton*?" Javier asks Melissa. She pops a carrot in her mouth, smiling still.

"Yeah, why? Does that surprise you?"

"A little," he says. "I love *reggaeton*."

"Well, so do I. As a matter of fact, I like a lot of things you don't know about," she replies.

Faith laughs at her friend. I pull my girl close, ignoring the school's PDA policy. She gives me a quick kiss. It is a brush, a tease. I need more.

"You want to go with me tonight, *mami*?" I ask in her ear.

"Yeah. It'd be fun," she replies.

She'll need to pick me up, since her father knows nothing about us yet. I can't make an appearance at her house—not that I have a car. Not that I care. I am caught in currents of gladness, gliding, floating. No more hiding. No more wishing. No more lying. No more restraint.

"Eight?" I ask.

"Sure. I'll meet you then."

Eight o'clock is celebrated by a minidress that shows off Faith's long legs. I almost beg her to forget the concert.

"*Oye, muñeca.* You look *maravillosa*."

We are standing by her Jeep outside my apartment.

"You, too," Faith replies. She pulls my head down for a kiss.

"You sure you don't want to stay?" I offer.

She licks her lips.

"Maybe for a second," she says.

I lean against the car and pull her to me. She parts my lips with her tongue and moves her hands to my back. My breathing is all wrong but I can't control it. Faith steals my air and gives it back in hot breaths. I am this close, this close, this close to walking back upstairs. Faith engulfs me in flames that I want to burn in until we are melting, dripping, molding into one.

"We need to go," she says against my ear.

I don't want to go.

She pulls away. I reluctantly hop in the car and watch her while she drives. I love the way she sees me for who I am, and likes me all the same.

Outside the club, *mis amigos* and Melissa are waiting.

"*¿Que pasa?*" Javier asks.

"*Nada,*" I answer.

Luis brought a girl I recognize from school. Esteban, Juan, and Rodolfo are checking out a group of ladies as they pass.

A girl who looks a lot like Melissa approaches us.

"*Oye, mira eso. Esa chica es sexy,*" Ramon says.

She stops and smiles at Melissa and Faith. "Hey, girls," she says.

"Monica, this is Faith's boyfriend, Diego, and some of his friends." Melissa introduces everyone.

Her sister leads us to a side door and gets us in for free. *Gracias a Dios*, because I don't have extra money.

The inside of the club is packed shoulder to shoulder. Loud music blares through speakers while everyone waits for the headlining musicians to take the stage. Faith's body automatically moves to the music. Not dancing full-blown, but not standing still either. Like she has an involuntary switch that turns on whenever she hears good music.

While we wait for the concert to start, I pull Faith against me.

"*Baila* with me," I say.

I don't have to ask her twice. She is eager to get on the floor, thirsty, drinking it in. Her moves are cautious, slowed by the boot on her foot, but she sways with my help, loving the music despite broken bones.

Melissa and Javier join us just as the music dies. The crowd yells. Lights dim. When they flare back to life, musicians have taken the stage and the club turns into a madhouse. Girls on the dance floor reach for the guys onstage, who cup their microphones. People shove to get closer.

Faith and I are pushed from all directions but I hold on to her, hoping no one steps on her injured foot. The clamor dies down after the first song as people get into the music. My body is a reckless thing. Pressing close to Faith. Her hips swing. My heart thuds. Our lips touch.

This is how it all started.

I remember our first night together in the club, the first time she kissed me.

We enjoy the music for a long time—both on the floor and off—until the concert ends. I round up all my *amigos*. Esteban, Juan, Rodolfo, and Ramon hop in a car together, while Luis and the girl he brought get into his car. Faith and I walk with Melissa and Javier to the parking lot.

It's raining outside, the drops cooling our skin. Faith is feeling playful; she lets me lift her into my arms, soaking wet. I hold her close, loving the way the rain drenches her completely. Beads drip from her hair and lashes. The moment is crazy sexy. Our lips crash together, hungry. She tastes like rain and peppermint.

I lose my edge, something I almost never do. I don't recognize the feeling inside, but it's like I have been submerged in darkness and someone has finally turned on a light. It flares dimly, almost nonexistent. It is nothing bright. It is almost not worth mentioning. It is everything to me.

What's the name for that?

I am too lost in Faith's embrace to see the danger.

The tone of Javier's voice as he calls my name stops me. I look toward him.

Figures huddle around Faith's Jeep, their backs to us. Melissa is parked in the next spot over.

I know before I see their faces. The air, the vibe, their stances tell me.

It's Wink.

And five of his *amigos.*

My stiff posture alerts Faith. I place her on her feet just as they look up.

"Thought I recognized this car," Wink says, taking a step toward me.

Javier is at my side.

"Go back to the club," I say to Faith. "You and Melissa."

I took out a few of them alone last time. This time I think they'll know to be more prepared. I need Javier's help. He's a good fighter. I would never want to involve him, but I don't see any other way. Especially since two of them have now pulled guns.

"Shit," Melissa says, noticing the Glocks.

"Now," I say, never taking my eyes off their guns.

"But I can't leave you," Faith pleads.

"Now!" I say with such authority that this time she doesn't question me. Faith and Melissa take off, Melissa helping Faith, like they fear for their lives. As they should. I concentrate all my attention on the MS-13s.

"Nice *gringas* you got there," Wink says menacingly. "Wouldn't want anything to happen to them. 'Specially now that we have her tag number and info."

"If you touch her, I swear to God—"

"Well, that depends on whether you've reconsidered our offer. You know what we want," he says.

I'm about to lose it, about to unleash every ounce of my fury, when his next words stop me dead in my tracks.

"Diego Alvarez."

My name. He knows my real name.

"What? You thought we wouldn't find out? *No soy estúpido,*" Wink says.

Javier doesn't leave my side. Without ever having to say a word, he has my back.

"We don't usually offer second chances, but your fighting would be an asset to us. You could become our *amigo* instead of our *enemigo. Únete a nosotros.*"

I'm at a disadvantage. I'm not close enough to strike him, but I am close enough for a bullet to strike me. I only need to stall him long enough for Faith to send reinforcements. I would even welcome *la policía* at this point.

"What makes you think I don't belong to someone else?" I say.

Wink's gaze travels to my hand, to the cartel tattoo. "If you join us, we can make that disappear," he says.

I have a bad feeling, like maybe he does know whom I belong to. And although their gang is powerful, taking on MS-13s is like taking on kindergarteners compared to the cartel's wrath.

"Last chance," Wink says.

I can't, won't join them.

"Fuck you," I say.

"Wrong choice," Wink replies as he raises the gun.

I run toward him. Faster than I've ever moved in my life.

Hopeful, hopeful, hopeful.

I need to make it in time. Every breath I draw, every beat of my heart, will be silenced if not.

I kick his arm as the gun goes off. Javier yells in pain. If I want to live, I can't look back. I must concentrate on the guys in front of me. But from the sound of it, Javier is hit.

One of the MS-13s runs toward Javier while I take on the majority of them. A scuffle breaks out to my right, which means Javier is okay enough to fight back. For now.

I knock the gun from Wink's hand. I have exactly one second to grab it. I'm hit hard over the head. My chance is gone, evaporated like residual rain puddles on a scorching day.

Now I'm wobbly, grasping for something in the blurry world around me. I blink back pain and try to stand. I land a few punches and kicks. Not on target, but effective nonetheless. Two guys go down, including the other one with the gun. His Glock slides across the pavement. I don't have time to reach it. Another MS-13 makes the mistake of running at me and I slam his head into Faith's metal bumper, knocking him out.

Wink pulls out a knife now that his gun is somewhere under one of the cars. That's when I hear sirens. Footsteps pound toward us like an oncoming freight train.

Wink charges me. I dodge him. Land a solid punch in his face. He comes at me again.

This time I feel the knife blade pierce my side, slicing into bloody velvet.

I hit pavement. I don't have to look down to know that the puncture is deep. Too deep.

I focus on Wink. I commit his mocking smile to memory. One day he will pay. For a moment I think he's going to stab me again, but before the cops can catch him, he runs off.

Leaving his knife buried in me.

45
faith

Ten hours forty-three minutes. Thirty-eight thousand five hundred eighty seconds appear and disappear like a cruel magic show that no one cares to see. I want to bottle up time and chuck it into the ocean and watch it sink to the murky depths where it will wait in darkness. The same kind of darkness it leaves me in.

Ten hours forty-three minutes.

That is how long it takes for Diego to open his eyes.

"Diego," I say, clutching his hand. My voice is emotion bleeding out, hemorrhaging at every syllable.

He grunts. Blinks. I wait for him to say something.

"What? Where?" His voice is gruff.

I remember how much it hurt for me to talk when I was lying in a hospital bed after surgery, just like him. I explain everything.

"You were stabbed." I try not to choke up. I swallow hundreds of tears. Still nothing will dislodge the panic that has taken residence in my throat. "The ambulance rushed you here as fast as possible, took you to surgery right away. Oh God. Diego, I should've come sooner. Maybe if I'd called the police quicker. I don't know."

Diego reaches for my hand. "Not your fault," he whispers.

I wipe a tear. "The blade pierced your spleen. They had to remove part of the organ. You almost bled to death, Diego."

I break down then, bury my head in his sheets. They look like roughly tossed waves.

Diego runs his fingers through my hair. "Almost doesn't count," he says.

I laugh through tears, attempt to wipe my face and look up at him.

"Where is Javier?" he asks.

"He's okay," I say. "Better than you. The bullet hit his arm but missed the bone and major blood vessels."

A white drape like whipped cream separates the room. I pull it back. Javier lies still, a blanket covering him up to his stomach.

"They made Javier my roommate?" Diego laughs, and winces from the exertion.

"Yes," I answer. "They gave him something powerful. Morphine, I think. Knocked him out so he can sleep through the pain. He was up most of the night with me, worrying about you. So was your dad. He went home to shower and change. He'll be back soon. You should probably know that the police have been here, Diego. They want to talk to you."

The fight wasn't his fault. But cops have a funny way of looking at things. I don't want him going to jail.

Diego watches me silently. "What?" I ask. "Why are you quiet? Are you in pain?"

"No," he answers. "I mean, yeah, but that's not why I'm quiet. Faith, please tell me they caught Wink."

I wish I could tell him that. "He got away. I'm sorry."

Diego curses.

"Do you remember anything?" I ask.

His lips are dry, cracking even. I want to wet them and suck them and make everything better and never let him go.

"Not anything past the stabbing. I blacked out," he answers. "Faith, I think you might be in danger."

"Don't worry about me," I say. I can't be concerned with that now.

"*Escúchame.* Wink has your personal information. Do not go outside at night. Lock all your doors and windows. Do you have a house alarm?" he asks.

I nod.

"Good. Engage it at all times. Keep your cell on you, too," he instructs. "Don't answer the door if you don't recognize the person, okay? Especially don't answer deliveries or people posing as repair guys."

I think of Grace. I can't let anything happen to her.

"Promise me," he says.

"I promise."

He sighs. "This is my fault. Maybe it would be better for you to stay away from me."

"No. Absolutely not. Don't even go there, Diego. You're not pushing me away again. I belong with you."

I lean over and kiss his lips.

"I belong with you," I repeat.

He nods, agreeing. "I can't push you away. I just don't know what to do. I'm desperate to keep you safe."

"I'm not going anywhere," I say as I kiss him again. "We'll find a way."

"Would you two get a room?"

I break from Diego to see Javier smiling at us.

"Some of us are tryin' to sleep, you know," he jokes. His words are a little slow, as if the medicine has stretched them out, slowing their exit from his mouth.

Diego grins. His face is richness and color and memories surfacing.

"Good to see you're alive," Javier says. His arm is bandaged, the rest of him intact.

"You, too, man," Diego replies. "*Lo siento,* cuz. Didn't mean to drag you into this."

They both look like someone took a marker to them: black and purple with tinges of green.

"That's what *familia* is for. I got your back," Javier says. "Though *mi mama* is another story. She said you're in trouble as soon as you feel better."

"Aw, man," Diego replies. "I hope it's not as bad as that time I broke her favorite vase."

They laugh and wince from the effort. I watch their interactions with love. They are family in the truest sense. They are family dealt a hard fate.

"It's a tough life," I mumble to myself. Though I'm glad to see them laughing about it now.

"What?" Diego asks.

"Nothing," I say.

Sitting on Diego's bed, my feet dangle toward the ground, the booted one feeling heavier. I contemplate lying back with him.

"Did you just say 'it's a tough life'?" he asks.

"Yes. Why?"

He grins. "No reason."

As Diego and his cousin talk, I decide on a chair between them. Diego holds my almost healed hand like he never wants to let me go. I hope he doesn't. He taught me to stop running from my heart. *Because of him,* I think as I gaze at Diego.

It's all because of him.

46
diego

One good thing about being stabbed is that it has given me more time in the last three weeks with Faith. She comes over nearly every day. She even told her dad that we're dating. He doesn't know that I'm Latino or that I have tattoos and scars. But he'll find out today.

"Are you sure you want to do this? Maybe we should put it off a little longer," Faith says for what I swear is the hundredth time.

I grab her hands so she'll stop fidgeting with her shirt. She pulls away.

"Dad already knows I'm benched from the dance team, and he's dealing with my wardrobe changes surprisingly well. He even supports my decision not to be with Jason, but I swear that any moment it'll all crumble and he'll change his mind," Faith says. She's talking fast. Too fast.

"Faith," I say, trying to get her attention. She won't look at me.

"What if he makes a scene?" she says. "He's done it before. Ninth grade, for example. Right before I met Jason, he caught Melissa and me out past curfew with boys. We only went to the bowling rink, but that didn't matter.

What mattered was that the boys weren't Caucasian. And they didn't attend our church."

She's pacing around my apartment like a caged mouse, looking for a way out of life's problems.

"Dad and one of his church friends found us there, in public, and humiliated me, told me to get in the car and warned the boys off. I wonder if he would have acted the same if he didn't have that church member to impress."

"Faith," I say again.

"He made a scene at the fair a couple years ago, too, when a nice guy hit on me. Sure, I was with Jason, and I planned on telling the guy that I was taken, but Dad beat me to it by telling him to back off."

It's unsettling for sure, but Faith is eighteen. Hopefully by now her father will allow his daughter to make decisions on her own. People need to fall sometimes to know how it feels to pick themselves up.

"He only tolerates Jason because he attends our church and his parents volunteer."

Maybe he can learn to tolerate me, too.

"I mean, it's a real possibility, him freaking out. It's my sister's sixth birthday. I don't want to ruin her party. There'll be people from church there. Not that I really care. It's my father's reputation I'm worried about. I just thought that this would be the best day to break the news. At least today he'll be happy and there will be distractions so he can't get too mad. This is a special day for Grace, though. I wasn't thinking about that. What if I cause problems on her special day?"

"*Mami,*" I say.

She's still not hearing me.

"What will we do if my dad starts yelling? If he kicks

you out, do I go with you? I love him and I'm crazy about you, Diego. What if I have to choose between you? I can't do that."

"Faith!" I yell.

She finally looks at me. I get off the couch and walk to her.

"Chill. Breathe," I say.

Her breaths are raw, ragged.

"Everything will be all right," I assure her. "Yes, he may get upset. So what? If I need to leave, I'll leave. You and I have seen each other through some serious stuff. This is nothin'."

"You're right," she says. Exhales deeply. "Okay. I can do this."

My hand slips silently into Faith's, desperate to soothe her.

"You can do this. And I'm not lettin' you back out."

"All right." She grins. "Hate it when you're right."

We walk to the door. I don't take my eyes off Faith, knowing that she needs someone to hold her accountable, someone to make sure she follows through.

"Ready?" I ask.

She nods. Nothing about her seems ready: restless, eyes too wide, hands clammy like she applied too much lotion. I know it's nerves. When we pull up to Faith's house, the street is lined with cars. We end up parking at Melissa's instead. The walk only takes a minute, but when we get there, Faith pauses on the lawn.

"You okay?" I ask.

"Mmm-hmm," she says. "Just give me a sec."

I'm nervous, too. But I won't tell Faith.

What guy ever looks forward to meeting his girl's father for the first time?

Though I met Mr. Watters at the hospital, I doubt he'll remember. I'm hoping he doesn't. That's easier than explaining Melissa's lie, that I was with her. Part, or maybe all, of this visit is bound to be uncomfortable.

"If he tells you to leave, I'm coming with you," Faith says.

"Okay," I agree. Javier is on backup in case I need a ride.

"And I want you to be yourself. You will hear a lot of 'yes, sir,' 'no, sir' from other people when they talk to my dad, but I don't want you acting like someone you're not. To them it's respect, but coming from you, it would be wrong," Faith says.

I don't have any problem with saying "sir," but I get what she's implying. Respect comes in different forms. She wants me to wear the one that fits me.

"Let's do this," I say, pulling her forward. I have a feeling we'll be standing here all day if I don't rush this along.

Inside Faith's house, I take a second to look around. It's not big, but it's not small, either. Squared pictures form a patchwork on the walls. Decorative pillows the color of lemonade and tangerines accent a beige couch and love seat.

At least she doesn't have to buy a new chair so I'll have a place to sit.

Balloons and streamers scream with brightness. A clown crouches in the corner, painting kids' faces. Grace's guests include twenty children under the age of seven. I grew up with Javier's family, so I'm used to *niños* being around all the time.

"Do the kids make you nervous?" Faith asks, noticing my stare.

"No," I answer with a smile. "If anything, they ease my worries."

Faith's dad is another story.

An older woman approaches, a hello jumping off her

lips ten feet before she reaches us. When Faith introduces me as her boyfriend, the woman's face suddenly looks as though she's sucking on a lime. Faith takes it as our cue to leave.

"Sorry about that," she says, as we walk to the backyard.

I stop walking. "Faith, *mírame*." When she looks at me, I continue. "I don't care what they think. Don't apologize for other people. This is about you and me. *¿Entiendes?*"

She gives my hand a squeeze and nods—just as her father approaches. His features remind me a little of Faith's. He has the same green eyes, but pinched at the corners. He is wearing jeans and a black polo shirt with a dark brown apron. I'm guessing he's the one manning the grill.

Faith's palm is still in mine. Her father's gaze drops from my face to our entwined hands.

"I believe we've met," he says, sticking out his hand.

He does remember.

"Yes. Diego," I say.

Faith looks confused.

"Carl Watters," he says, shaking my hand firmly.

Faith taps her foot nervously.

"So, you're Faith's new boyfriend?" her dad asks. Have to love a dude who gets straight to the point.

"Yes," I answer.

He eyes me for a second before speaking again. "Well, Diego, are you good on the grill?"

"Yeah."

I hope he doesn't intend to pull me aside and interrogate me, or order me to stay away from his daughter, because I really don't want to get into it with Faith's father.

Faith's brows furrow. "I'll help, too," she says.

"Not necessary," her dad replies, holding up his hand.

I'm guessing that's his way of telling Faith to give him a moment with me.

She does. I walk off with her father to the other side of the yard, where the grill stands, while Faith takes a seat near the door. She's not even close to being within earshot. That could be good or bad. Depends on what direction her old man wants to steer the conversation.

Mr. Watters hands me a spatula to flip the burgers. "Why didn't you tell me at the hospital that you were her boyfriend?" he asks.

"Honestly? I thought that was up to Faith, not me," I answer.

There are a lot of people around us, but no one pays attention to our conversation.

"How long have you been seeing each other?" he asks.

That depends on what he considers "seeing each other." "A few months."

Mr. Watters squirts some oil on the burgers to keep them from drying out.

"What's your story?" he asks.

Great, so this *is* going to be an interrogation.

"I moved from Cuba at the beginning of senior year. Faith was my peer helper—" I pause, smile, think about how Faith has helped me in more ways than one. Mr. Watters is staring at me. I clear my throat. "I live with my dad. I have other *familia* in the area, too."

"Why did you move from Cuba?" he asks.

I grit my teeth and try to aim for calm when I answer. "Things didn't go so well for me back there. Let's leave it at that."

He eyes the scar on my neck. "Listen, I don't know what kind of trouble you got into back home, and it's really none of my business, but when it comes to my daughter, I want to know that no harm will come to her. I'm not naïve enough to think that I can control her anymore. She's her own person, an adult, I know that. But I still want her to make good decisions. I'm not sure about you yet, but my personal feelings are irrelevant. All I need to know is that she's safe and happy. Do you plan on keeping her safe and happy, Diego?"

I don't hesitate. "With all that I am."

"Good," he says, flipping burgers over. I do the same. "Do you love her?" he asks.

Of course, but Faith's father shouldn't be the first one I admit that to.

"That's something I'd like to tell her first, if you don't mind."

He nods. "Be careful with my daughter, Diego. She's been through a lot."

Grease splatters on my shirt, leaving a stain. "I know," I reply.

He asks questions, but doesn't fret over the notion of Faith and me together.

"She thinks I don't understand her, that I can't see what's happening. But I do. You make her happy, happier than she's been in a long time. And I think she loves you."

My breath catches when he says the last part.

"I see the way you look at her," he continues. "I'm not going to pretend I like the tattoos. Don't take it personally. I don't like hers, either. But I also don't believe that a person should be judged by their appearance."

"Thank you," I say. I could never see me and this man being best friends, but we don't need to be best friends in order for me to make it work with Faith. As long as we have a mutual understanding that Faith's happiness is our main concern, I think we'll be good.

The burgers are done. I set the spatula down and wipe my hands on a towel.

"She may think I don't care about her feelings," Mr. Watters says, "but she's wrong. I know she worries about what the church will think. I wish she'd let me deal with the church and just enjoy being young. Do you think you could help her let go, Diego?"

"I wish she would," I say. "I've been tryin' to tell her that for a while."

Mr. Watters chuckles. "She's a stubborn one. She means well, though. It's tough for me to get used to the new clothes and a new boyfriend, but I think you might be good for her. Acting like the majority of the people at church isn't Faith. I'd rather take the true version of Faith over the fake one she's tried to be."

I am awed. "Have you told her this?"

"No," he replies. "Faith and I don't talk much. Plus, do you honestly think I'd make a difference?"

He's probably right. Still, all this time Faith thought she was doing right by her father when all her father really wants is for Faith to do right by herself. I have respect for him. He knows who, and what, Faith is.

And more importantly, what she isn't.

47

faith

"What did he say?"

The question does a somersault, tumbling out of my mouth as Diego makes his way across the backyard to me.

"That he loves you and he wants you safe," Diego says.

Come on. He's going to have to do better than that.

"What did he say about *us*?" I ask.

Diego shrugs. "He's not thrilled about me, but he's not mad, either. As long as I make you happy, he's okay with it."

Too good to be true. "Really?" I ask.

"Really." Diego smiles.

I throw my arms around his shoulders and hug him tightly.

He rubs my back. "See, what did I tell you? Piece of cake," he jokes.

I'm a little surprised it wasn't worse. They must've talked about more than me being happy and safe, but I'm not going to question Diego further.

"He's not as bad as you think," Diego says. "He wants you to leave the church issues and opinions to him. You should let it go, Faith. It's about time you lived for you."

When Diego leans in for a kiss, I forget everything but

him. His lips are soft and full, his mouth warm. His tongue never snakes out, much to my disappointment, but the kiss is intense all the same.

I feel a tug at my leg, breaking the two of us apart. I look down. Grace is smiling at me like a shiny penny that I must pick up.

"Hi, Gracie!" I say, swooping her into my arms.

"Hi, Faith," she sings sweetly. She turns to Diego. "Hey, D," she says nonchalantly.

It cracks me up.

Diego grins. "Hi," he says as he reaches for her. He sets my little sister on his hip and wraps an arm around her back.

I almost tear up at the sight of him holding Grace so gently, cradling the treasure that she is.

"Happy birthday," he says.

She giggles and reaches for his hand. I hope the tattoos don't scare her.

"I like your paintings," Grace comments.

"Thanks," Diego says. "I like yours, too."

He's referring to the star and cake painted on Grace's cheek.

"Want to meet my friends?" Grace asks.

Diego couldn't possibly be interested in the crowd of children. But surprisingly, he says yes and sits on the grass with the kids. They flock to him like a new toy. He's a natural. They love him, too. For the first time in a while, I feel a kind of giddy happiness that I thought abandoned me long ago. I am wishing on a star and watching it come true.

I'm about to join him when Mrs. Magg comes to my side.

"Hello, Faith," she says cordially.

"Hi, Mrs. Magg," I reply.

"Is this for my son's benefit?" she asks, gesturing at Diego.

I laugh. *Is she kidding me?*

"Jason has apologized many times. What does he have to do for you to take him back?" she asks, completely serious.

I stop laughing, but for the life of me I cannot wipe the grin off my face. It lingers like the bittersweet aftertaste of cranberries.

I honestly don't think her question deserves an answer. So I walk away instead, leaving a slack-jawed Mrs. Magg standing alone. Some people will never change.

"Hey," I say into Diego's ear. I sit on the ground beside him. Grass pricks and tickles my thighs.

He's laughing at one of the little boys, who is making funny faces. "Hey, *preciosa*," Diego replies.

Dad and Susan are bringing out Grace's princess castle birthday cake.

"Want some?" I ask, motioning to the gigantic pink-and-purple cake. They set it next to a leaning tower of gifts.

"Sure." Diego stands and extends a hand to help me up.

I love the way he looks in that moment: hair mussed from kids climbing on him, grass stuck to his clothes, completely and utterly happy.

After cake, Grace opens gifts. She tears into them with such excitement. I've never seen so many presents in one place in my life. Grace's face is lit like a firework. When the festivities die down and it's time to go, I give Dad a hug and say good-bye. My little sister gives Diego a kiss on the cheek, awakening a flutter in my heart.

I don't say anything on the way to Diego's apartment,

mostly because I'm replaying the evening in my mind. When Diego invites me in, I follow him to his room. I sink into the beanbag chair and imagine that's what it feels like to fall into a puff of clouds.

"It's good to see you happy," Diego says.

"It's your doing," I confess. "All of it. Everything."

Diego challenged my whole life. From the first moment in the office, he dared me to drop the mask. Thanks to him, I have.

"I'm lucky to have you," I say.

"Come to me," Diego commands.

I kneel on the carpet and lean over Diego.

He presses his mouth to mine. His kiss is a flame, sparking my insides. His passion is embers catching fire. Before I know it, I have abandoned the carpet and taken position on Diego's lap.

Diego says how good I feel in English and Spanish.

"*Que bonita. Te quiero. Te necesito,*" he says.

Diego is closer than my skin. Love forged into being. There is something about his touch, his fingers driving slowly over my ribs, that makes my heart thud as though it wants to break free of me and live in Diego's hands, where it belongs.

The air around us is two thousand degrees. His breath, my breath, becoming one. His body, my body, sharing space until there is no difference between where he starts and where I end.

More.

I need more.

His touch moves, wanders, discovers new places: my hip, my thigh, the spot behind my left ear. My fingers tickle the back of his neck. Make their way over the topographical map that is his body.

What lies underneath?

I want my hands on bare skin, but I'm afraid. What will happen? Will we be the same? Closer? I can't help the thoughts that enter my mind like a haunting whisper. Now is not the time for nerves.

Three, four, five fingers on my stomach. Six, seven, eight seconds until the thunder of pleasure allows me to move again. His breathing has climbed to new heights. I take the risk. My palm slides under his shirt. Muscles make his skin protrude in spots. Scars form craters in the unknown terrain I explore.

When Diego pulls away from me suddenly, I'm surprised.

"What's wrong?" I pant.

His look is that of pain.

"*Dios mío*, this is one of the hardest things I've ever had to do," he says.

Diego eases me off of him.

"Did I do something wrong?" I ask.

"No, definitely not. You're doin' everythin' right," he answers. "That's the problem. *Eres especial.* You have changed my life. I want our first time to be something you'll never forget, something that lasts all night."

My curfew is soon. Diego doesn't want to rush things. I smile at him. It must have taken a lot to pull away from me. I reach for his hand. Bring him to me, careful not to touch him the way he likes. I ease into his arms and let him hold me.

There are moments in life set apart from the rest. The *before* this moment, and the *after* this moment.

Diego is one of those moments for me.

48
diego

"Do you think she has a clue?"

Javier's excitement is met by my own. I'm jittery, as though I've gulped gallons of caffeine.

"No," I answer.

"Have to admit, it's a good plan," Javier says. "Never knew you were romantic."

"*Cállate*," I say, grinning.

"So you goin' to be down on one knee tellin' her how much you love her, or what?" Javier jokes.

"No," I answer. "I'm just goin' to be there, waiting for her. She won't expect it. Now, leave me alone so I can finish gettin' ready."

While Javier waits for me in the living room, I check the clock. Hands tick like a reminder of the time I almost didn't have. I throw on jeans and my only white button-down shirt.

"Come on," I say to my cousin.

Javier drives me to a giant fountain at the entrance of *La Plazita*: a stretch of about three blocks with Latino cuisine, culture, markets, dancing, and more. This is my world, without the danger.

People drift everywhere. My throat constricts slightly.

I'm suddenly flashing back to Cuba. A hundred memories cram together like pages in a book. I am aware of my scar, pulsing almost. I'm scared to remember that life.

Javier laughs and slaps me on the back as I'm getting out of the car. "*¡Buena suerte!*" he hollers.

I spend the next thirty minutes roaming the streets. For many, this is more than a fun getaway. This is a way of life. I wonder if any of them have escaped like me. Do they have dangerous secrets, too?

My phone chirps. It's Melissa, in on the surprise. Her text tells me that they are approaching the fountain. I stand to the side where Faith can't see me.

Faith wears a white spaghetti-strap dress that shimmers like an opal. When I walk around the corner, her eyes widen.

Melissa smiles, a best friend to the end, and leaves me and Faith to spend the evening alone.

"Did you plan this?" Faith asks.

"*Sí, mami.*"

I reach for her hips and pull her to me.

"Why?"

She can be who she wants to be here, who she truly is at heart.

"Because you let me into your world. Now I want to let you into mine."

She has tried so hard to be what everyone wants. She has tried and tried and tried not to let them down. But time and time again, unhappiness was her reward.

Where are they now? I wonder.

Where are those people who expect the world of Faith, who smile as her dreams slip through her fingers like dimes and clatter to the ground? Who judge whenever they want and leave her for dead if she doesn't meet their expectations?

She doesn't have to be that girl anymore.

I take her hand and lead her through the streets. So many places to stop, so many things to see: the market, trinkets, music. Sugar cane plants sprout around us, their tall stalks swaying in the gentle evening breeze. *La Plazita* is alive, moving in beautiful chaos. I buy an *annona cherimola,* custard apple, for Faith to try.

"This is delicious," Faith says around a mouthful. She hands it to me so we can share.

We pass several tents filled with everything you could think of—clothes, household items, artwork, instruments—all part of my world. Faith picks up half of the items, asking me what they are and what they're used for. She wants to know why nothing has price tags. I explain that the vendors expect you to name a price.

It's common for an item's price to be dependent on the purchaser. Salespeople throw out numbers; you counter with one of your own. If you're good, you'll barter them down to the bare minimum amount, like an auction, only instead of the price going up, it goes down. And unlike American markets, these sellers stay open well into the night.

La Plazita is mostly Cuban, but other cultures trickle in. I take a seat on a bench in front of a Mexican mariachi band. Faith laughs at their huge sombreros; they look like ants trying to balance something three times their size.

"What do you think?" I ask her.

Faith smiles. "I think I love it."

Streetlights shine dimly on her face like a waning candle.

"So beautiful," I whisper.

She leans toward me, her expression soft, so soft in the light. Warmth spreads just above my knee where her hand rests. Her lips part. It's an invitation that I happily accept.

"I'm glad you did this for me," she says. Her breath tickles my skin, raising gooseflesh. "I know you miss home. And I know you can never go back. It's probably hard to be around all this and not miss what used to be."

"It is," I admit. "But I'd never change a thing, 'cause coming here gave me you."

"And I'd never go back to my old life because the new one gave me you," she says.

"Well, isn't that *preciosa,*" a voice says from behind us.

I stand and whip around so fast that I nearly lose my balance. My body tenses. Faith jumps up, too, clutching my arm.

"Wink," I say.

Surely there are too many witnesses for him to fight me here. He's wanted by the police. It's taking a huge risk, showing up alone in a street full of people.

"*¿Qué quieres?*" I ask.

"What do I want?" He sneers. "I want revenge. You hurt *mis amigos, mis hermanos.* You insulted me and my offer for you to join us. It wasn't hard to follow you. I know your past, Alvarez. You should have listened to me."

I take a closer look. So many people surround us, but four stand out. It's the way they're perched, motionless, statues in a river of moving bodies. It's the way their eyes zoom in on us, oblivious to all else. They begin their march.

There are other men, too—aside from the four—dressed in normal clothes, acting like part of the crowd. I see the way they watch us.

"Leave," I tell Faith.

"No," she whispers. "Not again. Last time you almost died."

I have to convince her to leave. Her life depends on it.

"If you don't go, they'll use you against me. They'll kill you."

Steely hard eyes return my gaze. "I won't leave you again."

I don't have time for this.

"Please," I beg. I will do whatever it takes to get her to listen.

She doesn't waver.

The men stop several feet in front of me. "Hola, Diego. Remember me?" one of them asks in a deep accent.

It hits me like a tidal wave. My mind is churning, churning, beneath the memories. He smiles. A gun flashes at his side.

"Never thought you would survive that night," he says, eyeing the scar on my neck. "I'll be sure not to make the same mistake twice."

Faith stiffens and I know she understands. A diagonal scar protrudes proudly from his skin, traveling from the left side of his forehead to his chin. His nose is crooked, suggesting a severely misshapen bone beneath the surface.

My stomach turns to water, twisting and clenching. I look at Wink. He's smiling. This is because of him, because I didn't join his gang. My refusal dug up my past.

And now it will surely kill me.

I whisper under my breath so only Faith can hear. "When I say go, run."

"But—"

"Do it." I smile for one second, the briefest flicker of

love. I want to convey everything I feel into one moment, like she will somehow remember that last look every time she visits the memory of us.

"Say *adiós* to your precious *mujer,*" he says with a smile. He doesn't want Faith, but he'll kill her to hurt me.

"Go!" I yell.

It happens so fast. Faith turns to run best as she can with her nearly healed foot. I jump to the spot where she once stood, blocking a direct shot at her. The bullet has already left the gun. Pain rips through my chest, tearing, clawing my flesh open on its way inside. I cry out. People start running through the streets like mad, deranged animals. As a herd, they don't know where to go, unsure from which direction the gunshot rang.

My body sways slightly, a pendulum swinging with one final effort.

My time is up.

I collapse. The air has been punched out of my lungs. My vision is filled with calves and feet. Some of them are stepping on me on their way to safety. My ears ring from shouts and the rushing of wind. I grab at my chest. My hands come away covered in blood.

Suddenly Faith is at my side. People are running over her, too. Blood blossoms across my shirt.

"Diego," she says, tears streaming down her face. "No!" She is racked with sobs.

"Don't cry," I say. My voice is raspy. The pain is nearly unbearable. I concentrate on Faith. Only Faith.

She tries to apply pressure to my chest, but I scream in agony. She stops.

"What do I do?" she asks desperately.

"Let me go," I say. At least she is safe. I took the bullet

that was meant for her. The men got what they truly wanted—me.

"No, Diego. No. I can't. You'll be okay. It'll be okay."

I am dying. She knows it.

"I love you. *Te amo*," I say. "That's what I brought you here for tonight. I wanted to tell you that I love you, Faith."

My eyes are heavy, so heavy. I take one last cherishing look before my final words escape me.

"*Te amo eternamente,*" I whisper.

49

faith

"I love you, too, Diego."

I choke on a sob, barely getting the words out.

"Just keep breathing," I tell him. "Help!" I scream.

Diego's eyes are closing. Sirens blare closer and closer.

"Please!" I wail.

I shake his shoulders. "Stay awake."

I kiss his lips. He is barely breathing. And the blood, there's so much blood.

Please don't let him die, I pray. *I'll do anything. Just don't let him die.*

I press my hands to his chest again. This time he doesn't protest. He is fading, graying before my eyes.

"No!" I scream.

I cannot lose Diego. I finally found a love that ignites every part of me, a love that lives in the soul.

Forever love.

"No." I sob into Diego's shirt. He is drenched, soaked in blood, blood seeping across his chest like the stains of ink on his skin. Not him. Not my Diego. *No.*

My strength is nearly gone. I feel it spilling out of me like Diego's life out of him.

I look back up at his face. We are both covered in the red stain of death. His lids are closed. I would give anything to look into his beautiful eyes again.

I want to freeze everything at the moment before chaos erupted, the moment when Diego was about to confess his love for me. If only time could be a snapshot, be held still for eternity.

And then I feel it. The last beat of his heart. Barely a flutter, really. But I love that flutter. I love it with all that I am. It's Diego's heart's way of telling me what his lips already said. I love you. *Te amo.* His heart's way of telling me that he will die for me, a thousand and one times if necessary.

Shh, listen. Can you hear it? Fluttering, flapping softly like broken wings daring to fly. It's saying good-bye.

I don't want to let him go, but I have no choice. Silence descends. The lack of beating—the void—pounds the loudest.

I'm being pulled away from Diego. Or maybe I'm being pushed. It's all the same, either way. He's gone. Gone.

Emergency workers surround Diego, attaching pads to his skin, yelling "Clear!" They shock him, his limbs flinching from the introduction of electricity. Diego is put on a board, strapped down. His shirt is ripped open.

And yet all I want to do is curl up next to him. I want them to take me wherever they're taking him. I belong with him. He is bloody and motionless, and yet I don't think I have ever, never in my life, seen anyone as beautiful as he is.

Out of the corner of my eye, I spot something moving like a shadow on the outskirts of my vision. It's him. The shooter. He's pretending to be part of the crowd, but I know better. There are other men, too, following him. The shooter smiles at me as I hear the worst word of my life. He hears it, too, I know. And finally, the man with the gun is satisfied. It's what he wanted all along.

I look back to Diego as the shooter disappears from sight.

They're closing the ambulance doors and somehow I know this is the end. But no matter what, I will love Diego forever. For the first time, I truly understand sacrifice.

"DOA."

That's the word that came out of the emergency worker's mouth, the word that made Diego's killer smile.

"DOA."

Dead on arrival.

50

faith

It's been six months since Diego died. I didn't try to find out about his funeral because I didn't want to remember him that way, in a casket, or maybe burned to ashes. I want to remember Diego smiling, touching me.

Every day is still as excruciating as the last. It feels as though I've been tossed off a ledge and I'm desperately trying to climb back up, hopelessly grabbing on to jagged rocks, pain lancing through me with each beat of my heart.

A heart that was meant to stop with the bullet that killed my love.

I miss him. God, how I miss him. He died right before Christmas. I've spent every holiday since thinking about him, wishing I could feel his arms around me, screaming at the sky, begging someone to listen.

Even winning Prediction couldn't make me smile, though it surprised Melissa when they called her name for homecoming queen. And I still remember the look on her face as she threw away the last of her cigarettes, never to pick them up again. High school graduation was torture. It was supposed to be one of the most joyous times of my life, but it was misery. I kept thinking that Diego should've been there, walking the stage.

I cannot, even for one hour, stop imagining the way his lips used to curl like a wave whenever he saw me, or the sound of his laughter, or even his moments of silence. Nothing is ever silent now. I dream about him constantly. It's the only place where I can see him in vivid colors. I don't want to forget.

I refuse to forget.

It took me until the day Diego died to realize that I no longer have autophobia. Because of him, I don't worry about being alone. Diego is with me always.

People don't understand why I left Florida, why I moved to Estelí, Nicaragua, as soon as I graduated. All I can say is that it felt right. I've been here one month, and I've already done more for, and with, these people than I ever did in America.

Dad helped me find this place, knowing I needed to leave the States. It was then that Dad and I had a long talk for the first time. Things were said that have been locked away in a box, rusting, dying. He brought them to life. I learned that he only ever wanted the best for me, that he regrets not communicating better, that my clothes and the church's opinions do not count for more than his daughter's well-being.

I'm to blame, as well. I should've asked how he felt about things instead of assuming. I should've taken the initiative. I'm the only one who can be me, who can choose my destiny. Fate was waiting silently, like a dusty relic, for me to grab it, to polish it, to make it mine.

When I mentioned leaving, Dad told me about American missionaries who built schools and helped out local people in a poor part of Estelí. They were looking for another person to join them, so I did. I don't plan to be here forever, but it's a start. I want to travel to other places. Help more.

People back in the States think I'm running away. They're wrong. I'm running *to,* not *away,* from Diego. I want to be somewhere I can make a difference. I want to carry out the dream that Diego and I shared. A dream to make this world a better place. To love in the face of hate. To laugh in the midst of turmoil. To create hope instead of fear.

Diego never gave up on me. This is my way of never giving up on him.

As I unpack the new shipment of supplies—medicine, water, packaged and canned food—I hear Raymond, one of the American missionaries, entering the building.

"Hi, Faith," he says to me. "*Hola,* Faith."

He's teaching me Spanish, the native language in Nicaragua. He says things to me in English, then Spanish. I always thought Diego would be the one to teach me. He'd be proud of my progress. I allow myself a small smile.

"*Hola*," I say.

My story is an open book to Raymond and his wife. They share my need to help others, a need that motivates me to place one foot in front of the other, to wake up each morning. Maybe I can plant seeds of hope in young people, water them, watch them grow.

Every time I tell Diego's story to a young person, every time I help build a new school, or help a local build a home, or give the community food and water, I have a chance of reaching them. If I help save even one life, it's worth it. Maybe in the future, the streets can be a safer place. Maybe kids will see that there is always another choice besides hate and fear and violence.

Raymond asks me to go to the backyard—which is more like a tropical paradise considering that the year-round temperature is eighty degrees—to hand out food. I pick up the box of food and head out back. There can be anywhere from two to twenty kids at once. Parents are usually working in the middle of the day, so I only expect children.

I walk outside, squint, pause on the back step to let my vision adjust to the bright midday sun. Trees block little of the glaring sun. Using my hand as a visor, I take a few steps and stop dead in my tracks. The box of food drops from my hand.

This can't be.

It's impossible.

There aren't children waiting for me. In fact, only one person waits and he looks just like—

"Diego?" I say.

I must be dreaming because when I say his name, he smiles and walks toward me. He wears a plain blue shirt and jeans, his hair mussed. He looks angelic, sun bursting around the outline of his body, filling in the cracks between his arms and torso.

"Faith," he says.

I run to him like I'm chasing the past. Dream or not, I want to feel him. I need to feel him.

"I've missed you, *mami*," he says.

I back up. I haven't heard that word since before he died.

"How? But . . . I saw . . . they said you were—"

"Dead?" he finishes.

I nod.

"I was. For three minutes and two seconds, apparently," he answers. "They restarted my heart in the ambulance."

"This whole time," I say.

Diego rubs one thumb tenderly across my cheek.

"I'm sorry I couldn't tell you. The government wouldn't let me. For your safety. For mine, as well."

"Government?"

He holds me close. "They've been watching *El Cartel de Habana*. When some of its members entered the U.S., American operatives followed, which led them to me. They were there, in *La Plazita*."

"They should've stopped them," I say, touching the spot above Diego's heart.

His thumb strokes my jaw, then my lips. "The crowd was too thick. By the time they made it, well, you know."

I do. I always will. The image haunts me.

"Like I said, it wasn't safe," Diego continues. "Will you forgive me?"

Safety. He hid from me, to protect me. He took a bullet for me, to protect me. *Will I forgive him?* There's no question. I will.

"Yes, of course, yes. But what about the guy with the gun? The gang? They'll come for you," I say.

He brushes hair away from my face. "Don't worry about that. They think I'm dead. *La policía* covered all tracks. I am invisible. Forgotten. They took me to a government hospital, hoping for my help when, if, I awoke. I've spent the last six months recuperating. If you thought I had bad scars before, you don't want to see my chest now."

I love his cocky grin. He knows I don't care about his scars.

"What about Wink? The others?" I ask.

I know by the way Diego winces that Wink was never found.

"I'm okay now," is all he says.

Diego is okay.

I wrap my arms around him. He never takes his eyes off me. I always said I would give anything to look at him again.

Here's my chance.

"Stay with me," I say.

"I wish I could," he replies. "I don't have much time. The government didn't want to approve this trip, but I refused to help unless they did."

Diego pulls me to a shaded area under an awning of trees. I sit next to him, leaning into his warmth.

"Here's the deal," he says. "For the next three months, the American government wants me to work with them. They want to know everything I know about *El Cartel Habana.* And they won't put me on the frontline. I can't tell you any more than that, I'm sorry. They've offered me protection and a free pass out of America. I can go anywhere I want when I'm done."

"What's the catch?" I ask. There's always a catch.

He takes a deep breath. "The catch is that I can't be with you at all during those three months. They've approved phone calls from protected lines only." He pulls out a small cell phone. "Keep this on you at all times. I'll call you."

I take the phone and put it in my back pocket, hating that I have to pull my hands away from Diego for even one second.

"But I just got you back," I say. "How can I watch you go again?"

"It'll be torture," he agrees. "But if I do it, I'm free. Afterward I can be with you, no limits. If I don't cooperate, they can rack up gun possession and drug affiliation charges and send me away, eventually deport me back to Cuba. If I'm deported, the cartel will know in no time."

He doesn't have to say the rest. I understand. The cartel won't just find him, they'll kill him.

"Looks like we have no other choice," I say.

"You know what they say about long-distance relationships, right?" Diego says with a grin. "They make for a great first night back."

He winks at me and I laugh.

We stay like that for a while. Laughing. Talking. Wrapped in each other's arms. Wrapped in the hope of a future together.

"I have to go," Diego finally says.

I am reluctant to let him leave. His lips brush the bridge of my nose. It's intimate in the sweetest way.

"If we can make it through death, we can make it through anything," he says, standing.

Men in black suits await him. He kisses me lightly, touching my heart once before he goes. When the car door opens, he waves to me. I wave back.

Diego—the love of my life, the light of my heart—is alive.

51
diego

It has been three months to the day since I saw Faith in Nicaragua.

I'm dying to get back to her. Every late hour spent awake talking to her on the phone, each agonizing second working for the government, is all worth it. I'm free.

The driver opens the door to my car. Faith waits for me. She looks tanned from the paradise she now calls home. Her smile shines brighter than a million lights. The sun sets behind her, giving the illusion of a fiery-red halo above her head.

Mi ángel.

And then she runs to me.

I wrap my arms around her and draw in a deep, long breath, inhaling the scent of strawberry hair. I've always loved strawberries, but never more than I do right now.

"It's good to see you," she says.

I don't have words. I let my lips do the talking. I kiss her softly at first, then harder. I miss her. I love her. I never have to leave her again.

I am a juxtaposition of emotions, all lining up, then falling together like dominos.

Faith's hands slide up my shirt. I play with the hem of

hers. I don't care that we are standing in the yard, that people may be watching. I don't care about anything but Faith.

Only Faith.

"Come inside," Faith says.

I follow her. She leads me to a small, round bungalow made of wood the color of sand. Decorations are sparse—a small bookshelf, a two-seater love seat, a tiny kitchen. A curtain of beads separates an area that houses a queen bed and a nightstand. It's about the size of my old apartment, the one *mi padre* still lives in.

No one except *mi padre* knows I'm alive. I want to tell Javier, but it's not wise. The less he knows, the better. It kills me to leave him in the dark, especially after he took a bullet for me, but that's exactly why I don't inform him. If by some small chance the cartel found out about my involvement with the U.S. government, they would go after anyone close to me. It's better, safer, for Javier to be uninformed.

I cannot think about any of that. I have been gone from Faith far too long to give an ounce of energy to anyone else.

She is *mi vida*.

"Like you always wanted," I say, commenting on her bungalow. Less is more for her.

She grins and takes my hand. "Glad you like it. It's your home now, too," she says.

My eyes slide to the queen bed. I want nothing more than to lay her down on that bed and show her exactly how much I've missed her, but first there's something I have to do.

"Show me the school," I say.

Faith watches me.

Did she see my eyes on the bed?

Does she want me like I want her?

"I want to see what my *princesa* built with her own hands," I insist.

"Okay," she replies.

We walk out of the bungalow and down a narrow path that winds like a twist tie. Our way is paved by uneven bricks that lead to a small gray structure made of concrete blocks. The inside has one long table with foldout chairs. There are no decorations. Just a simple desk that I imagine the teacher sits behind.

"Isn't it perfect?" Faith says.

It really is.

"Yes," I answer, truth lacing my tone. "You did this?" I motion to our surroundings, trying to imagine Faith up to her elbows in dirt and cement and dust, working her hands till they are calloused and bruised. *She did this*.

"Yes." She smiles proudly.

I want to feel proud like that, too. I want to be strong like my girl, not getting paid a penny but still rich in other ways that matter more than money ever could.

"I can't wait to do this with you," I say.

"Soon," Faith replies. "We'll be building another one, a few miles east, next month."

I take her hand. She leads me out of the school toward her favorite spot; a canopy of leaves sways above us. I make sure to keep Faith in front of me so she can't see the nervousness in my face. Under the trees, flowers and vines wrap around each other in a natural embrace.

"This is where I come to think of you," Faith says.

The temperature is slightly cooler here, in the shaded garden, moonlight taking over.

"I mean, I think of you all the time, but this is the spot where I can lose myself in our memories," she says. "This is the spot that got me through the last three months, through missing you."

I see it, how time could rewind here, how thoughts could be lost in the beauty surrounding us.

I reach into my pocket and pull out a small box, taking Faith by surprise.

She looks as though she wants to say something. Her mouth opens. Shuts. Opens again. She reminds me of a cute little fish.

"Faith, I love you," I say. "I hate any pain I caused you. And I know I don't deserve you, but I can't imagine living this life without you."

I open the box. A silver ring glints inside. She smiles a huge, earth-splitting smile.

The ring doesn't have a big diamond. As a matter of fact, there is no diamond at all. But it does have two small, defined wings engraved on it.

"*Te amo con todo mi corazón.* I want you to be mine forever," I say.

She touches the ring. Time stills. We lock eyes.

"Will you marry me, *muñeca*?"

She tries to speak, but her voice is caught by emotion. She clears her throat and tries again.

"Yes," she whispers. "Forever yes."

EPILOGUE
diego

I am the eye of a hurricane. So much destruction all around me, and nothing but calm within. Silence. Floating. Mercy. Awe.

Faith said yes.

I pull the ring out of the box and place it on her finger. She twirls the silver band. It catches a flicker of moonlight and shimmers more beautifully than any jewel ever could.

"It's gorgeous, Diego," she whispers.

Her lips touch mine. We are passion and love and hope, hope, hope.

I carry Faith in my arms back to the bungalow. She laughs all the while. I only stop once we reach the curtain of beads. The careless moon spills itself into the bedroom, covering Faith in its silver hue like wet paint. I kiss her lips. Soft. Sweet. Mine.

Mine.

Gently I lay her on the bed. She kisses me tenderly, like we have all the time in the world. And we do. I ease her shirt over her head, tracing the outline of her bra before removing that, too. I kiss down her shoulders, up her stomach. She is beautiful. In every way.

Faith takes off my shirt. Her gaze travels to the scar; it

spans the distance from my chest to my stomach like railroad tracks. Then she does the best thing. She kisses me. My scar, I mean. She kisses all the way down my wound. My eyes almost water. The emotion I feel when she kisses my weakness is intense.

"I love you," she says.

I cover her lips with mine. I kiss her with all that I have, every emotion. I wonder if she can feel my heart beating. She gasps when I hold her close. Gooseflesh covers both of us. When she touches me, I lose it.

"I want you, *mi amor*," I say in a raspy voice.

"I am yours," she whispers.

And I am hers, too. She is the key that unlocked my darkness. She poured in millions and millions of kilowatts of sunshine. I've never really thought about it before, but it's amazing how dark I once was. I see it now that I have such brightness in my life.

I randomly remember a saying about two people becoming one. Now I get it. I feel it, as though *mi alma* is literally merging with hers.

And I will never be the same.

Bliss. Making love to my girl was pure bliss. Afterward, she curls into and around me. I hold her close, breathing in the smell of strawberries. They will always remind me of Faith. She smiles.

"*Te amo, preciosa*," I say.

"I love you, too," she replies.

That is all I need in this life.

Faith.

Hope.

A future.

Thanks to another chance at life, I can give her everything I have, every ounce of love and passion flowing through my Cuban blood. And then some.

I briefly remember the pain, the struggle, the losses.

But.

"No matter how tough life gets," I say as I lean in to kiss Faith's lips, "I'm glad to be livin' it."

In that moment, one thing is blatantly clear to me: some stuff lasts forever. Like love. Even when the world says no, even when no one else believes but you, some things linger. They ebb and flow like an echo off the walls of infinity. Over and over again. Because not even death can kill them.

And the forever moment is a lot like flying freely on broken wings made new.

Read on for a sneak peek at *After Us,*
the sequel to *Before You,*
available next January.

1

melissa

The beach is a moving canvas of people.

Cabanas and waves and bathing suits and sand castles all blend together to create a serene picture of life on the coast. The sky is on fire with blues and yellows and oranges. Tiny puffs of clouds like wisps of cream. Sunscreen lotion saturates the air, smelling like SPF and sweat. I squint through the blaring sun and walk toward a crowd of girls lying on their bellies with the strings to their tops undone. Bare backs naked of tan lines.

"Frozen margarita, extra salt," I say, giving the drink to a girl with blond hair a shade darker than mine.

I balance the tray on one palm. Hand off drinks with another. Like a machine dispensing snacks.

"Piña colada." Next girl. "Sex on the beach." Next. "Vodka and tonic." Last. "Rum and Coke."

I smile. Compliment one of the girls on her leg tattoo. Girls love compliments. Eat them up like sugar.

I don't know these girls. I don't know most of the people splayed out on the beach like a deck of cards. Ordering alcohol like water, trying any reprieve to cool themselves down from rays that bake them to burnt crisps.

It's too hot to be alive today. It's burning. The air is

breathing fire all over me. The sun is pressing so hard into my skin that it's turning red. If I close my eyes, I can imagine my skin melting off like wax. I'm dripping sweat. Body glistening as though I've jumped in the water. I haven't.

"Thanks," the girl with the leg tattoo says.

One of the girls ties her top and flips over, insistent on showing me her low hip tats. Two pink bows wrapping up the package of a perfect body.

I remember what it was like to have a perfect body.

"Love it," I say. And I do.

I can never get a tattoo there.

I don't wear bikinis anymore. My swimwear is a collection of one-pieces. Covering certain fragments of me that I'm not willing to show. Holding me together. Though admittedly still racy, especially the one I've got on today, the suit that hugs me like a glove, fitting my every muscle and curve. It's white with wavy ruffles like sea foam over the material around my breasts, plumping them up. A simple tie in the back to support the front. A small triangle covering my backside. Nothing but tiny pieces coming together, exposing skin. A runway of fabric lining my stomach and down, down. About four inches wide. Just enough.

My tray is still stacked full of drinks for another group of people. They look like towers. Like a whole miniature city of skyscrapers and small circular buildings crammed together. Drowning in liquid.

I wait for cash.

A quick glance tells me that the five girls have tipped me something close to fifteen bucks. Not bad.

"Enjoy the heat," I tell them by way of good-bye.

On to the next customer.

All around me, sun tints skin a soft brown, sometimes red. Corners of beach towels flutter in the slight breeze like stingray wings. It hurts to look at the ocean, glittery and reflecting light.

I've already checked IDs for the five guys waiting on drinks. Each tall and muscular, with the sort of deliciously ripped bodies that belong in a place like this. Each ordering Corona bottlenecks. I hand out the beers and accept their cash. Flirt a little. Makes for better tips.

"What are you guys doing out here today?" I ask. Grin.

"*Nada, mami*," one says in a Latino accent, taking a seat on a lounge chair. The others follow suit. "Just enjoying this weather. Wanna enjoy it with me?"

He pats his lap. Like I'd actually sit on it.

"Can't," I say. Wink at him. "Have to work."

The guy leans forward. Checks me out. I check him out right back. Shaved head, nice lips.

His friends look, too. Except for one. I can't see the face of the one looking toward the water with dark sunglasses on.

"I'll have one, too," he says, still not glancing my way.

What is so interesting that you can't look a person in the eye?

I check the water. Nothing out of the ordinary.

"ID, please," I say. Nothing personal—can't serve underage. Even though I'm eighteen and understand. It isn't worth losing a prime job at the busiest hotel on the beach. A job that pays really well, with customers who tip even better.

He hands it to me, still not looking up. I glance at it. I don't need to see his full face to know that it's not him. Looks more like the guy sitting next to him than the guy handing it to me.

"Gonna have to do better than that," I say.

I need the money that this job provides. With three sisters away at college and Mom working double nursing shifts to support them, I need whatever I can get. Everything we have is stretched thin. A bubble about to pop.

His rough sigh says he's not happy with my response. He turns to me.

Tick, tick, tock.

Boom.

Time breaks into a million shards. Tiny slivers of moments. Trapping me. My breath catches.

He sees me then. Moves his sunglasses to the top of his head to get a better look. Eyes narrow. Unbelieving.

I can't find enough seconds to understand what's happening here. I heard that he moved away. I'm searching desperately for a breath of fresh air, but I can't find one.

Wavy brown hair that's almost black. Thick lips that I've kissed once before.

I'm staring at tattoos that wrap around his shoulders, hugging him. A hundred different images, all black and white. Photographic. I'm looking at a sun over his left collarbone, the only bit of light shining into the chest piece. Clouds ripple under his neck like waves. His shirt is off and I'm staring too hard, I realize, because his friends start laughing.

It's a memorial. The piece is to remember someone he lost.

"Melissa?"

There's a timber in his voice that makes my insides gooey. I'm melting ice cream on this hideously hot day. He says my name like it's painful for him, looking at me with those incredulous eyes. Willing me to say something, anything, but I can't. I can't.

I run away instead. My feet propel me forward, fast, churning sand beneath my heels. I don't care when a shell cuts the underside of my foot. Or when tiny grains of sea bottom become a natural Band-Aid.

I need to breathe.

I hate that he is here right now.

I love that I've been given another chance to see his face.

"Wait," he calls from behind me.

I won't stop.

Fast, fast, faster.

He won't stop.

Just go, just go, just go.

I'm not quick enough.

"Wait," he says again, grabbing my arm lightly.

Five fingers that burn memories into my skin.

I turn to the sound of his voice.

"Javier," I say, choking on his name. Choking on the memories.

Me and Faith, my best friend. At this same beach. Months ago.

Javier and his cousin Diego, in the water. Faith needed to get Diego's attention. Faith needed Diego in so many ways. I needed to know what Javier's mouth tasted like. I told myself that it'd be fun.

Love was Faith's style. Fun was mine.

I try to shut out the memory. Can't.

Javier's lips were every bit as amazing as I'd thought. Plump and gentle and rough and perfect.

We never did more than that. Never talked about the fun day at the beach. Never pursued what we left behind.

I never told him that I've wanted him ever since.

READER QUESTIONS

1. Both Faith and Diego begin their journey by running from their pasts. How important is it to overcome past obstacles? Is there anything in your past that troubles you still?

2. From the start, misfortune finds Diego. What would you do if a gang approached you for initiation? Do you agree with Diego's decision to fight the gang members? Would you have handled the situation differently?

3. Faith doesn't learn about the gang, or Diego's past involvement with a cartel, right away. Diego chooses to keep that from Faith to protect her. Just as Diego joined the cartel to protect and provide for his family. To what lengths would you go to protect and provide for the ones you love? Is there such a thing as too far?

4. Diego is judged by his appearance—tattoos, scars, ethnicity. Likewise, Faith is judged by the appearance she projects—top student, daughter of a pastor, conservative clothes. How important are appearances? What are your thoughts on stereotypes?

5. Cultural differences show throughout the book. Do you think culture shapes a person? What do you think of the scene where Diego shows Faith the Cuban market? Is it important to learn about other cultures? Should culture ever be a barrier between people?

6. The loss of a parent is something no teen should have to face, but many do. Faith never knows what became of her mom. Do you think this is a good or bad thing? Can it possibly be both? And what about Diego's mom? Do you think having closure makes letting go any easier?
7. Faith turned to drugs to numb her emotional pain. What would you do if someone offered you drugs? What if you were like Melissa and knew someone struggling with drugs? Would you get them help?
8. In the end, Diego is offered a second chance at a clean life, and Faith decides to help people in underprivileged countries. Do you believe Diego deserves a second chance? How can you help those in need?
9. Though they both have difficult pasts, despite the fact that they've made mistakes, through their cultural differences, Faith and Diego fall in love. What does love mean to you? Do you think that their dream of a brighter future is possible? What does it mean to fly on broken wings?

WITHDRAWN